Finest Hour
The Exiled Fleet Book 3

Richard Fox

ISBN: 9781698190518

CHAPTER 1

Commodore Gage stepped out of a lift and onto the *Orion*'s bridge as battle-station sirens wailed. His Genevan bodyguard, Thorvald, brushed past him, the larger man's armored bulk blocking Gage's view of the crew as he made his way up to the holo tank on the command dais.

The ship's XO, Price, was already at the tank. She brushed her blond hair back from her face and held it, her other hand on a helmet resting on the circular control panel around the hologram showing New Madras and the local void. She glanced at Gage's helmet, waiting for him at his station.

"Protocol." Gage tapped his helmet with one

hand while the other jabbed at icons within the tank. Indus ships vectored red diamonds blinking not far from the main star fort protecting the northern hemisphere.

He had to lean back to see around Thorvald, who'd put himself between the commodore and the crew, and the rest of the sailors had yet to don their helmets before void combat. "I'm in command. I button up last. What's everyone waiting for?"

"Protocol," Price said softly to keep her words just for Gage. "You're Albion's regent, sir. I mean 'sire.' By tradition, everyone is to ensure that the royal family—or their representatives are to—"

"Blast it." Gage put on his helmet and keyed the air seals. His ears popped as the void suit beneath his uniform locked onto his helmet and stale air wafted over his face. Price took the cue and followed suit. He heard the snap of more helmets being donned, but could only see the rest of Thorvald's back.

"Take your place by the lift." Gage rapped knuckles against the dragon-scale-like armor plates on Thorvald's suit. "The crew is no threat."

"Apologies." Thorvald turned slightly, the front of his helmet closed and modeled after a medieval knight's. "The AI within my suit is…insistent. The bonding process has been—"

"Later," Gage snapped. "There's a battle unfolding and the crew needs to see me ready and unafraid. Can't do that if I'm peeking over your shoulder. Move."

Thorvald stepped off the dais, taking up a position by the lift doors and shifting a carbine off his back to hold against his waist.

"We're going to have a discussion on what me being the regent means aboard this ship. After the current crisis. Fleet status?" Gage shifted the holo view to the star fort *Amritsar*. The structure was shaped like a compass rosette—four long planes studded with weapon batteries around a squat inner ring, but with two more up and down the z-axis (north-south in Albion naval terminology). Plasma cannons lit up with heat from the ship's passive scans, but there was no telemetry data coming from the guns to know which direction they were facing.

Gage frowned. Squeezing the fingertips of

one hand together, he poked them into the fort and popped his hand open. The command should have displayed all information feeds coming from the fort, but he got a red error message instead.

"All ships have made the transition from slip space," Price said. "Forming a standard battle line with shields oriented toward the Daegon incursion." She poked hard on a screen and mumbled a curse. "The data for which just shut off. In fact, none of the Indus channels are…they're broadcasting, but we don't have the crypto to read any of it."

"Even in the void there's a fog of war," Gage said. "Have the fleet hold a screen formation over the planet but don't join shields into a wall just yet. Have the *Hephaestus* position between us and New Madras. We can't afford to lose her. Let's get a better picture of this battle before we lock down for a fight."

He brought up data feeds from his fleet and added them to the holo. Sensor feeds from the *Fairbairn* flashed with priority traffic, and he swiped it up and into the tank. Up came video of Daegon ships—the distinctive linked-diamond hull sections in stark contrast to the Albion and Indus vessels—firing in several directions at once. One Daegon ship, one of their smaller destroyers, took a direct hit at the join between the first and second hull sections and snapped apart, flames grasping at the void as the internal atmosphere bled out.

"These are all escorts," Gage frowned. "Where's the battleship-sized command vessel?"

"We're not reading anything of that size…wait a second." Price shifted the holo up and a gold square pulsed along a projected flight path from the *Orion* to Theni City. "Cobra squadron is escorting Prince Aidan. We don't have any identify friend-or-foe transponders from the Indus. If we don't have theirs, they don't have ours."

Gage's face went pale as he realized his mistake. Assumptions were the mother of all foul-ups, and he'd assumed the Indus and Albion IFF would remain linked after his first contact with Admiral Chadda, the New Madras military commander.

Without the right IFF transponders, the fighters of the Cobra squadron would appear as blips on New Madras defense screens. Even if the weapon batteries did a visual check to ensure they weren't firing on their own ships that might not be broadcasting IFF due to battle damage or other malfunctions, the Albion Typhoons didn't look much like the Indus Chakram void fighters. It would take only one scared weapon crewman to panic and assume the new, unfamiliar ships were the enemy.

"Let me guess," Gage said, "we lost IFF the second the Daegon arrived in system."

"That's…that's correct, sir. We're trying to hail the *Amritsar,* but all we're getting is noise," Price said.

"They switched encryption without telling us," Gage said. "We had this problem during the Reach War. They mentioned this at the academy—how they…should work. Keep hailing the Indus."

Gage opened a channel to the Cobra squadron commander, call sign Marksman.

"Cobra actual, we've got a slight situation here," Gage said.

"Would that be the lack of IFF, Commodore?" Marksman's head and shoulders, his face obscured by his helmet, came up in the holo.

"Because the pucker factor's been especially tight since we noticed. Getting shot down by Daegon's one thing. Getting hit by 'friendlies' is downright embarrassing. Especially since we've got—"

"Hold your course for Theni City," Gage said. "You're expected. I'll have this commo issue sorted…Fly casual."

In the holo tank, dozens and dozens of torpedo icons sprang from the *Amritsar* and arced toward the Daegon ships.

"Too many," Gage said. "By our sensor count they just emptied every tube on that fort."

"Overkill." Price nibbled her bottom lip. "Indus systems are notoriously out-of-date. Why would they release a death blossom like that?"

"Because they panicked," Gage said. "And the Daegon were counting on it. Any response to our repeated hails? Didn't think so. No time for subtlety. Guns!" Gage shouted.

"Sir!" came back from the targeting section.

"One plasma shot, forward battery two, firing data coming from my station." Gage tapped a pad, then dragged and dropped a file onto the gunnery section's icon.

"Sir…the target is the Indus star fort," the gunnery officer said.

"Commodore," Price said, frowning, "there's a lack of subtlety and then there's…poking the proverbial bear."

"We are firing *at* the fort," Gage said, "not *on* the fort. Important difference. The round will just miss their shields. Engage."

The gunnery officer paused for a moment, then shrugged.

Gage felt a slight tremor through the deck plates and watched the holo as the bolt streaked away from the *Orion*, past the fort, and into the void. The round would dissipate into waste heat and photons before it cleared the orbit of the outermost moon.

"We're being hailed." Price nodded slowly.

"Figured that would do it," Gage said. "To me."

A window slid up in the holo of a man in a blue and yellow vac suit, his face visible through a clear visor, his beard scrunched to his face by smart wires, a helmet with a large metal ring askew over one side of his head.

"Admiral Gage," Chadda said. "Did your ship have a weapons malfunction? Or did your IFF systems not…" His brow furrowed as he glanced down, then he turned to speak terse-sounding Indus over one shoulder. Looking back at Gage, his face slightly flush with embarrassment, he said, "We didn't update our crypto measures with you when the Daegon entered the system. Standard practice for us. Sharing with allies is not as standard."

"I gathered as much," Gage said. "Now that I have your attention, can we fix this problem?"

Chadda nodded quickly and waved a hand at Gage. New data feeds slowly populated the holo tank.

"You've got an entire squadron of fighters en route to Theni?" Chadda asked.

Gage's eyes hardened. "A number of critically wounded in need of medical care our ships can't provide," Gage said. "And I thought the sight of Albion fighters overhead would show our joint resolve, decades of friendship between our people, to the citizens of Theni."

Price leaned back slightly, surprised to hear

12

the Commodore lying.

"Yes, excellent idea," Chadda said. "With this victory, Albion allies in the skies above, this will go a long way toward settling the near panic the planet's been in for the past few days."

"I don't believe this fight is over," Gage said. "We've fought the Daegon before. They're not afraid to take casualties. What you destroyed weren't their ships of the line. Keep your ships on high alert until—"

"Ashtekar particle spike!" the conn officer shouted. "Locus over…the northern magnetic pole. It's skewed off normal, Commodore. They're coming in over the ocean a few hundred miles from Theni City."

"So close to the gravity well," Chadda said as one hand went to stroke his beard and bumped off his visor. "That's impossible."

"We saw this when they assaulted Albion," Gage said. He twisted the globe in the holo around and laid a quick intercept heading for his fleet. "My ships can be in weapons range in minutes. I suggest you vector the battle group you have over the equator to engage from the south. We'll have them in our cross fire."

"I am quite capable of defending my own skies, Commodore." Chadda paused. "And I agree with your suggestion. IFF has synced. Any strikes on my ships or soil from Albion guns will not be excused so lightly as the last time." He wagged a finger at Gage and the channel closed.

"Yes, he has this well in hand," Gage deadpanned. "XO, reorient the fleet to a lance formation. *Orion* at for fore."

"Aye aye," Price said and the ship lurched ahead toward the slip-space exit point forming over New Madras. The rest of the fleet formed into a cone with the carrier as the point. "Why did you lie to him, sir?"

"Trust is in short supply," Gage said. "We just killed one Faceless assassin that was murdering his way through my crew to Prince Aidan. I don't know if everyone around Chadda can be trusted. As such, the fewer people that know where the Crown Prince is, the less of a chance the Daegon will know where to go after him. I'm quite content to have the enemy think Aidan is aboard the *Orion*. He's safer that way, even if we—as a result—are not."

"You think Ambassador Carruthers can keep it a secret?" Price asked.

"Our diplomatic corps aren't fools," Gage said. "And she understood my instructions when I spoke to her over a secure line."

"And the Cobra squadron…"

"Will remain in Theni City as a gesture of goodwill…and to evacuate Aidan should the need arise," Gage said.

"Rather adept of you, sir," Price said. "Tolan would be impressed."

"Speaking of, where are he and the *Joaquim*?"

"Made slip space back to the Kigeli Nebula a few minutes ago," she said. "There's no quick way out of this system to anywhere else since all the New Madras nav buoys were sabotaged prior to our arrival. Tolan's ship made a back plot over our way in just before the lay line collapsed."

"And he took most of the pirates we had in the brig with him," Gage said. "One less headache to deal with."

"Slip arrival!" the gunnery officer called out.

In the holo, dozens of Daegon ships materialized. Gage ceded targeting authority to his bridge officers and concentrated on the tactical problem unfolding before him. Again, the Daegon had sent through their smaller, less capable ships. They'd come through slip space in an irregular formation, none close enough to support the others with their shields.

"Sloppy," Gage said. "Damn sloppy." He zoomed in on one of the ships and found open hangar bays on the diamond faces. A shape blurred out of the hangar and Gage zoomed back out and tagged the exiting object. It vectored toward a city on the coast of the northern ocean.

Hundreds more plots erupted from the Daegon fleet and followed the same path.

"It's an invasion fleet," Gage said and opened a channel to Admiral Chadda. "*Amritsar*, target the carriers and destroy them before they can unload everything. Easier to kill their soldiers aboard ship than when they get to the ground."

Chadda spoke quickly in Indus to someone

offscreen, and a chorus of panicky voices answered.

"Our torpedo systems…aren't back online yet," he said hesitantly. "Our magazines suffered a number of malfunctions. We overloaded their capabilities when we wiped out their initial force."

"Which is what our Daegon enemy anticipated," Gage said. "My fleet will be within firing range soon. We'll do our best to stem the tide." He muted sound and video on the channel to Chadda and looked through the holo to Price.

"XO, ready a full torpedo salvo. Target the troop carriers," Gage said.

"Aye aye." Price worked commands into her panel as Gage zoomed the tank in on Aidan's shuttle heading to the planet. The Daegon force was close to the Crown Prince and icons for Daegon fighters appeared around their ships.

"We're low on torps, Commodore," Price said. "Targeting solution is working through the fleet but if we lose them all, we'll—"

"Make the same mistake the Indus just did," Gage said. "The irony isn't lost on me. But the Daegon don't know how many torpedoes we have left. The throw weight of that star fort is known. We need to appear as dangerous as possible, Price. Gain and maintain their attention so they don't try for the shuttle."

"We could recall them…"

"By the time they make it back we'll be in the thick of the fight." He shook his head. "There are no good options here. Just less-bad decisions to make."

More and more drop ships and landing pods shot out from the Daegon ships, their lethal cargo raining down on the coastal city. Gage watched as enemy craft blinked out of existence as ground defenses engaged, but with each passing minute, more and more invaders made it to their beachheads.

"We're at the outer edge of effective torpedo range," Price said.

"Fire at will. Let our destroyers off the leash, have them interdict the Daegon landers. The rest of the fleet closes to cannon range to finish off their ships," Gage said.

The *Orion* shuddered as weapons blasted out of launchers. The torpedoes accelerated straight off the dorsal and ventral tubes, then curved toward the

Daegon troop carriers. More torpedoes from the fleet's cruisers and frigates joined the swarm and alert icons pinged next to each ship: empty torpedo magazines.

Gage skewed the holo to one side, checking on Prince Aidan's progress. The shuttle's position slowed from its projected course, coming almost to a standstill.

"What the hell…" Gage tapped a screen to open a channel, but the connection didn't go through.

"Commodore," Price said, snapping the holo back to show the entire battle. Albion torpedoes hurtled through a swarm of counter fire from the troop carriers. Gage swallowed hard as more than half were destroyed before they could begin their terminal acceleration. The remaining weapons sprang forward, like the closing jaws of a trap, and hit home.

Daegon ships fell out of formation, bleeding air and broken hull fragments as they succumbed to the planet's gravity. One carrier kept disgorging drop pods, but haphazardly, sending troops into the void or on trajectories through the atmosphere that guaranteed they'd burn to a crisp before they ever made it to the ground.

The surviving ships lurched forward, engines roaring, and made straight for the *Orion*.

"Helm!" Price called out. "Get us clear!"

Gage gripped his console as the ship canted to one side, and a groan from the stressed superstructure carried through the bridge.

The *Orion*'s cannons opened fire, striking the prow of the lead Daegon troop carrier and blowing it apart. Another ship charged through the debris and its hull was shredded like a fist punching through glass. The damaged ship faltered and spun end over end as its engines malfunctioned. A broadside from the *Ajax* blew it into a fireball that flashed out before being snuffed by the void.

"They're closing on us," Price said.

Gage ignored her and zoomed in on Aidan. His shuttle and escort were circling high over Theni City…and a pack of Daegon fighters were closing on them.

"Marksman," Gage said into the open channel. "Marksman, what are you doing? Get into the city's anti-air envelope now!"

No response.

"Brace for impact!" came from a bridge officer.

The holo tank flashed red and overrode Gage's control. A wire diagram of his ships appeared, with a red-outlined Daegon ship barreling straight toward it. The *Orion*'s forward batteries fired in sequence, each plasma bolt striking just below the enemy's prow and angling it up ever so slightly with each hit.

The Daegon ship pierced through the ship's shields and glanced off the upper hull, tearing through a point defense battery. Gage looked out the forward windows and watched the troop carrier rumble past the bridge's superstructure. The deck shuddered so hard he was almost thrown off his feet.

Red light flooded the bridge as the Daegon's engines passed by.

Damage alerts pulsed in the holo tank, an ugly scar across the top of the *Orion*'s hull.

"That was too close," Price said.

The troop carrier exploded and a piece of the hull struck the bridge, ripping out the windows and the forward stations. The men and women at their posts didn't even know what killed them.

Thorvald was there, pressing Gage to the deck and protecting him with his own body as bits of the hull careened around the command dais.

"Aidan!" Gage struggled against the Genevan's grip, but he was pinned. "Get help to the prince!"

CHAPTER 2

"If we had the clearance codes, we would've given them to you by now!" Marksman yelled into comms net.

Nick "Freak Show" Wyman rolled his eyes and did another visual scan from his Typhoon's cockpit. The Cobra squadron, and the shuttle they escorted, were flying racetrack patterns above Theni City, still above the upper atmosphere.

The flash of a distant ship-to-ship battle made his hand clench against his control stick. Part of him wanted to be in that fight, but another part of him remembered the absolute terror of his last tangle with a Daegon ship, where he'd destroyed a capital ship's shield emitter through flying best described as "suicidal tendencies" and a series of lucky shots.

"This is ridiculous," said his wingman, Betty "Rosy" Ivor. "Indus want to get all formal and proper in the middle of a goddamn invasion? Who the hell do they think they are?" She brought her fighter alongside Wyman's wingtip and waggled her craft slightly. "Let's call their bluff and just dive in. Get this over with and get back to the *Orion*."

"We got wounded in the shuttle," Wyman said. "You think they can take the g's of a rapid descent?"

"*They* don't have to do a hell dive," Ivor said. "*We* can do it and that way Marksman will know the Indus aren't going to light us up."

"Too risky." Wyman craned his neck around to see explosions from the Daegon invasion fleet. "You really want to piss off the new CO that badly? We just got assigned to the Cobras. Let's stay off the shit list for a little while, yeah?"

"You're no fun," Ivor said, and her fighter drifted away.

"*No. Nothing to declare!*" Marksman shouted. He'd kept dual commo lines open so his squadron could "lean forward in the cockpit" and be ready for the signal to finally escort the shuttle to the spaceport.

"Got bogies on the scope," announced Sparks, a pilot on the outer perimeter. *"Least a dozen. Coming in fast."*

Wyman's heartbeat accelerated and the cold chill of adrenaline hit his system. He double-checked his missile loadout and charge to his plasma cannons. His fighter was loaded for bear, but that proved to be little comfort.

"Yes, yes, we will submit to customs inspection," Marksman said. *"Now, you going to clear us for descent before these Daegon catch up to us? Because I guarantee they won't fill out your goddamn forms…you are? You are. Thank you. We'll be right down."*

"I'm going to love this planet," Briar said. "I can tell already."

"Cobras," the squadron commander said, "blue flight with me on escort. Red flight hang back and deal with the Daegon that think we're an easy target."

Wyman's ears perked up at the order. He was the red flight leader.

"Go for orbital interdiction or hit them on the way down, sir?" Wyman asked.

"Our Shrike guidance systems turn to shit in the upper atmosphere," Marksman said. "Delay them in vacuum and we'll be low enough to feed them a missile if they catch up to us. But don't let that happen, Freak Show."

"Aye aye." Wyman banked his fighter around and vectored toward the oncoming Daegon fighters. The teardrop-shaped fighters were mere blips on his HUD, but they were closing fast.

"Rosy, Sparks, Flame Out, on my wing. Let's get set for a tilt."

"We're not jousting," Ivor said. "We're about to go three-to-one in near vacuum. These are crap odds."

"We've been through worse." Wyman linked his targeting computers to the other Typhoons and assigned targets to each. "Watch the edges, boys and girls. These guys can surprise you. Set for full spread, double Shrikes to each bogie."

"That's our whole loadout," Flame Out said. "The foundry that makes Shrikes is back on Albion and I doubt there's any fresh munition deliveries on the way."

"Just do it," Wyman said. "Marksman said there's wounded in that shuttle, but Rosy and I have a bit of experience escorting VIPs. Very VIPs, you get me?"

Even with their encrypted comms, Wyman didn't want to voice his suspicion of just who really was on that shuttle.

"I get you," Freak Show said. "Target's locked."

Blue bolts from the Daegon fighters snapped past Wyman's cockpit. He jinked from side to side, confident that the enemy didn't have a solid bead on him, but that they were shooting just to throw him off. He looked down, and the HUD on his visor showed him where the shuttle and the rest of his squadron were, like he could see through the bottom of his cockpit.

"Single launch ready," Wyman said. "Prep for a dead drop soon as we pass."

"Are you nuts?" Sparks asked. "We've got the range. Just do a—"

"Launch!" Wyman hit a trigger and a single Shrike sprang off his fuselage. Three more missiles joined it, closing fast on the enemy. He tapped an override command onto his targeting computer, and the grips on the rest of his missiles loosened ever so slightly.

Thin white beams came off the edge of the Daegon fighters, destroying each of the missiles with ease.

"Go for guns, and ready drop," Wyman said, an edge of panic to his words. Swallowing hard, he opened fire. Green plasma pulsed out from under his nose and he rolled to one side, still firing as return fire from the enemy seared his undercarriage. An error alert pinged from one of his missiles and he found himself trying to cancel the firing solution for that Shrike, dodge incoming fire, and ready his attack all at the same time.

There was a brief cry on the radio, then the Daegon squadron roared past him. He slapped a palm against his targeting panel and all his Shrikes ejected off his fighter. He dove toward the planet, the sudden acceleration pulling blood from his head and graying out his vision.

"Come on, work. Work!" He looked up and saw a dozen starbursts as his flight's missiles activated. Entering into a dogfight, even in the void, meant hard maneuvers after the initial pass as pilots attempted to come in behind their foes for a kill shot. These sudden turns greatly reduced their forward velocity…and made them easy targets for the missiles he and the other Typhoons had dropped like mines in their wake.

The Shrikes accelerated at speeds no human pilot could tolerate and destroyed most of the Daegon fighters within seconds.

Wyman ignored Ivor's shout of triumph and rapid-fired his plasma cannon along the path of an enemy survivor, throwing up a cloud of bolts in its path. The Daegon did a barrel roll and dodged two of Wyman's shots, but a third clipped the edge and sent the fighter tumbling end over end.

Wyman fired again, but his control stick buzzed. His capacitor was spent, and he was defenseless for another good thirty seconds.

The damaged enemy righted itself and spun

its nose toward Wyman. One side of the firing arc traced around the ship's edge lit up.

Ivor shot over Wyman's canopy and destroyed the Daegon with a quick burst.

"That's five for me," she said. "Guess you got an assist on that one."

Wyman dove his fighter toward Theni City and checked his scope. No Daegon…but only three Typhoons.

"Lost Flame Out," Sparks said. "No ejection. No pilot."

Wyman looked up to the void as wisps of clouds carried past his fighter. Traces of burning debris cast lines through the sky as he descended deeper and deeper into the atmosphere. There would be nothing of Flame Out to recover. Nothing to return to his family or properly bury.

What would remain was doubt—doubt that Wyman could've come up with a better plan that would have beaten all the Daegon and kept all four of them alive for the next fight.

"Roger, keep gun-camera footage intact for graves registration," Wyman said. "Vector in on

Marksman's beacon. We'll join up with them at the spaceport…head on swivels. There may be enemy stragglers that made it down."

"So who's in that shuttle?" Sparks asked.

"Whoever it is, it's our mission to get them to the ground safe and in one piece," Wyman said. "We're not there yet. Mission's still going. Don't forget it."

"If Flame Out knew," Ivor said, "he'd know it was worth it."

"Oh…" Sparks said. "Oh, that's who it…never mind. Five by five to the beacon."

"Five by five," Wyman said.

CHAPTER 3

Gage stared into the flickering holo tank. Crewmen were already repairing the bridge's hull, and the sunspot of plasma torches and chatter at the gash were the only other signs of activity around him. He'd sent Price and the rest of the survivors to the auxiliary bridge while he readied for what he anticipated would be a difficult discussion.

The last of the Daegon ships had been destroyed nearly half an hour ago, but Admiral Chadda and the rest of New Madras were scrambling to contain the Daegon troops landing at Punam, the city on the coast. The isthmus had been sealed off in short order; it seemed the Indus ground troops were better organized than the void forces. This didn't surprise Gage as the citizens were of the Neo Sikh faith and more militant that the average Indus.

From what Gage could glean from the New Madras interlink, the official story was of a great victory in orbit, and a minor incursion to the ground that would be eliminated shortly. Gage had his doubts about that, but he had his own problems to worry about.

Through the gap, he could see the long scar across the *Orion*'s hull. The entire top deck had lost pressure and the casualty list grew longer every time he looked at it. Turrets annihilated. Torpedo tubes destroyed. At least they'd all been empty when the Daegon ship had tried to ram her, else the accidental detonation would have made the damage even worse.

Captains from the rest of the fleet appeared in the holo. All looked tired, strung out from the extended nightmare that had been the retreat from Siam and the pursuit by the Daegon through the Kigeli Nebula.

"11th," Gage said. "Albion's light burns. You've all done well today."

"How is the *Orion*?" asked Vult of the battle cruiser *Ajax*. "Do you need to transfer the flag?"

"The damage looks worse than it really is." Gage's jaw worked from side to side, as if the half-truth left a bad taste in his mouth. "Damage control estimates all systems will be back online within the hour. Replacement components are already being fabricated aboard the *Helga*."

"And what exactly are we still doing here?" asked Arlyss of the *Renown*, a hint of derision to his tone. "New Madras clearly isn't a safe harbor for us—treaty with the Indus or not. There is a plan, isn't there, Commodore?"

Erskine, the captain of the *Valiant* gave Arlyss a dirty look.

"The nav buoys linking New Madras to Vishuddha and Cathay Dynasty space were destroyed before we arrived," Gage said. "It will take at least two weeks of constant Ashtekar particle survey before any ship can enter slip space."

"Then we do a hard bore to Vishuddha," Arlyss said. "The Daegon can't touch us in slip space and—"

"Eight months," Gage snapped. "Eight months it'll take us to do a hard bore to Vishuddha. Thirteen to Lantau in Cathay space. Other systems that are closer are already under Daegon control. None of our ships can spend that much time in slip space, not with the damage we've taken. We're supplied to do hard bores from Albion to our colonies. The most we were ever meant to move beyond our supply chain is three weeks. And as you have figured out by now," he glanced at Arlyss, "this is as far as we can go until a proper course through slip space can be charted. The path back to the Kigeli Nebula has collapsed, not that I think any of us want to go back there."

"Then what are your orders, Commodore?" Vult asked.

"Turn to, make ready for battle," Gage said. "I want a full readiness workup from every ship in the next three hours. Priorities to the *Helga's* foundries will be assigned and then we'll cross-level crews as needed." He raised a hand as the captains stirred. "As needed. I know every ship is shorthanded right now, but I need every warship on the line that I can get. I don't know when the Daegon will return, but what we just fought was a recon force. They'll be back, sooner than any of us would like and with enough force to take the entire planet. At least that's what I would do if I were the Daegon and had just sacrificed so many ships and lives."

"They'll likely know we're here," Vult said.

"Yes. Perhaps the beating we just gave them in the Kigeli will make them think twice about attacking us here—here with a sizable Indus navy at our side," He half smiled, almost believing his feigned confidence.

"And the Indus are still our erstwhile allies?" Arlyss asked. "They've been…flaky in the past."

"Leave the Indus to me. The rest of you worry about your ships. Stay on close alert until further notice. We don't know when—or where—the Daegon will return. Albion's light—"

"The Crown Prince," Arlyss interjected just as Gage was about to close out. "Where is Prince Aidan?"

Gage's grip tightened on the console, his anger rising. "The prince is safe. We will leave it at that." Gage tapped a key and muted Arlyss, who continued talking. "If there is nothing else?"

Arlyss, visibly agitated, raised a finger next to his face as his mouth moved but no one heard him.

"Next meeting in three hours for ship status update. Albion's light burns." Gage ended the conference. The holo switched back to an orbital view of New Madras. Red icons marked where a ground battle raged at Punam, a few hundred miles from Theni City where Aidan had landed not too long ago.

The city—and the Albion embassy there— was the safest place for the boy, Gage told himself. The *Orion* had come so close to being lost…the city had to be the best place for Aidan. Even though there'd been a close call on the way down.

He looked over to the wounded bridge and shook his head. There was no perfect solution. All he had were the decisions he could make and the consequences that followed, intended or not.

****

Clouds surrounded Wyman's fighter in an endless gray as his and the other two Typhoons descended on Theni City. Sunlike glows from their engines marked their positions as turbulence rattled his cockpit.

"Scope's clear," Ivor said. "Least something's going right for a change."

"You just jinxed us," Sparks said. "We're going to land and the locals will shoot us on sight because we look like Daegon."

"I heard the Daegon—the real ones, not their infiltrators—have blue or green skin," Ivor said.

"Where'd you hear that nonsense?" Wyman asked as his HUD pinged with a new flight plan from Marksman. He frowned as the new route was to fly several circuits over Theni City before landing at Bathinda Spaceport. There was a large no-fly zone over the center of the city and the route had them skirting too close to the zone for his taste…and the change struck him as entirely unnecessary.

"Clarke told me," Ivor said. "He's on the bridge staff and he saw the Commodore talking to one of the Daegon in the holo tanks and…blue skin.

Then Darren in sick bay saw the gene profile of the steward that poisoned all the captains and—"

"Stow the scuttlebutt, Rosy," Wyman said. "We've got a new flight plan. Sending it now."

"Does Marksman know we're running on fumes?" Sparks asked. "I've got three shots left in my magazines before I'm down to using passive-aggressive flying and rude hand gestures against the Daegon."

"Show the flag," Wyman said. "Altitudes not much higher than the drone ceiling for the city. We're meant to be seen."

They broke through the cloud cover and Wyman did a double take at the expanse of Theni City. The urban sprawl stretched for miles between two snow-covered mountain ranges, far larger and far more densely packed than any city on Albion. They banked onto their flight path and went right over the wide circular plane of Bathinda Spaceport, itself ringed by defenses and a tall circular wall.

"Cut air speed," Wyman said. "Just enough velocity to keep us airborne."

"If they wanted an aerial display team," Ivor

said, "they should've sent the White Cats team from Exeter. Marksman want us to do a barrel roll for the peasants?"

"Bit harsh, Rosy," Wyman said. "We'll be wheels down in a couple minutes."

"What's that to our nine o'clock?" Sparks asked.

At the center of the city was a golden building in the middle of a river running through Theni.

"It's smack-dab in the no-fly zone," Wyman said. "Guess it's a temple or something. Indus religion can be very different from planet to planet, if I remember my grade school history lessons right. They don't want us to fly near it, we don't fly near it."

He glanced over the side of his cockpit and saw poles bearing yellow triangle flags scattered through the city. There were people in the streets, mostly standing still and watching them pass.

"Think we'll get some actual shore leave?" Ivor asked.

"Are you always thinking about booze or partying?" Wyman asked.

"Hey, you got to go paint the town red on

Sicani. That must have been a hell of a shore excursion. Even the Commodore got stabbed," she said.

"And I got shot at, almost blown up, then chased off that horseshit of a planet with Tolan. That creep," Wyman said. "Next time a 'hey you' task like that comes up, it'll be *your* turn, Rosy."

"You got to go on shore leave?" Sparks asked. "Assuming the Daegon don't show up in the next couple hours…are these the kind of Indus that drink or the kind that don't drink?"

"Let's finish this circuit before you start the clock on liver damage, OK?" Wyman shook his head.

A few minutes later, the three fighters set down at the spaceport and Wyman popped the seal on his cockpit. A rush of cold, dry air assaulted him, catching his breath and freezing the snot in his nose. He considered putting his helmet back on, but opted to cover his mouth with his glove to warm up the air ever so slightly before he had to breathe it.

A ladder snapped into place next to him and he stood up. Two Indus, both men with beards and turbans, held the bottom of the ladder firm. A third man—taller, with a long black beard and wearing a padded flight suit—waited near the bottom, his hands clasped behind his back.

Wyman touched the frost-grimed handle of the ladder and made his way down, his eyes locking on an impressive-looking curved knife at the taller man's waist. His turban was more compact, and made of light blue cloth.

He pressed his hands together and said, "*Sat sri akal*," slightly bowing his head.

Wyman extended a hand and the other man shook it. "I'll just mess that up if I try it," he said. "I'm Freak Show. Wyman."

"No problem, sir. I am Captain Ranbir Singh, New Madras Air Defense Force. Welcome to Theni City. I am your liaison while you are our guests here." He smiled, and his frost-stiffened beard rustled.

"If you're my liaison," Wyman said, waving Ivor and Sparks over to him, "then let's get started on repairs." He ducked under his Typhoon where a black gash cut a diagonal line, just missing the landing-gear housings.

Ranbir sank to his knees next to Wyman. "We

will remold the armor plating," Ranbir said. "Recharge your capacitors and outfit you with our own version of your Shrikes. The software isn't too different and Lieutenant Commander Marksman has already opened your data cores to us. We'll have your ship ready to fly in less than an hour." He snapped his finger gently next to his face.

"That's...very kind of you." Wyman reached the back of his hand to the trail left by the Daegon energy blast and felt residual heat through his glove. A few more inches the other way and...

"Come, I doubt you are used to this cold." Ranbir waved him out from under the fighter.

As the Indus man stood, Wyman reached for his turban. "Careful. Don't want to—"

Ranbir grabbed Wyman by the wrist, a metal bracelet jangling on the Indus' arm. The other two ground crewmen had their hands on the handles of knives at their waists, and Ivor and Sparks had frozen, unsure what was happening.

Ranbir let go of Wyman's wrist. "I am very sorry." Ranbir backed out from under the fighter. "You are so new to Theni and New Madras. You do not know our ways and I overreacted. But please, in the future, do not touch the turban of any baptized Sikh. It is an affront to God."

"I didn't know," Wyman said.

"And that is why no offense was taken." Ranbir put a hand on Wyman's shoulder. "Come, we have a short walk to the embassy where you'll be staying. Mr. Marksman is there waiting for you."

"Give me a minute," Sparks said, wiping a hand across his eyes and turning to the three Albion fighters. He looked to an empty space, where Flame Out would have landed, and went to one knee. With the knuckles of one hand pressed to the ground, he bent his head in prayer.

"Sorry," Wyman said quietly to Ranbir. "He's of the Order of Saint George…so was his wingman." Wyman looked to the sky and kissed the back of his fingers then raised his hand up for a moment. "Lost a pilot in orbit."

"My condolences," Ranbir said. "What Albion has been through…"

"We won't give up," Wyman said. "No matter what happens. Albion's light burns. Never give up."

He looked away to the mountains and the gray skies as snow began to fall.

Sparks got up, his head hung low, and Ivor put an arm over his shoulder.

Ranbir led them toward an open gate, he and Wyman a few steps ahead of the other two.

"You don't have…" Wyman flapped his arms against his flight suit as he began shivering, "a ground car or something?"

"All nonessential automation has been taken off-line for the duration," Ranbir said. "It's not a far walk. The circulation will warm you up. It's actually rather tepid for this time of year."

"Says the guy in the padded flight suit," Wyman muttered. "Old Earth geography wasn't my strongest subject, but Madras on the Indian subcontinent was a coastal city south of…south of someplace the Sikhs are from."

"Ah ha." Ranbir smiled, white teeth flashing within his bushy beard. "You're quite knowledgeable. My people are from Punjab, which is now under the Himalayan ice sheet. We tried to fight back the glaciers from the sacred Golden Temple, but in the end, God willed us to remove the place and use its bricks as the foundation for new temples across the stars. As for this planet's name of New Madras, there were not a lot of Sikhs in that city before the diaspora—there is a funny story to that. You know how the Second Reach War ended?"

"With the Reich conquering Francia and their navy on the ropes after Albion and the Indus crushed them at the Battle of Gamma Dargis. Peace talks broke down after some bombing killed most of the diplomats. I think we're still technically at war with the Reich…That's all we need. Those tin spurs and the Daegon against us."

The two stepped onto a sidewalk, passing boarded-up shops with signs in an alphabet Wyman couldn't read.

"The borders of several star nations were redrawn," Ranbir said, nodding, "and the Indus High Congress decided that New Madras would be their fortress world along the fringe of wild space. And Albion. Which we never considered like the pirate worlds. But New Madras was originally…farther from the Indus borders. The Reich managed to seize a number of our worlds as well during the war. When the High Congress wishes to settle a world that will not fall to invaders, they send my people, the Neo Sikh, to settle it first. We have a more martial tradition than most of the Indus."

"You're being polite," Wyman said. "The Reich steamrolled over the Indus with a less 'martial tradition' at the beginning of the war."

Ranbir sniffed. "And then my ancestors had to hold the line. But there is no bitterness or resentment here on New Madras, I assure you."

"I can tell." Wyman put his hands to his ears, the outer edges stinging with pain from the cold.

"The Daegon made a mistake if they think New Madras will surrender as easily as Bengal or the Cathay worlds," Ranbir said. "We will fight."

Wyman's mind went back to Albion and the first few hours of the Daegon's surprise attack on the planet. Ships burning in space. Cities alight from orbital bombardment. The armada the Daegon arrived with that seemed to fill the entire sky…

"You'll get one," Wyman said. "My pilots and I have tangled with the Daegon fighters. What do you fly? Chakrams?"

"That's correct." He tapped a badge sewn onto his flight suit.

"Then let us share what works against them with you all," Wyman said as they turned a corner.

The Albion embassy was surrounded by armored vehicles and Indus troops in light body armor. The metal coverings over their turbans almost struck Wyman as comical, but the brown stones of the embassy tugged at Wyman's heart strings; it almost looked like home.

"Yes, excellent." Ranbir handed him a plastic box the thickness of a finger. "A phone. Call me when you're free. And perhaps find some warmer clothes first. The run to the spaceport is fast during an alert, but if you wish to take your time getting to and from…"

"I'm going to be dressed like a damn polar bear next time you see me," Wyman said, his teeth chattering. "Pleasure meeting you. Now how the hell do I…"

An Albion Marine in combat armor and with a half mask over his mouth and nose waved at him at a turnstile gate.

"Warmth," Ivor said, pushing past Wyman and breaking into a run, "sweet heat, save me!"

Wyman and Sparks jogged after her.

CHAPTER 4

A man with deep blue skin and a wide, almost atavistic face glowered at a holo of New Madras as a cape clasped to his shoulders with golden chains grazed the deck of his ship, the *Medusa*. Lord Eubulus, a massive man even without his imposing armor—the glossy black of its polish trimmed with small punch spikes—ground his jaw, the teeth snapping as they passed each other.

In the holo, Albion ships arrived over the Indus planet and demolished the Daegon landing craft. He re-watched the destruction several more times, the sequence of events speeding up.

"This…is your fault, brother." Eubulus

turned to another Daegon, one with a more athletic build and black hair tied back with platinum thread.

"The *themata* are chaff," Tiberian said. "They're meant to be fed into the grinder to preserve better lives—Daegon lives."

"They should have landed five entire divisions on New Madras," Eubulus said, thrusting a hand at the holo. "Instead they barely managed six brigades in the initial landing zone. The ferals will beat them in short order and then they will have an asset on their side, Tiberian, an asset you were charged with destroying. Hope. They will see this battle as a victory, an easy one, and then it will be that much harder for me," his face flushed with anger, "and my men, to secure the planet. All because of you."

"I did not command the themata force you sent to Madras." Tiberian lifted his chin slightly.

"No. You were sent to kill the Albion royal family, which you did but except for a single child. A child! This child slipped out of your grasp again and again and now the child is on Madras and with a fleet from Albion." Eubulus flicked a small iron box hanging from Tiberian's neck. "Your writ from the

Baroness goes unfulfilled." He touched a similar box, one made of gold, hanging around his own neck. "My task remains, and now my chance to accomplish it quickly and easily is in jeopardy. Because of your failure."

"My writ remains." Tiberian grasped the box. "I will go to Madras and find Prince Aidan and capture him. Then I will bring him back to his world and parade him before his people so that they will lose the will to resist."

Eubulus shook his head and turned his attention back to the holo.

"Do you understand why the Baroness gave you such a task? One so important that it warranted the gold when it was first given? And it's not just because you are her favorite plaything in bed," Eubulus said.

"Albion is the template for our crusade," Tiberian said. "A proud kingdom, one with a long history of defiance and glory. Once it is laid low and the entire population bends the knee to us, other ferals will follow suit."

"So you do know," Eubulus said. "Then you

must know why your failure up to this point is putting the entire crusade at risk."

"Quit being so dramatic." Tiberian shook his head slightly. "Albion and its colonies are in compliance. Their young are being drafted into the themata. The cowards in their 'nobility' have pledged themselves to our cause. The Baroness has most of what she wanted…just not all of it. Not yet."

"Hope has spread." Eubulus lifted his chin to the holo. "The Albion ships you let get away have fought you. Beaten you. They know how we fight, our capabilities. They will teach these Indus what they've learned. These ships should be stragglers, the last survivors begging for safety and carrying tales of total defeat from world to world. Instead…they bear good news. Hope."

"Then we must take it away from them," Tiberian said.

"Hope that will spread to other systems. To the gathering of their leaders on Vishuddha. To the other star nations. Our House was ordered to break the ferals' will, to disorganize and fracture them for the rest of the Daegon families to seize with ease once they cross the Veil. If they arrive and encounter a unified resistance…they will make the Baroness pay. Even she has a writ from the Order."

Tiberian walked around the holo globe of New Madras. He touched a projected screen and data flowed across the planet's surface.

"You're…hesitating." Tiberian raised an eyebrow at his older brother. "The ferals have a child's grasp of slip-space travel. They thought destroying their nav buoys would slow our advance, but what they've done is back themselves into a corner. You see it the same as I do. The Albion ships are trapped in that star system. You can launch a full-scale assault from this system, Malout, right now…and be done with it. No false hope to spread. You'll have New Madras, and Vishuddha, within the timetable the Order has for our House. Yet here you are…whining."

"Bah," Eubulus huffed.

"You complain that the Albians destroyed so many of your themata in orbit, but they were the screen for the infiltration teams. They were the first to make it to the planet. They will sabotage every critical system on the planet within days. What are you waiting for? Launch the assault. So what if we have to burn a few more cities to bring them into compliance? There are always more ferals for the yoke."

"New Madras is not my only target, Tiberian." Eubulus swiped a palm across the holo and it dissolved and reformed into a local star cluster around the Indus world. "The Albians escaped from you, and their jaunt through ley lines unknown to us in wild space has changed the strategy. We can't risk the ferals doubling back on us through pathways unknown to us. The Baroness wants our gains secured…not at risk."

Locations of Daegon forces popped up through the stars.

"The spies we sent years ago gathered slip-space data for the major populated systems." Tiberian crossed his arms. "Not to the fringe systems…"

"Even our resources are limited…and time was not—and is not—on the Order's side," Eubulus said. "I'm forced to divide my fleets to secure these other systems and establish garrisons—*lingchi,* as

House Tang likes to call it. Death by a thousand cuts. And I am bleeding."

"Hardly," Tiberian sneered. "You have the ships to take New Madras now. Right now. And my *Minotaur* is with you."

"If we enter slip space to chase after your writ, I'll conquer New Madras—I'm sure of that," Eubulus said. "But at a significant loss of ships and Daegon lives. So significant that I will have to beg our cousins for help to push on to Vishuddha. They're having difficulty with the Cathay worlds...don't think they can spare ships and soldiers like I could do for you."

"You wait here and it will only get harder," Tiberian said. "They'll reorganize. Learn from the Albians. Bring in more ships and—"

"Nothing is getting into that system from Indus space." Eubulus reached into the holo and snipped the ley lines connecting New Madras to other major systems. "Lady Assaria granted me a flotilla of battleships from the Albion garrison force. They are en route now. While we wait, our specters will sow chaos."

"I want command of the battleships," Tiberian said. "I will use them to finish off the Albians and—"

Eubulus laughed—a deep, unkind noise that seemed to emanate from his dark heart. "The beggar demands to be the chooser," Eubulus said. "You and the *Minotaur* are under my command. The Albion ships are not my priority, only the boy prince as your writ is Assaria's will. Don't worry, brother. I'll let you loose once the time is right. Tug at your chain too hard and I'll see Gustavus take your ship."

"I could have left your son to die…" Tiberian said.

"I know, that's why I still tolerate you. The boy likes you, for some reason. He'll stay with you for a time. Teach him how to win for once, yes?"

"Thank our forefathers that the child looks like his mother," Tiberian said, "though his new scars make him almost as ugly as you."

"Ha!" Eubulus put a meaty hand on the back of Tiberian's neck and closed just tight enough to threaten. "Go repair your ship. A disorderly appearance is a sign of weakness."

Tiberian shoved the arm away, flicking the blades along the edge of his armor just enough to scratch the chain mail on Eubulus' under arm.

"Then I'll await your order to enter slip space...and then I can end this business for us both." Tiberian tapped the box hanging from his neck and bowed slightly.

CHAPTER 5

Captain Loussan of the Harlequin pirate clan pushed past one of his crewmen, keeping a close eye on the man's hands as he did so. Unpopular captains had a bad habit of catching a knife between the ribs when they weren't careful—and judging by the "accidental" shove he got from the crewman, Loussan was losing what little authority he had left over them. But given that they weren't even aboard his ship, being considered a "captain" was tenuous at best.

"By your leave, sir." Chavez smiled at Loussan and touched the brim on an imaginary hat. "Close quarters aboard this lovely vessel being what they are."

"Not as cramped as an Albion brig cell, now is it?" Loussan glanced around the interior of the *Joaquim,* the small cargo ship that he and most of his crew boarded to leave the New Madras system just before the ley line collapsed. His observation was obvious; what was unsaid—that he had got Chavez out of that brig cell—was also heavily implied.

"She's no *Carlin.*" With a bigger smile, Chavez revealed a few missing teeth and turned away.

Bringing up their last vessel, destroyed by the Daegon, stung Loussan. He hurried toward the ship's bridge, casting a furtive glance over his shoulder. Reaching the sealed door, he knocked out a quick code.

"Anyone else there?" came over a speaker.

"Tolan, we've done this so many time by now that—"

"Then you know the procedure."

Loussan rolled his eyes. "Eighteen crewmembers accounted for and not within rushing distance of the cabin door. Now let me in."

"And your nightmare toy?"

"Ruprecht is still powered down and still locked in a cargo pod. You have cameras all over the ship, Tolan. Just bloody look at them." Loussan put his hands on his hips.

There was a click and Loussan opened the heavy door just enough to squeeze himself through. He pulled it shut and the locks reengaged.

"Ugh…" Loussan wafted a hand beneath his nose and turned to Tolan sitting at the bridge controls. "When are you going to leave this place? You reek, Tolan. And coming from a man of my profession, that's saying something."

Tolan sat at one of two command seats, his bare feet up on the control panel. He wore a dirty bathrobe that might have been white once, but had gone gray after too many washings with other laundry. His boxer shorts with printed smiley faces and a sleeveless undershirt with some questionable stains had also seen better days.

Tolan's face was off—his nose soft, jawline loose and lips almost drooping. One eye seemed to have sunk slightly lower than the other.

"Pull yourself together, for shit's sake,"

Loussan said. "At least pretend to have a clue. It makes it easier to keep the others in line if I don't have to fake my confidence in you. I wouldn't throw you a shilling on Sicani if I saw you out on the street looking like that."

"You're the only one I let in here." Tolan pulled at his loose face and it snapped back like rubber. "And your opinion of me is not on my list of major concerns. What I do need is the name of a Reich tech expert on Bucky Station."

"We're going to Concord?" Loussan leaned against the bulkhead. "What happened to returning to Sicani to drop off my crew?"

"I ran into some folks that didn't have my best interests at heart the last time I was there." Tolan picked up a plastic cup from the deck and sipped from a straw.

"You owe them money."

"And they were all upset about it." Tolan raised a hand. "But now some blood's been spilled on top of a few late invoices. Not my fault, by the way, totally on them. As for Bucky Station, I need a Reich tech expert to make some repairs to a few off-market systems I have on this ship. Don't worry. I know the tech. But I do need your connections to get something else...new IFF codes. Clean IFF codes. From there, Concord has ley-line connections back to Albion space. Get me there and I'll make sure Commodore Gage commutes your entire sentence."

"Don't think the results of some *in absentia* trial mean a damn thing anymore," Loussan said. "I need a ride back to wild space."

Tolan glanced at the porthole.

"And my crew needs a ride back to wild space," Loussan added. "They're expecting Sicani."

"Sicani isn't happening for reasons already disclosed. It's Bucky Station in the Coventry system. Best I can do," Tolan said.

"I can dismiss my crew on Bucky...but I have to pay them off." Loussan raised a palm.

"Do I look like a man of means?" Tolan scratched his crotch.

"Commodore Gage is no fool. He knows spies like you need money to operate. And if you think you're going to secure the labor of a specialist Reich tech *and* a clean IFF transponder without cash...don't insult me. We both know how life works in wild space."

"OK." Tolan shifted in his seat. "Maybe I have a couple Albion-stamped troy ounces of gold aboard the ship. I can do five a head."

"You trying to get me killed?" Loussan asked. "Five troys won't last a week on Bucky. They need time to find a new ship to crew, and I don't know if anyone's hiring."

"Five troys is good for a couple months of room and board at a middling fleabag of a hotel. It won't last if they're drinking and whoring. Tell your crew not to be such a bunch of degenerates."

Loussan raised an eyebrow.

"Fine." Tolan slammed his cup on the control panel and blue slush jumped out and landed on his sleeve. "I can do seven."

"Ten or they'll mutiny."

"Busting my balls here...nine and you tell them you gave up your share to get it that high," Tolan said. "Which you are."

"Now wait just a second—"

Tolan rapped on the control panel. "You're

getting this fine ship, and all her tech, soon as my mission to Albion is done and I've linked back up with Gage. She's worth a lot more than a couple of troys, I'll tell you that much. And what will you do with her? Go back to the Harlequins?"

Loussan looked out the forward windows to the star swirl of slip space and said, "Don't think you understand family politics. Things are always complicated. The last big war was a boon time for us. Francia ships and crews coming in from the cold of Reich rule. Star nations focused on killing each other more than our extralegal capitalism…everyone got fat and rich. These Daegon, though…they seem like the type that'll turn a blind eye to free-space poaching?"

"Nope," Tolan said. "Seem like a bunch of right bastards to me. 'Free' space won't stay that way with them around."

"Used to be a good captain, good crew, good ship could always find another opportunity. Can't raid? Smuggle. Can't smuggle? Go freelance until you've got the resources…if nothing else you could always point your ship at a star with a habitable world and become a colonist," said Loussan. "True freedom is having a choice to make. I doubt we have a choice to fight the Daegon. I'll get your ship, Faceless, but I'll also know what you do about those bastards. Knowing an enemy is the first step in fighting them."

"Wow." Tolan sipped from his drink and the last of it burbled up the straw. "A pirate with a vision. Didn't think you guys could plan past your next bender and breakup with an exotic dancer."

"That's why I'm the captain," Loussan said, tapping his chest. "Now if you'll excuse me, I have to go sugarcoat the news about Bucky's and Concord. Just don't set down on the planet. Bunch of fanatics down there. Not our type. And I don't suggest you leave the bridge."

Tolan belched, then reached to one side of his seat and gave a pack of rations a quick pat.

"Have fun out there," he said and waggled his fingers at Loussan as he left.

CHAPTER 6

As Bertram wheeled a heavy suitcase behind him and followed a well-dressed woman on the edge of advanced age down a hallway, he glanced at a painting of Albion and the New Exeter palace on the walls.

A younger woman in a naval uniform followed right behind him, her back straight, her attention on the doors down the hallway.

"I'm sure Commodore Gage will appreciate the guest quarters," the older woman said. "The last senior military guest was here many years ago for joint exercises with the Indus, but budget constraints led to the last several iterations being cancelled, then it was indefinitely postponed. The locals would ask me about them every year like clockwork. Now there are Albion ships in orbit and my inbox is overflowing with—"

"Madam Ambassador, the quarters…" Bertram said, on the verge of wheezing, "they're close?"

"Here." She waved a hand across a sensor and a door slid open.

Bertram pulled the case inside then set it down very gently. The sailor walked the room, eyeing each power outlet and light fixture.

"Will the Commodore need any particular refreshment once he leaves his ship? The locals make excellent bedding if he'd prefer that to the Albion cloth we have here," Ambassador Carruthers asked.

"He won't be down long enough to sleep, even if he does leave the bridge," Bertram said, wiping sweat from his face.

"Then why did he—"

The sailor's uniform ripped away as Salis' armor flowed up and around her body from her back. The T-shaped glowing line formed on the front of her helm and diodes rippled up and down her arms.

Carruthers backed against the wall, one hand slapping at a button on her shirt.

"This room is clear," Salis said. "Let him out."

"Finally." Bertram popped open the suitcase and a puff of air escaped into the room. A little boy began wailing.

"Oh, I'm so sorry my Prince." Bertram picked Aidan up and bounced him against his knee. "I know it was dark and scary, but we had to—"

"Noooooo!" Aidan pushed his palms toward Salis, then buried his head against Bertram's shoulder. Bertram continued to try to calm the boy, whose cries degenerated to near-hyperventilation.

"That's…" Carruthers moved away from the wall. "That's Prince Aidan. Why didn't the Commodore tell me he was coming down here?"

"Because the prince is a target," Salis said. "The more people who think that the Crown Prince is aboard the *Orion*, the safer he'll be down here. You'll put this floor off-limits to your staff. All meals and items will be delivered to the elevator and received by Bertram or myself. But first, you'll do an immediate blood-panel test of all personnel with access to this embassy and give me—and only me—the results."

Still crying, Aidan swung his arms around Bertram's neck.

"Now wait a moment," Carruthers said. "This is my embassy and I will not take orders from some Genevan on a power trip. Exactly how old are you, young lady?"

"Old enough to give my last dying breath for Prince Aidan. Do you need Gage to put these orders in writing, have them transported to you digitally so every spy in the system can take a glance at such suspicious orders and then draw an obvious conclusion and put the prince at risk, or do you want to do what I tell you?" Salis' T-line glowed a little brighter.

"I'll see your requests are followed," Carruthers said, her face flushed. "If anyone asks, I'll insinuate he's keeping a mistress in here."

"Commodore Gage would never—" Bertram had raised a finger to protest and Aidan squirmed so hard that Bertram almost dropped him.

"Do either of you even know what you're

doing?" Carruthers took Aidan and sat him down on the bed. She reached out and touched Aidan's nose, prompting Salis to take a step forward. Bertram waved her off.

"Boop!" Carruthers wagged a bit of her thumb stuck between her fingers. "Got your nose."

Aidan stopped crying and chuckled. He wiped tears away and smiled at the ambassador.

"You have children?" Salis asked.

"Four," Carruthers said, stroking the back of her hand down the side of Aidan's face. "Seven grandkids. All on Albion. The better question is if I still have them, isn't it?" She leaned closer to Aidan and smiled. "Been a tough time, Your Highness? Every time things got scary…what happened?"

Aidan pointed at Salis, then buried his head in Carruthers' lap.

"He associates my armor with trauma," Salis said. "There's nothing I can do about it."

"They never taught you how to be with kids at your dojos or monasteries or whatever they are on Geneva, did they?" Carruthers asked, the words almost an accusation. "What he must have gone through…seen?" She tilted a head to a painting of King Randolph and Queen Calista.

Salis slapped Bertram on the arm and pointed at the painting. The steward took it off the wall, then removed every other bit of art depicting the royal family.

"That bad…" Carruthers stroked Aidan's hair. "I prayed it wouldn't be that bad…"

"Commodore Gage has things well in hand," Bertram said. "Well as can be, all things considered."

"Geneva is…three systems away by ley line," Carruthers said to Salis. "Would your people take him in?"

Salis' visor flowed back, the thin sheets forming a helmet around her head. "Geneva maintains strict neutrality in all conflicts," she said. "If we brought him to my home world…they would refuse him. Not my decision, that is the way of the Houses."

"This isn't another Reach War," Carruthers said. "These Daegon are a different beast entirely. The House Council would change their policy, if prompted."

"It doesn't matter to me where the Crown Prince is," Salis said. "I will be with him. Bertram, get the rest of the bags. Aidan's blood-sugar levels will bottom out in the next ninety minutes. He'll need to eat."

"Aren't you just a ray of sunshine," Carruthers said. "I can't imagine why Aidan doesn't like you around."

"I'm not a nanny. I'm his protector." Salis canted her head slightly.

"A child needs more than physical safety," Carruthers said. "So much more. We have a number of Albian women working as tutors for some of the wealthier Indus here in Theni. I can put out feelers for—"

"You've got the job," Salis said, nodding slightly.

"I'm the Albion ambassador." Carruthers' mouth was set in a firm line.

"You have a staff. You have a duty to the Crown and the prince. Whatever the Indus need from Albion, they will ask from Gage. Seems simple to me." Salis tapped on a wall. "We'll need the other side reinforced and a direct route to the bomb shelters. It will take me forty-nine seconds to get the prince into safety with the current layout. Genevan standard is thirty or less."

"Four decades in service and here I am taking orders from a whelp," Carruthers muttered.

"Where's the kitchen?" Bertram asked as he put clothes from the case into a dresser. "Do the locals have anything in the way of chicken nuggets with barbeque sauce?"

"They're all vegetarians down here," Carruthers said. "But we have proper food in the freezers."

Bertram shut a drawer, his mouth slightly open. "They don't eat…meat? Maybe we should go back into orbit." Bertram raised an eyebrow at Salis, who stared daggers back at him.

"Frozen food it is then."

****

Wyman held a hand over a panel in his

Typhoon's cockpit, his breath fogging with the canopy open and untreated air breezing past his face.

"Anytime?" He half leaned over one side to glance down at Indus technicians working under his fighter.

"Almost." A man wiped a hand through a beard thick with frost, then kicked a generator. "Activate your phase variance couplings."

"I told you," Wyman said, rolling his eyes, "we don't *have* phase variance couplings. We use mulita-phase inverters to cross the electron exchange and—"

"Yes, yes…" The tech waved a hand at him. "I meant this."

"You meant it last time and we fried aileron controls," Wyman deadpanned.

"Push the button! Aren't you cold?"

"Damn right I'm cold in this frigging snow cone of a planet," he muttered. "Activating!" He mashed a thumb against a button and his cockpit came to life. "Holy—it's working! No one touch anything!"

Wyman ran system diagnostics and closed the

canopy. Hot air rushed through vents and he loosened the top of his borrowed jacket and sighed, like he'd stepped into a sauna after a long day.

There was a knock on the canopy. Ranbir was there, slashing fingertips across his throat to tell Wyman to cut the power.

Wyman mimed not being able to hear, and Ranbir waved his hand harder.

"Never a minute off with these guys." Wyman shut his Typhoon down and reopened the canopy.

"Your systems check out," Ranbir said. "My techs will get your bird green across the board, but they will work faster if you're not around distracting them."

"No need to make fancy excuses to get me into someplace warmer." Wyman lurched out of the cockpit, his muscular frame leaving little room for maneuvering. "Where's Ivor?"

"Waiting for us," Ranbir said as the two walked toward the exit where armed soldiers stood ready, all huddled near a portable heater. "She invited me to your embassy for dinner, but I've no taste for Albion food. Everything is boiled in a pot and everything has meat in it. Won't you two come with me to *langar?*"

"If it's someplace warm, I'm all for it." Wyman pressed a gloved finger against the side of his nose, feeling the frozen snot creak against the touch.

"Certainly," Ranbir said. They passed a shop and Ivor came out, nearly slipping on the ice.

"I'm getting the hang of this," she said as she shuffled toward them, keeping her feet as flat against the sidewalk as she could. "Busting your ass a couple times will teach you the right way."

"There." Ranbir pointed down the street to a gold-wrapped flagpole with a yellow triangle at the top. "That Gurdwara has langar in the next few minutes. You are always welcome to come here, but it's best I accompany you this first time."

"Vouch that we're not Daegon?" Wyman asked, glancing up at the darkening sky.

"If the Daegon came in peace, they would be welcome at langar," Ranbir said. "Tell me, why New Madras? Why did your fleet come here?"

"There's no sugarcoating it," Wyman said. "We were on the run and thought we'd find friends here…and we have, by all accounts."

"Indus and Albion have been allies for centuries," Ranbir said. "If things were different, if the Daegon had come for our worlds first…I believe Albion would have welcomed us."

"It's not like we or you are the Reich," Ivor said. "They gave a raw deal to any Francia military they captured. And you ever hear about that convoy from the Elko colony that ran from the last Mechanix incursion? Hit Reich space and vanished."

"Rumors for children," Ranbir said.

"Two hundred forty thousand people don't just 'vanish,'" Wyman said. "Albion was with the Indus when things were dicey during the Second Reach War. Things are sure dicey now."

"The fighting at Punam is nearly over," Ranbir said. "Many martyrs, but every one is a gift to keep this community free."

"That's one way to look at it," Wyman said as they entered the Gurdwara, a smaller temple than the one in the center of the city. Many Indus were already there, handing over coats to a man behind a counter and taking small plastic tabs in exchange.

"Shoes," Ranbir said and pointed to the Albion pilots' feet. "Remove them please. Leave the dirt outside."

"If there's an alert, we'll be running back to the flight line in bare feet," Ivor said, giving Wyman a worried glance.

"Military personnel have their own storage. The *sewadars*—volunteers—know the drill," Ranbir said.

"Smells good," Ivor said as she pulled off a boot and knocked packed snow off over a grate in the floor. "Anything's better than the emergency rations the embassy had. Tea from concentrate this morning…how far we've fallen."

Wyman got his boots off and Ranbir took them away. The two Albians stood close together, both looking out of place in their flight suits of foreign make and both with complexions and hair colors at odds with the locals, who seemed oddly benign to their presence.

"You know what *langar* means, don't you?" Ivor asked. "Because it doesn't translate to 'barbecue the foreigners,' right?"

"Really, Ivor? This is hospitality. Show some class…and if they were going to eat us, they wouldn't bother fixing our fighters." Wyman said.

"And these," Ranbir said, handing Wyman a yellow bit of cloth. "Over your head, please. And for you…" He gave Ivor a head scarf covered in embroidered flowers.

Wyman tugged at the elastic band, then put the simple cap over his hair. Ivor looked at the unintimidating pattern of the scarf, raised an eyebrow at Wyman, then wrapped it over her head and down one shoulder like the other women entering the Gurdwara.

"Is there a wedding?" Ivor asked as more people filed past them into a larger room.

"No…but there are more people here than usual," Ranbir said as they joined the crowd. The larger room was devoid of pews as Wyman expected for a church. Instead, long lines of rugs ran down the length of the space. At the far end were several men playing simple wooden instruments and a raised platform with an open book.

Indus moved past them, already knowing

where to go.

"Where…is there an officers' mess?" Wyman asked Ranbir.

"At a langar? No, no." Ranbir gestured to one of the rugs. "Here beggars eat next to kings, and all are equal before the Guru Granth. Come." He led them to a rug and they sat between two sets of families with small children, mothers and grandmothers watching over them all.

The kids stared wide-eyed up at Wyman and Ivor as they sat down. One of the children spoke to Ranbir and reached for Ivor's hair. A grandmother pulled him away and chided the boy.

"What?" Ivor asked.

"Your hair." Ranbir rolled his eyes. "He's never seen gold hair before. He doesn't think it's real."

"Better be real, you know how much trouble I go through to keep it conditioned? Too easy to just shave it all like this scrotum." She elbowed Wyman.

"Everyone eats here?" Wyman asked, giving a volunteer a quick wave as a plate was set down in front of him. "Just like this?"

"And all are welcomed," Ranbir said. "No one is ever turned away. This is part of the Guru's message—we are all equal before God and all are worthy of respect."

"Doubt our VIP could ever come here," Ivor said. "The minder would lose her damn mind at being around so many people."

"Shame," Wyman said, "he—the VIP—could use a break. Poor kid."

Flatbread with a strong odor of garlic was set onto Wyman's plate, then a volunteer with a trolley wheeled past and ladled onto it, beside the bread, scoops of lentils in green sauce, then cauliflower covered in orange spices, then yogurt. The volunteer smiled at Wyman and held up another ladle.

"You're so big," Ranbir said. "He thinks you're hungry."

Wyman looked down the line to see many more children, all looking expectantly at the cart.

"No need." Wyman waved a hand over his plate and the server moved along.

"It's different." Ivor poked her flatbread into her lentils. "Being on the ships, we never see the people on the ground…never really know who we're fighting for. Makes me…" She sniffed and wiped a sleeve across her eyes. "My God…all those people back on Albion. We just…we just cut and run, didn't we, Freak Show?"

Wyman put an arm around her shoulders and conversation died down.

"You know why we had to leave…who we were protecting." He gave her a squeeze and she nodded quickly.

"But you all wouldn't do that?" she asked Ranbir. "You wouldn't sacrifice others for one person. Not when everyone is perfectly equal."

"Equal in the eyes of God is one thing." Ranbir's face turned down. "Equal before men…is another. Our leaders have bodyguards. We lock our doors at night. We will kill the Daegon to save Indus and Albion. No one here judges you. And please…no touching."

Wyman lifted his arm up and scooted away from Ivor.

"We didn't just get married, did we?" Ivor asked, her face going pale.

"No, no, that's the Kongs. The Cathay Dynasty has very odd customs," Ranbir said.

"Oh, that's a relief," Wyman said.

"That's...a relief to you too." Ivor's face scrunched in anger. "Not that I want to—you know what I mean. Shut up, Wyman. This green stuff is yummy. What do you call it?"

"Dahl," Ranbir said. He looked over a shoulder to the front of the room, where a pair of soldiers spoke to an elderly man with a beard so long it almost reached his waist. "Hurry up and eat...I think there's a storm on the horizon."

CHAPTER 7

Thorvald tapped into his shuttle's telemetry data and an overlay cast onto the HUD on the inside of his visor. They were still on course for Theni City, with two squadrons of Typhoons from the *Orion* as escort. The Genevan glanced at Commodore Gage where he sat on a rough bench bolted to the side of the cargo bay. The Commodore leaned against a corner, his eyes closed, his respiration and body temperature indicating he was still awake.

The AI within Thorvald's armor nudged his attention to the escape pod.

Easy, Grynau, plenty of time to save our principal if there's an issue.

+Alert+ came from the AI.

I am. I am. Monitor escort frequencies for anything amiss. The Daegon wreckage was swept for survivors, but something may have been missed.

He felt a bit of warmth through his armor. The AI was happiest when it had a task. Older intelligences like Grynau were known to be temperamental, and given the difficulty he'd had bonding with the AI, he was thankful for any progress in their relationship.

"Thorvald," Gage said, yawning and stretching one leg out at a time. He wore formal dress of a red tunic and riding boots, and he had a sheathed sword across his lap.

"Sir."

"I'm grateful for your and Salis' protection. I doubt we would have been able to stop that Faceless assassin aboard my ship without your help, but something's been gnawing at me. Haven't had time to process it until now." Gage stood and checked his hair in a mirror, then stepped back and touched his ribbons.

"By the king, they're upside down." He

unzipped his tunic, revealing a thin vac suit beneath, and set the top onto the bench. "Bertram would have never let me out of my quarters looking like this."

"My apologies," Thorvald said.

"Not your job." Gage unsnapped the ribbons from the inside of his tunic and set them right. "But as to your job…I'm no expert on Genevans or your technology. I know you keep some of the finer details as trade secrets and you're forbidden from telling me anything about our operation by the terms of your employment…unless there's an issue that would affect my safety. Or Prince Aidan's."

+Truth+

Always. Always truth with him.

"You and your armor…seem to be at odds," Gage continued, not privy to the discussion between Thorvald and the AI. "That was Captain Royce's suit, correct?"

Sorrow washed over Thorvald, and he felt sympathetic emotion from Grynau.

"That is correct, sir."

"And you had to don that suit during the Daegon attack…but why weren't you in your own armor when that attack came?" Gage asked.

+Traitor+

"I…I was bare due to…" His armor tightened around his jaw, warning him against a lie. Thorvald rubbed his chin. "I broke my oath to the King. This is why. I broke my oath and I was caught and Captain Royce stripped me of my Yarvisha—my suit AI—and was to send me back to Geneva in chains…and he was right to do it."

Gage leaned toward Thorvald, elbows on his knees. "I need all the details, Thorvald. I'm not an expert on your planet or your contracts, but being stripped of your…AI strikes me as a serious issue. So serious that I don't understand how Captain Royce's suit can tolerate you."

"There have been…issues," Thorvald said, "but this AI and I share the same purpose: to protect the Albion royal family. An oath I will honor to my last dying breath—even if I lapsed in my duties. What happened was that I…fell in love." A cold pit opened in Thorvald's stomach. "We are to have no relations during our contracts, and after almost twenty years on Albion, I grew lonely. Then I met an off-world woman named Helena. A chance encounter in the palace. Small talk that I should never have entered into grew into a temptation to speak further…and I took it."

"I have a hard time believing Captain Royce took such umbrage against something like small talk," Gage said.

"Violating protocol would not have voided my contract with the King, but I compromised the palace's communications security to speak with Helena. After almost two decades helping to oversee all aspects of the family's safety and security, I found a number of vulnerabilities. We constantly challenge other Genevans to find ways to infiltrate the grounds or otherwise endanger our principals…we don't really have hobbies…and I kept a few flaws close to my chest to assist in our games. When I wanted to speak with Helena, I used one of those flaws."

"And you were caught," Gage said.

"Helena was not as careful as I was. Someone piggybacked off her messages to me and almost compromised the entire cyber-protection suite. While the techs were fighting off the hacker…they found me. I don't deny what I did. It was stupid. My actions put the royal family at risk and that is unforgiveable to a Genevan. To anyone."

+Traitor…fool+

"And what of Helena?" Gage asked.

"Killed on Albion during the Daegon attack is my guess." Thorvald shifted his weight from foot to foot. "She no longer matters. My oath to Albion, and to you as regent and to Prince Aidan, remains. To my last dying breath."

"And I thought Genevan guards were incorruptible." Gage leaned back, his palms flat on his thighs. "If I'd known of this when you first arrived aboard the *Orion*…I don't know if you'd still be in service. But I saw what you did to protect Aidan when that Faceless was loose aboard my ship. And you fought your way out of the palace with the prince. I have your correct actions as a bodyguard on one hand," he turned a palm up, "and your indiscretions on the other." He mimed a scale between both hands. "Which weighs more, Thorvald?"

+Protect him. Protect him at all costs+ The

AI tightened the armor against his chest and back, squeezing him like a vice.

"My life is yours," Thorvald said. "If you have doubts, then my AI will abandon me and you can leave me on the planet to fend for myself. I only ask that you send Grynau to Geneva. My House will reward you for its safe return."

"Sent on to Geneva…there's food for thought. No, Thorvald, you'll stay with me. With Aidan. But as this war with the Daegon goes on…I may not have any choice. The bounty your House offers on the AI and armor you wear is substantial," Gage said.

"I don't understand," Thorvald said, a cold blade of fear against his heart.

Gage removed a small tablet from a pocket and tapped the screen.

"Fleets cost money. The operations cost of just entering slip space to go from one system to another is substantial. Factor in repairs, munitions manufacture and even payroll and it's pretty obvious why stateless ships turn pirate so quickly—like the Francia military did after the Reich rolled through their systems. If I have to decide between keeping you and Salis around and losing capabilities for lack of funds…it's not a choice I want to make, but if it comes to that…"

"I understand, sir," Thorvald said. "We serve at your discretion."

"Which is why we're even bothering to go dirtside," Gage said. "The Indus have been generous since we arrived, but that goodwill dried up pretty quick after they fought their first Daegon. Their promise of equipment and repair docks has yet to materialize. So a little public-relations campaign is in order. Whatever resources I can glean from them are resources we don't have to conjure up on our own."

"I thought the *Helga's Fury* could sustain the fleet indefinitely," Thorvald said.

"The *Helga* and the *Mukhlos* could, but the loss of one ship hobbled our sustainment capabilities." Gage rubbed his face. "And even the *Helga* needs access to raw materials. What she's got aboard will be exhausted in a few more days. I could be the finest tactical commander in settled space, but if I don't have the logistics to back me up, then I'm essentially useless. But let's not lose sight of the bigger picture. You and Salis…you risked your lives and you saved Prince Aidan on more than one occasion. You kept Albion's last hope alive, and you have my gratitude."

"I can never redeem myself for what I've done," Thorvald said. "All I have left is service…and penance."

"I doubt your security breach led to the Daegon attack on my home. I'm going to guess that your error isn't going to amount to much in the long run, so let's put it behind us. Agreed?"

+Oath breaker…coward+

Thorvald willed away his AI's emotions and did his best to smile, the corners of his mouth moving unevenly.

"I serve to my last dying breath," Thorvald said, bowing slightly.

"And I could not ask for more." Gage stood and smoothed out his uniform. "Ever been to an Indus social function? They're something else."

****

Gage walked down the shuttle ramp, his breath fogging. Two columns of Indus troops in almost-gaudy blue uniforms with yellow and gold trim formed a cordon to a waiting ground car. The car was of Old Earth style, with garlands of flowers strung up on the sides.

Ambassador Carruthers waited next to the car, bundled up against the cold.

The Indus soldiers brought rifles up, slapped them against white-gloved hands, and rendered a salute as Gage's first step touched New Madras soil.

"Who authorized this?" Thorvald said, tension in his words.

"I'm a head of state, technically," Gage said and lengthened his stride slightly to reach the waiting car faster. Carruthers opened the door and Gage slid into the much warmer interior. Thorvald went to the front seat as the ambassador joined Gage in the back.

Gage blew warm air on his hands as the car drove forward.

"Pleasure to meet you in person, sir," Carruthers said. "Our guest has settled in, but there are a number of…concerns."

"Bertram can handle anything he needs."
Gage looked out the window as the car left the
spaceport and joined an escort of Indus armored
vehicles, drones buzzing overhead.

"Bertram is doing his best, but he lacks any
sort of psychological training," Carruthers said. She
touched a button and a screen went up between the
passenger seats and the front. Thorvald looked over
his shoulder to them, and Gage raised a hand to calm
the bodyguard.

"The boy needs a psychologist," Carruthers
said. "He's shutting down emotionally and that is not
the way little boys should be."

"He's gone through a lot that most little boys
haven't," Gage said. "You bring in someone from the
Indus, that puts him at risk. There's not…there's not
much else I can do, Ambassador."

"Do you think the embassy is the only Albion
presence on New Madras?" She furrowed her brows
at Gage. "We've had a presence here for over two
hundred years. Between expat teachers,
businessmen—let me show you." She picked up a

tablet from the side of her seat and handed it to Gage. "There is a comprehensive list of every known Albion citizen in this star system. The Indus immigration department gave this to me, and almost all of them have been in contact with my staff since word of the invasion hit. They all want answers and I've had *nothing* for them until you arrived."

Gage swiped the list of names up, scanning the occupations. "I take it there's a psychologist on here that can help your guest?"

"There are five," she said.

"Then pick the best and bring them in. Once they enter the embassy, they don't leave. No contact with anyone outside. That understood?" Gage asked.

"Commodore—I mean Regent—Gage, that's a tall order. All five have families and—"

Gage rapped the corner of the tablet against the door.

"As you wish." Carruthers raised her chin slightly. "Worse comes to worse, I'll just have to move the family into the embassy as well. Not that we have room for any more after your security detail was added to our Marine complement."

"Send a copy of this up to Captain Price, my executive officer," Gage said. "Any and all with military experience will be reactivated under the Emergency Decrees. The fleet needs every able body it can find."

"Naturally," Carruthers said. "And when will you address the Albians here? You are the Regent, after all. You are the Crown."

"How many are there?"

"Fifteen thousand, four hundred and twelve," she said. "Not counting spouses or children with Indus citizenship."

"Another priority for me," Gage said. "How did King Randolph deal with an entire planet and colonies?"

"He was raised for the job from birth. You're still used to being just a naval officer, isn't that right? Now you have head of state, chief of law enforcement…could you imagine if Congress was still in session?"

"I'd rather not. I have enough headaches as it is. Bring whatever Albian citizens you can to the spaceport. I'll speak to them on my way back to the

Orion. Fair enough?"

"Easy enough," she said. "We'll be at the governor's palace in a few minutes. How much do you know of Indus culture? Neo Sikh culture in particular?"

"I was going to read the primer your office sent over, but I fell asleep on the shuttle."

"Then you need to listen to me very carefully…"

****

The car pulled beneath a gold-plated arch adorned with carvings of elephants and script Gage couldn't read. Thorvald was out of the car before it came to a complete stop, his fierce appearance as an almost-medieval armored knight in stark contrast to the Indus soldiers arrayed around the entrance to the palace.

An Indus steward in a richly embroidered tunic opened the door for Gage, his head bowed as Gage exited. The Commodore adjusted the sword at his hip and followed Thorvald inside, Carruthers just behind him. The interior was done up in bright colors, and massive murals depicting holy men on Old Earth took up the walls.

Admiral Chadda, wearing a sword on both hips, bowed quickly to Gage, then offered his hand. The Indus man was shorter than Gage anticipated, the top of his turban barely reaching Gage's chin. Every inch of him struck Gage as a warrior, even though his feet were bare.

"Commodore, a pleasure, welcome to Theni palace," Chadda said. "We have food waiting for you. Please come with me."

"Admiral, time is of the essence," Gage said. "If we could—"

Carruthers cleared her throat.

"If we could please hurry," Gage said.

"Certainly, but we must continue in a manner that is rightly guided, don't you agree?" Chadda motioned to a set of double doors and they opened as they neared. Inside was a crowd of Indus military officers and others who Gage assumed were key political leaders. All the men had full beards. The women wore bright-colored sarongs over insulated body gloves. He wondered what effect the curved knives on every hip—man and woman—had on Thorvald.

A long table was set with food that smelled spicier than anything Bertram made in the small kitchen attached to Gage's quarters aboard the *Orion*.

On a raised dais, three men in white robes holding simple musical instruments sat behind a table covered in a white sheet.

"Let us receive wisdom from Guru Granth Sahib," Chadda said. The sheet came off the table, revealing an open book so big it looked like it needed two men to carry it.

"Who is the Guru?" Gage asked, pointing at the men behind the dais.

"The Guru is the scripture," Chadda said.

The Indus sat down without prompting, and when Carruthers pulled against Gage's elbow, he followed suit, shifting his sword across his lap. Two men came over to Gage and gripped the heels of his boots.

"You *were* serious about this part," Gage said under his breath to Carruthers and let them remove his boots.

Chadda looked at Thorvald, who went to one knee. The armor around his feet and ankles flowed back and bunched around his shins.

The musicians played a gentle tune and a man opened the massive book to a seemingly random page and recited in tune with the music. A few minutes later he closed the book and replaced the sheet.

Gage stood up with Chadda and the same two men replaced Gage's boots with practiced efficiency. A woman with henna tattoos up and down her hands handed Gage a plate of food. Thorvald passed a palm over the plate and blue flight glowed from the seams of his glove.

"We would never—" Chadda began, angry.

"I lost my admiral to one we trusted," Gage said. "These are difficult times for everyone. Please excuse his tenacity." He looked at the food: a simple mix of flat bread, a green paste he couldn't identify, and a small mound of nuts.

A scrum of officers and civilians formed around Chadda, all speaking to him rapidly. Chadda raised both hands up next to his turban and said stern words in the local dialect.

Gage glanced at Carruthers.

"They've lost their appetite and want to get to brass tacks, sir," she said.

"Finally." Gage reached his plate toward the table, but Carruthers pushed his arm back to him as the Indus stood in silence, watching Gage. Dipping the bread in the paste, Gage took a bite.

"Now we can go." Carruthers took the plate from him and Chadda ushered him to a set of hidden doors that opened from the wall.

Inside was a command center, with a single holo table in the center and tired-looking Indus men and women at workstations arrayed in expanding rings around the holo.

"The battle for Punam City continues," Chadda said as he led Gage to the center of the room. "The Daegon dropped troops, but with very little means of support. Their soldiers fight on even after they've run out of ammunition. We've taken no prisoners."

"By choice?" Gage asked as he walked down the small corridor between rings. The Indus all had their eyes on him, their tired gaze filled with hope.

"We are merciful, even to the most merciless of enemies," Chadda said. "The Daegon do not surrender. The wounded we come across kill themselves before we can treat them. Those too badly injured to resist are finished off by other Daegon or a…" he gestured to his neck, "some sort of a choker around their necks that cuts their arteries."

"Not all their dead have the chokers," said an Indus officer in the white uniform of their Medical Corps. "We've found a number of them that…there's something wrong with them." He touched a panel and holo plates appeared in the tank, each showing the corpse of a Daegon, their helmets removed and faces exposed, their skin in green, blue or purple hues.

"Are they aliens?" Chadda asked. "We've run a genome analysis and—"

"They're human," Gage said. "Just as human as we are. You found they had significant radiation-exposure traits?" The medical officer nodded. "That's consistent with the dead we've examined. Their leadership caste is…apart from their foot soldiers. The Daegon repeat '*nobis regiray*' as either a command

103

or a battle cry. It's derived from Latin for 'you will be ruled' or words to that effect. It's the only real clue we have to their culture. One of my agents brought a tech sample to a Martian and found a connection to Earth from just before the Mount Edziza disaster that sent the home world into an Ice Age and wrecked civilization for nearly two hundred years. Their evil is all too human. We need to accept that."

"There is no evil," Chadda said, "only the karma that we reap for ourselves. These Daegon are a new test from God, through *dhiraj* and *nioan* will we defeat—"

"Are those weapon systems?" Gage asked.

Chadda tugged at his beard. "You do not understand. This is not a simple clash of void ships that we are fighting, but a battle of the spirit."

"Admiral, you may fight the spiritual battle as you see fit. I can only help you fight the Daegon on the material plane. Can we focus on that?" Gage asked, trying to stifle his annoyance even as Carruthers gasped faintly.

"Please," Chadda said and gestured to the holo tank.

Gage reached into the tank and zoomed out to see all of New Madras and the two nearby moons.

"The enemy prefers to fight at very close range," Gage said. "Their control of slip space is far superior to our own and when they attack again, we won't have much time to respond. I suggest moving your fleets to cover the *Amritsar* and screen above the major population centers."

He moved icons of Indus units to new positions over the planet, with three fleets very close to the star fort.

"We do that and we've got a ball and chain around our ankle," Chadda said. "Maneuvering so close to the gravity well is difficult. We're practically stationary targets." The Admiral touched the holo and the icons returned to their original spots. "This is how we've defended our star systems since the First Reach War. We protect the high orbitals to deny any enemy the chance to bombard the cities."

"And traditionally a planet will surrender once an enemy has the orbitals," Gage said, "as they're helpless against the destruction that would rain down on them from the ships that control their skies. I'm aware of this, Admiral, but the Daegon are not an enemy that holds to the same rules the Reich or the Mechanix do. They...they overran Albion's defenses in hours. And they did it because our Home Fleet was arrayed just as you're suggesting. The Daegon came in close to the atmosphere and our ships farther away couldn't respond with long-range munitions for fear of hitting their homes on the surface. The Daegon use our own cities as shields. They count on us being unwilling to kill our own civilians...and they're right about that. We won't trade those lives."

"And this is why the Indus have been allied with Albion for so long," Chadda touched Gage's arm. "We aren't that different from each other."

"We can't fight this enemy the way we want to fight them," Gage said. "They have their own tactics, and our way to victory is to exploit their vulnerabilities. They don't have many options to use their blitz tactics on New Madras. Move our ships closer to the planet. Be there with guns ready to blow them out of the void the moment they appear."

Chadda clicked his tongue. "But if we are not as close...the Daegon will offer us battle there. A slugging match over a city guarantees collateral damage to the city. Don't forget what happened to Locronan when the Reich attacked the Francia as they were evacuating the city."

"I'm aware of what happened. Millions killed when a shell hit a dam and flooded the city. Naturally the Reich and Franks blames each other. But what I'm telling you, Admiral, is that a fight in the low orbitals is unavoidable. The Daegon have already attacked Punam using these same tactics and—"

"And they're nearly defeated," Chadda said. "Our Army is second to none. If the few remaining Daegon have some way to communicate to their commanders, then they know it is futile to try and beat us on the ground. We have the spirit of Havaldar Ishar Singh."

"I don't know who…you're not listening." Gage took a slow breath to calm himself.

"Your assessment of the Daegon holds for their initial attack." Chadda crossed his arms over his chest. "But I must respectfully disagree with you as to their next steps. They will carry out a more conventional attack. My fleets will remain farther from the gravity well to respond to any Daegon incursion."

Gage looked over Chadda's shoulder to the Indus officers behind him. They nodded and spoke amongst themselves, seemingly in agreement with the Admiral.

Gage clasped his hands behind his back. Continuing to argue with Chadda would only make things worse. He'd taken a position in front of his staff—and, by proxy, every soldier and sailor under his command. To change after such a pronouncement would appear weak and indecisive. While Gage didn't hold the same rank as Chadda, he knew when a commander could not be moved from a decision. Call it tunnel vision, call it obstinacy…it was a fact of leadership that Gage could recognize, but one he knew he couldn't change quickly and easily.

But to defend this planet, and give his fleet and Prince Aidan a chance to survive, he had to bring Chadda around.

"Admiral, this is your command and your responsibility," Gage said. "I and the Albion fleet are your allies…but we are your guests as well. May I suggest we carry out war games in the holo? Perhaps we can glean better tactics, together, that way."

"While a ground battle is still on going?" Chadda shook his head. "While the Daegon could return at any moment? We can't afford time for 'games,' Commodore."

Gage's jaw clenched, but he forced himself to relax. Further argument would only damage his relationship with the Indus.

"Then let us discuss repairs to my ships," Gage said. "You have nine mobile void docks in orbit. I need three of them to bring my destroyer force to full strength."

"This I can do." Chadda smiled. "Some tea?"

Gage nodded slowly as worst-case scenarios played out in the back of his mind.

****

Gage tapped the tip of his sword scabbard against the floorboard of his ground car as it drove back to the spaceport. He eyes passed over Indus on the streets, civilians going about their lives as seemingly normal as ever.

His face was hard, and he ground his teeth ever so slightly.

"That bad?" Carruthers asked.

"Fool," Gage said. "Myopic. Close-minded. Fool."

"From a diplomat's point of view, you did great," she said. "We had to fight the first half of the Second Reach War without the Indus. They do come around...just takes them awhile."

"Their ships will be flaming comets over these skies and their cities will be on fire before they 'come around,' Ambassador," Gage said. "Albion has paid the blood price to know how the Daegon fight, and Chadda doesn't seem to care."

"Then what do we do, Regent?" she asked.

"I can't evacuate every Albian on this planet," Gage said. "And if I could, where would we go? Our colonies and our home world are under Daegon rule. We've been reduced to an itinerant people. I was raised such that Albion was—is—the bright light of civilization on the edge of settled space. Now that light is here on New Madras and...and it's flickering,

Carruthers. I'm no Admiral Sartorius. He knew the Indus better than I. He would have left that room with more than dock time on ship tenders and a half promise for our staff—not commanders—to carry out war games."

"Again, you did very well from where I stood," she said. "Chadda isn't known for his competence among the senior leaders of this planet, but all the criticism for him evaporated as soon as the first Daegon ship came in through slip space. Indus aren't the types to try to wrest away military control at the first sign of trouble. They view that as on par with shuttle passengers trying to take over the cockpit when turbulence hits mid-flight."

Gage mumbled.

"And what will you do once the nav systems have enough data to make the slip-space journey out of this system?" she asked.

"Vishuddha," Gage said. "Meet with the rest of the League, organize a counteroffensive to liberate Albion…something that'll be easier to do if I can show up with a victory here on New Madras."

"The League…the mutual defense pact of the

treaty was meant to convince the Reich from starting a third Reach War. The Daegon are a new threat, whoever or whatever they are," Carruthers said. "Do we even know how strong they are? How many ships they have?"

"You think the League is a waste of time?"

"No, Regent, I'm saying that convincing the League to launch an offensive to retake Albion isn't going to be easy. You think the Cathay emperor will just give you his Golden Fleet and leave the Forbidden Planet unguarded when there could be a Daegon armada on the way to his throne world?"

"The Daegon will defeat us in detail, take us out one by one, if the League doesn't act as one and hit back. That's the reasoning behind the entire mutual defense pact. There are enough rational leaders through the League to realize this," Gage said.

"Not in my decades of politics. People are people, and when they're afraid rationality is an early casualty. And what of your subjects here?" she asked. "You need an answer to that, sire, because Albians are waiting for you at the star port."

"'Sire?' I'm no noble, Carruthers. I'm as

common born as they come," he said.

"You are the Regent. We see you as the Crown, like it or not…and you need an answer in the next few minutes. We're almost there."

"Blast it." Gage looked through the front windshield to see a crowd gathered around a hangar. "I forgot all about…can we…" He seemed to shrink into his seat. "I did agree to meet with them, didn't I?"

"You did, sire," she said.

"Stop calling me that, feels wrong. Just 'Commodore,' all right?"

"Yes, sire. May I suggest you tell them something to quell their fear?"

"I'll tell them the truth, no matter how painful it may be," Gage said. "Chadda was all about karma. I may not believe in it, but I can see the value in not telling them the situation is all milk and honey then being contradicted by a Daegon attack minutes later."

"I'm just glad it's you that has to do this," Carruthers said. "I'm getting too old to keep a happy face on all the time."

"The crowd scans clear of any weapons,"

Thorvald said over his shoulder. "Remember the mob protocols."

"These are Albians, Thorvald," Gage said. "They're our people."

"Remember the protocols." The Genevan got out of the car before it rolled to a stop. A throng of people, their skin tones running a different spectrum than the generally darker complexion of the Indus, stood just beyond a single line of local soldiers.

Gage steadied himself, then got out as Thorvald opened the door for him. A wave of questions and shouts met him, and Gage's heart broke as he heard so many familiar accents. One set of parents held up a squalling infant, the father waving frantically at Gage.

Gage put one hand on the engine compartment of the car and vaulted onto the hood, his boot heels denting the metal.

"Stop!" Gage held up the hilt of his sword. "Stop," he repeated louder and the din died down. He looked over the faces in the crowd, a knot forming in his chest.

"I am Commodore Thomas Gage,

Commander of the 11th Fleet," he said. "What you've heard of Albion, that the Daegon attacked without cause or mercy, that they took the planet and the colonies...is true."

A wail started in the crowd.

"I have no specific information about your loved ones back home, forgive me. The 11th Fleet, and all of you on New Madras and the rest of our countrymen across settled space...we are the light. We are what remains free. And while just one of us is alive, Albion will not die. We must fight on until we stand on free Albion soil and look to skies that belong only to us. This was the first promise of King George when he founded the Kingdom and, as Regent, that promise lives on."

"Get us out of here!" someone shouted.

"I have warships in orbit," Gage said, shaking his head, "not colony ships or passenger liners. You are safer here, on New Madras. Stay here and keep the light burning. I will fight to keep you alive. I will not stop until we can return home, but for now I need you all here."

"What of King Randolph? Prince Jarred?"

came from the crowd.

"Dead." Gage swallowed hard. "But the royal family still lives and I serve as Regent."

"Who put you in charge?" asked a heavyset man in the back.

"King Randolph's succession plan is part of the Genevan oaths." Gage pointed to Thorvald. "If I am wrong to take on the mantle of Regent, than he will treat me as a threat to the Crown. And if I am a threat to the Crown?"

Thorvald mimed crushing a skull.

"And I couldn't stop him if I tried," Gage said. "Regent or not, I am in command of the 11th Fleet. The Emergency Decrees are in effect. Those of you with prior military service will be brought back into uniform to—"

Thorvald's head cocked to one side and he swung around to face Gage. He motioned for Gage to lean down, then whispered into his ear.

Gage stood and buckled his sword belt around his waist.

"To the shelters," he told the crowd. "All of you get to the shelters. Now."

CHAPTER 8

Gage stepped onto the *Orion*'s bridge, one hand zipping up the side of his vac suit as he hopped up onto the command dais. Price was there, her helmet perched on the command console.

"Any change?" he asked.

"Negative, sir," she said, "which bothers me more than anything. Fifty minutes ago there was an Ashtekar spike at a Lagrange point near Isana, the outer moon. The slip-space disturbance indicated a translation mass equivalent to most of our fleet, but nothing's appeared on the scopes."

"Has astrogation run a back trace on the slip signature?" Gage touched the side of his collar and the vac suit tightened slightly around his neck.

"Three times, all pointing back to the Theonis

system," she said.

"Theonis...Theonis?" Gage's eyes narrowed.

"Nothing there but low-scale asteroid mining." Price shrugged. "Three jumps from any relevant star system. No known Daegon presence. If I may, trying to get sneaky through Podunk systems doesn't seem to fit their style. They've taken the bulldozer approach thus far."

"I agree with you." Gage's hands moved through the holo and a least-time course from the translation point to New Madras appeared. "Why haven't the Indus sent recon probes to get eyes on?"

"They have. Every unit they send sends back nothing or goes off-line. It's weird and I think the locals are starting to get scared," she said.

"That's all we need now, isn't it? A ghost fleet on our doorstep," Gage said. Alerts flashed in the tank as Indus fleets began moving outward from the planet. "No, no, no, Chadda, what are you doing?"

"Did they not listen to you when you laid out how the Daegon assault planets?" Price put a hand on top of her helmet.

"They heard me...but they didn't listen,"

Gage said.

A channel request pinged in the holo and Gage touched it. Admiral Chadda appeared in a window. "Commodore Gage, this is more in line with what we expect from a Daegon attack, is it not?" The Indus man gave him a derisive smile.

"We've yet to encounter Daegon that can go invisible to sensors," Gage said. "I suggest a reconnaissance in force to see what we're dealing with."

"A good suggestion…in fact, why don't you do it? It is your idea," Chadda said.

Gage paused, realizing he'd essentially volunteered for the mission. "In the interest of cooperation, the 11th Albion Fleet will go," he said. "Though I need to leave behind my two destroyers currently void-docked with tenders to complete their repairs."

"Certainly. Find out what we're dealing with and report back. I'll decide how to engage from there. Chadda out." The window flipped off.

"What's his problem?" Price asked.

"Seems he sees us as the junior partner in this

alliance. Hard to disagree as he has so many more ships. Make ready to weigh anchor and set us on an intercept course on the least-time plot from the slip-space detection," Gage said.

"Not to denigrate our hosts…but if we were on Albion and survivors of a new enemy showed up and told us how to fight them, I'd shut up and listen," Price said. "Plotting course now."

"Vicarious learning is the best way to grow from painful lessons." Gage brought up the comm menu for the destroyer *Cutlass*. "But knowing that can be a lesson in and of itself."

He opened a secure, private channel to the ship's commander, Lieutenant Commander Timmons.

"Commodore?" Timmons wiped sweat from her brow. "My engineering section is open to vacuum while work crews replace the capacitor relays. It'll take me—"

"At least four hours to be functional," Gage said. "Which is faster than the *Stiletto* in the berth next to you. Four hours is long enough. The rest of the fleet and I are moving to scout out this disturbance.

Should anything…drastic happen, you are to retrieve a VIP in the Theni embassy and take said VIP to Geneva. Even in a hard bore, your destroyer can make that trip."

"A bore to Geneva? We'd be on emergency rations before…but the math works. Aye aye," she said as concern grew on her face. "What do you think is out there, sir?"

"We're doing this recon face-first," Gage said, shaking his head, "which is not how I want to do it, but needs must. Are your instructions clear?"

"Crystal."

"Gage, out." He closed the channel as the *Orion* lurched out of orbit and turned toward the distant moon.

"You made it back from the shore party without being stabbed this time," Price said. "An improvement, wouldn't you say?"

"I accomplished more getting stabbed by a pirate than I did being polite to the Indus." Gage rubbed his arm and chest where Loussan had hurt him. "Maybe there's something to more aggressive diplomacy. Ten hours to the moon. Take some time off your feet, XO."

"With all due respect," she said, "when was the last time you slept?"

"I had at least an hour on the shuttle down. I'm good for days," he said.

"You take three hours to sleep and then I'll take three hours," she said.

"No."

"Fine. I take three hours then *you* take three hours."

"Acceptable." Gage nodded and began reading through repair and personnel status messages in his inbox. "But one sign of the enemy and the deal's off."

CHAPTER 9

The interior lights of the *Joaquim* were low for the ship's night cycle. Pirates slept against crates and each other, the rough-and-tumble types used to a lack of luxury. One, a woman with a headscarf adorned with small coins along the edge, stood up and stretched.

She glanced up at a rail-thin man with tattoos running up and down his arms and creeping up his neck who was standing on a catwalk that ran along the cargo bay. He puffed on a nic-stick and scratched beneath his nose with his thumbnail. The woman went around a cargo pod and nudged the shoulder of three men sleeping in a corner.

"What is it, Tatiana?" asked a dark-skinned man as he pushed another off his shoulder.

"Ahn, Jurl, Smitty…you're the last ones." She squatted down and continued at a low hush. "Any of you happy with getting all of eight troys for this cruise?"

"Straight-up bollocks is what it is," Smitty said as he wiped sleep from his face. "Lose all our stuff on the *Carlin*, jackboots' cell, then we get marooned on that bloody Bucky's place? Eight troys…should get at least twenty. That's the Harlequin minimum."

"Least we get something," said Jurl, the dark-skinned man. "Better alive with some clink in our pocket than dead in the void."

"It's all Loussan's fault." The third looked up at the man on the catwalk, then narrowed his eyes at Tatiana. "You feeling froggy, my girl?"

"Slight worse than froggy, Ahn. Loussan's bent the knee to the jackboots. Lost his ship. Lost the lives of our fellow Harleys. Lost my respect for him as captain. Any of you feel different?" she asked.

Ahn and Smitty shook their heads, then looked at Jurl.

"You talking an honor duel?" Jurl asked. "How's that work in the code? This technically isn't Loussan's ship. Someone challenges him, official-like, he'll just have Ruprecht stand in for him."

"We're not doing this by the code," Tatiana hissed. "This ain't no Harley ship. No family ship. Code don't apply here...so we do things our own way. We take this ship, void that freak on the bridge, and leave Loussan on Bucky's with *one* troy to his name so he can beg on the docks for the rest of his life. No one will ever take him on again, especially after we let the families know what he's been up to with the jackboots."

"And him?" Jurl looked over at the sealed container that held the Katar assassin, Ruprecht.

"We take him back to Lord Moineau on Sicani. He loves his Katars. Couple tweaks to Ruprecht's code and he'll never even remember Loussan...or us," Tatiana said.

"I don't know..." Jurl frowned.

"You want to try and make your way on Bucky's?" Smitty asked. "Or you want to give the jackboot and Loussan what's coming to them and we head back to free space like proper Harlequins?"

"How would we even get control of this bucket?" Jurl asked.

"Geet found a skeleton cipher in one of the empty bunk rooms." She nodded at the lookout.

"You think he found an actual skeleton cipher?" Smitty asked. "He's dumber than a box of rocks. Bet he thought it was a drive full of dirty movies."

"I've got it," Tatiana said, touching a pocket on her loose pants, "and I know it's legit. He's been a sharp cookie lately. Guess seeing the inside of a jackboot cell convinced him to start putting a little effort into being a proper Harlequin."

"Maybe he put smarter rocks in the box," Ahn said, nodding his head slowly. The other pirates looked at him for a moment, then back at Tatiana.

"You were the last ones I had to ask. Everyone else is on board. Here's the plan…" she said.

****

Tatiana, Smitty and Jurl walked down the catwalk, and she opened the door of a crew cabin slightly, then slipped inside. Three pirates on four of the bunks sat right up, crude knives and heavy bludgeoning tools in hand. The fourth was still snoring.

"Geet!" Tatiana kicked the man's ankles and he sat bolt upright, his head hitting the bunk overhead.

"Ow! I wasn't sleeping, Chief. On my duties as proper." He rubbed his forehead quickly and blinked hard at the rest of the pirates in the small room. "What's this then?"

"'What's this then'?" Tatiana reached under his bunk and tossed him an emergency hood. "What do you think it is? We're almost to the Concord system. Time to be about our duties, Geet. You're with me. Rest of you lot make for Loussan's cabin and get him tied up soon as we've the bridge. Simple as that."

Lifting the side of her blouse, she revealed an emergency-hood pack on her belt. Then she tucked the edge of her garment into her belt and palmed a small data stick in one hand, a sharpened bit of ceramic with a cloth handle in the other.

"We're true Harlequins, none of you forget that," she said. "That's why we're doing this."

"Here, here," the rest said in unison—all but Geet, who was still fighting sleep.

"Sorry, what do we—" Geet stopped talking when Ahn shoved a small hatchet from the ship's tool chest into his hands.

"Mouth shut. Head down. Ears open, you tosser," Ahn said. "Just like aboard the *Carlin*."

"If you say so…" Geet frowned at the hatchet.

Tatiana left the bunk room, Smitty and Geet behind her. She glanced over her shoulder and smiled at Smitty as they neared the mess area.

"You boys ready for another exciting meal of expired oatmeal? Rehydrated just this—" She bolted to one side, made straight for the bridge door, flipped a latch up and jammed the cipher into the port. One glance into the porthole and she smiled. She could see the back of Tolan's head, canted to one side of the command seat. Asleep.

"Come on, come on…" She felt a thrum through the cipher and the bolts on the door popped open.

Tatiana kicked the door open and lunged forward, Smitty on her heels. Her shiv arced down and stabbed into the base of Tolan's neck. Instead of blood, a puff of downy feathers floated into the air.

"The hell?" Tatiana drew her knife back and a hologram flickered around a man-shaped bundle of pillows and blankets.

The door to the bridge slammed shut, cutting Geet off from the other two.

"Get control! Get control of the ship!" Tatiana hit Smitty on the shoulder and went to the door. When the handle wouldn't budge, she tried the cipher key, but nothing happened.

Geet tapped on the glass with the butt of his hatchet. "Do I just guard the door, ma'am?" he asked, his words dampened.

"Bloody idiot." Tatiana whirled around. Smitty looked dumbfounded, staring at a bank of blank control panels.

An alarm klaxon sounded and an environmental alert flashed next to the door. She felt a rush of cool air against her face from a vent over the door as "O2 MIX" flashed on and off around the door. Gunshots rang out from elsewhere in the ship and Geet's face went pale.

"Ah, ah, ah." Tolan appeared on all the bridge screens. "You've all been bad pirates. I really don't have the time or energy to rub your noses in the mess you've made, so enjoy some lovely pure nitrogen flooding the entire ship. Amazing stuff, nitrogen. It's in every breath you take, but you never really care about it. It's the oxygen that matters. And the more nitrogen in the air you breathe, the less oxygen's actually getting into your bloodstream. Not a bad way to die, all things considered."

"You freak asshole." Tatiana slipped the emergency hood from its case and put it on. A press of a button later and stale air with a note of sweetness filled her nose. "You think we don't know that trick? It's as old as void piracy. Bunch of whimpering civilians locked away in a ship? Foul their air until they give up or get dead and compliant."

Smitty already had his mask on, but Tatiana had to knock on the porthole and point to her hood to get Geet to don his.

"Where are you?" she asked, looking at Tolan on all the screens. He had a rebreather to his mouth. "Where are you, you Faceless freak? Don't make this any harder than it should be and we'll let you off at that shit hole of a spaceport you had in mind for us. You'll live, just with a few more bruises than you'd like."

"I'm going to have to pass on that on, toots," Tolan said. "People to see. Things to do...and I really am at my wits' end with you bunch of criminals. All those years I spent in wild space gave me some real trust issues. Oh, by the way, notice a faint strawberry scent in your hoods? That's a nifty little poison called Lisbon's Kiss. I picked it up back when I was doing the whole Faceless-for-hire routine. You should note some slight tingling in your extremities by now."

Tatiana held up a hand. Her fingers had gone numb. She ripped the hood off her face and gagged. Smitty slumped against the control panel, his eyes watering, snot pouring from his nose.

"Real gamut of physiological reactions to the Lisbon," Tolan said. "But cardiovascular shutdown takes about two minutes from initial exposure. Your hoods were spiked with the poison. So yes, I did know that old trick about fouling the air."

Geet banged against the porthole with the handle of his hatchet, yelling as he waffled between having his hood on or off.

Tatiana's legs went numb and she fell to the deck, her vision going dark as she gasped like a fish.

"All in all, not a great way to go. But not too terrible," Tolan said. "See you all in hell."

The door to the bridge opened and Geet stumbled inside, hatchet raised and one hand over his mouth.

"Tati?" he nudged her with his foot and she coughed up a bit of phlegm, then let out a slow death rattle.

"Smitty?"

The other pirate sat on the deck, his legs stretched out, back to the control panel, head lolled to one side and one foot twitching.

Geet tossed his hood away with a high-pitched shriek, then turned around.

Tolan was at the end of the short hallway leading to the bridge. He had a pistol trained on Geet, his face blank and nearly featureless. Loussan appeared behind him, a sad look on his face.

"Drop the axe, buddy," Tolan said. "Drop it real slow so we can have the most important conversation of your entire life."

Geet let the hatchet fall and the blade tip punctured the top of his boot. He knocked the weapon away and fell back on his haunches. When his hand touched Tatiana's shiv, he tossed it back at Smitty's body and began whimpering.

"He didn't know anything," Loussan said. "Leave him alone."

"He really is as dumb as you say he is." Tolan shook his head.

"I didn't know!" Geet held his hands up in front of his face. "They just…just woke me up and told me to be a good sailor and do what I was told. Tati can be mean if you don't…just shoot me before the poison gets me, please, sir!"

"Oh, shut up." Tolan lowered his gun. "Look

at your left forearm. That tattoo of what's either a guitar or some sort of totemic phallus. See those two little pricks? One's the tranquilizer that kept you out of the planning sessions. The other's the antidote to the Lisbon Kiss. You're fine."

"The bad air?" Geet scratched at his arm.

"I just turned the AC up to max," Tolan said with a shrug. "That alarm goes off every time. Haven't had the time to replace the scrubbers or the sensor. I'm not sure which is broken. Anyway. You're not going to suffocate either. You're welcome."

"I…" Geet scrambled away from Tatiana's body. "What did I do? She said I—"

"You…" Tolan put a palm up in front of his face and flipped it to one side. Geet saw a mirror reflection. His skin morphed to match all the tattoos. "You have some serious issues, kiddo. Legit question, did you get some of this ink for losing a bet? I'm just glad I got to keep my shirt on because even I would be embarrassed for anyone to see what's on your inner thigh."

"He borrowed your face for a bit and hid you in one of his many smuggler compartments," Loussan

134

said. "Then Tatiana pitched her little mutiny idea to the crew. You were never actually approached to join in this plot."

"But she said—"

Tolan—his face still Geet's—flashed his teeth at the cowering pirate.

"Loussan," Tolan said, pinching the bridge of his nose as his countenance reverted to that of a man in his early thirties with thin features, "you've quite the mess to clean up. Do gather up all those bodies and dump them in the air lock for a quick-and-dirty void dump. This ship smells bad enough as it is. Leave this one here for a minute while I explain just what his duties on *my* ship will be from here on out. Yes?"

"Shame this happened," Loussan sighed. "What kind of a world do we live in where you can't trust your fellow pirates?" He grabbed Tatiana and Smitty by the ankles and dragged them away.

"Now, you, my wonderful little patsy," Tolan said, squatting down next to Geet. "You and I need to get our stories straight. You were asleep and the head mutineer woke you up and said to come help her take the bridge. You did what you were told and are *very* sorry you took part in an attempt on my life. Got it?"

"But Tatiana said I gave her the cipher—"

Tolan bopped Geet on the top of his head with his pistol. "You were asleep," Tolan said firmly, "and then—"

"I don't know nothing else." Geet shook his head. "Nothing at all, Master Tolan. Nothing."

"There. And to think everyone thought you were a dummy. You can figure things out after a bit. Good news is that you're on the crew. Bad news is that you're the lowest rung on a short totem pole. Get out there and clean up the bodies. Then start cleaning everything else. Don't stop. This place is a pigsty." Tolan reached into his bathrobe and removed a small metal case. "Shoo. You bother me. I've got just enough time for some bliss before we hit Bucky's."

He jerked a thumb over his shoulder and Geet scrambled out on his hands and feet, making it through the door just before it slammed shut. He brushed himself off and looked through the porthole.

Tolan was in the command seat, his feet

kicked up. He pressed a small capsule to his throat and flinched, then his hand fell to one side and his body shuddered. Tolan's face went soft, collapsing into a mound of putty with an open mouth.

Geet turned, trying not to retch.

"Geet!" Loussan called from the lower deck. "Find a mop!"

"Yes, Captain." Geet lowered his head and went to work.

CHAPTER 10

The moon Isana loomed ahead of the *Orion*, three ancient craters across the northern hemisphere striking Gage as dead, empty eye sockets forever watching New Madras.

"Launch drones," Gage said. "All ships make ready for combat."

"Drones away. Batteries report ready," Price said. "Sixty percent of torpedo tubes are green. We've got one volley in the magazines...still waiting on that resupply from the Indus."

"I'm sure they'll have it waiting for us when we return," Gage deadpanned.

In the holo, two drone tracks curved around

the moon. A cloud of sensor data appeared on the far side, then cut off.

"If it's the Daegon," Price said, "why are they just sitting there? Shall we do a recon by fire? Torpedoes can be sent without active guidance."

"We need to shake the tree to see what's in it, not try and chop it down…bring us around in a wide orbit. The *Orion* at the fore of the fleet formation. I have a suspicion…" Gage said.

"Aye aye, we'll lead from the front on this one." Price grimaced and the *Orion* swung around the moon.

Gage keyed battle stations and waited for the rest of the bridge crew to don their helmets. When they kept looking back at him, not readying for void combat, he grumbled and put his own helmet on first.

"I tried telling them you want things done the traditional way," Price said as she slipped her helmet on and sealed it. "But they just don't listen. Must be something about the Indus system."

"Must be." Gage watched the moon as the *Orion* came around. A blur formed behind Isana, phantom images of vessels appearing and disappearing. Then the distortion cut out. A massive warship snapped into focus, still surrounded by interference.

The ship was almost twice as long as the *Orion* and half again as wide. The maw of a spinal cannon pointed at the *Orion* and main gun turrets up and down the ship's hull slewed toward the Albion ships. The red hull gleamed like spilled blood in the system's starlight.

Gage froze, caught flat-footed by the dreadnought.

"Shields, sire?" Price asked, palm poised to slap the emergency activation.

"They've got us dead-bang," Gage said. "And they're not Daegon…are they?"

"That's…oh no, it's the Reich," Price said, her shoulders slumping. "Anyone but them. And now they're hailing us. Maintain combat alert?"

"Disperse the fleet and get us out of the line of fire of that spine cannon. If they try and bring it back onto us, activate shields and have your finger ready to fire torpedoes," Gage said.

"It's already there, sire," Price said.

"Stop calling me that." Gage removed his helmet and waved down the rest of the bridge crew as they were about to follow suit.

Gage ran a hand through his short hair and answered the hail.

A young man in a slate-gray vac suit, a thin crimson sash over one shoulder and a six-pointed badge on his chest, greeted Gage with a smile.

"On behalf of Kaiserina Washington the 30th, I greet you in the name of the Reich. I am Unter-Duke Klaven, thirty-seventh successor to the throne. My vessel, the *Castle Itter*, is inviable Reich territory and any assault on her is an assault on the Kaiserina. Do remember this." He smiled, one cheek marred by a dueling scar.

Gage's response caught in his throat. Double-checking the IFF transponder from the ship, he saw the hull markings…it was indeed the *Castle Itter*.

"I am Commodore Gage of His Majesty's ship *Orion*. Let us point our guns elsewhere in the name of cooperation, yes?" Gage glanced at Price and she gave orders to the gunnery officer.

"Of course, of course…you're not *the* Gage,

141

are you?" Klaven turned one eye closer to his camera. "Of Volera II fame?"

"One and the same," Gage said.

"Ha! What luck. I always wanted to meet you. Such a maneuver you pulled off against those Harlequins. Did you know we study that battle at the Imperial academy? No, why would you…what is it, Diaz?" Klaven leaned back and looked to one side. "Yes, I was just getting to that. Amusing that we keep picking them up wherever we go."

"Duke Klaven," Gage said, his hand going to the fire controls, anger seething in his heart at the sight of the Reich ship. "you have intruded into Indus space. The use of cloak technology during slip travel is considered a hostile act by the League, and if you don't drop the rest of your sensor interference, I will—"

"As you wish," Klaven said. "After being chased out of Theonis by the Daegon, it seemed prudent to arrive as unnoticed as possible here. But imagine my surprise when an Albion fleet came to say hello. I kept the field up just so as not to spoil the surprise for you. Diaz? Bring her over. Nothing more

142

to hide."

The interference around the *Castle Itter* faded away, and a half-dozen smaller ships materialized slowly in the sensor feed.

"A red-letter day for you all," Klaven said. "I for one am glad for your kingdom. Such difficult times deserve victories, even if they're small ones."

"Klaven, what are you getting at?" Gage asked.

"Sir…look," Price said.

In the holo, new IFF transponders pinged from the other ships around the *Castle Itter*.

Albion ships.

"It's the *Sterling*…and the *Adamant*," Price said. "They're ships from 2nd fleet!" A buzz rose from the bridge crew as more and more ships became clear.

"Not just your ships," Klaven said, raising one hand and stepping aside. A heavyset woman with short hair and wearing an Albion uniform stepped into view. "But I have your Regent, Countess Christina, heir to the Albion throne."

Almost as one, the entire bridge and Price

looked to Gage.

"Don't thank me all at once," Klaven said.

"Commodore Gage?" Christina frowned. "Commodore? If I remember correctly, you were Sartorious' little project. How is it you're a Commodore? And where is the good Admiral? And why…why are you broadcasting code vermillion in your IFF. That should only be for the *Adamant*."

"My lady…we have much to discuss," Gage said.

"Wonderful." Klaven turned the camera to him. "I simply must insist you come aboard the *Castle Itter* as my guest. The reunification of Albion forces, such a wonderful moment. I want to see it with my own eyes. Shall we make haste to New Madras?"

"Allow me to inform Admiral Chadda that…neutral forces are in system. He will decide if a Reich ship can approach his world," Gage said.

"Semantics," Klaven said, waving a hand at him, "but do what you need to. I'll make things ready aboard the *Itter*. Arrive at your leisure."

The channel cut out.

Gage stared into the holo tank and lowered

his head, touching one brow as a headache formed.

"Lady Christina." Price removed her helmet and ran fingers through her hair. "*That* Lady Christina."

"Don't, Price."

"The same Lady Christina that failed out of Sanquay Academy. Twice."

"Price."

"The Lady Christina that had to be given a merchant marine commission, then called onto active duty by special order of the Admiralty so she could finally hold a navy rank."

"I know who she is."

"The Lady Christina that misfired a torpedo into the void docks over Uffernau."

"The investigation was inconclusive." Gage felt his headache growing stronger.

"The same Lady Christina that now thinks she's the Regent." Price put her hands on her hips.

"It will get sorted," Gage said. "But I need to get over to that Reich ship, no matter how much I'd rather blow it into flames and twisted metal right now."

"You don't care for Klaven?" she asked.

"The ship. The *Castle Itter*. She was at the Battle of Turnbull, toward the end of the last war," Gage said.

"I don't understand," Price said.

"That's where my father died. And it was the *Castle Itter* that killed him."

****

Gage took a deep breath at the top of the shuttle ramp. Air hissed through the cabin as the atmosphere equalized with the *Castle Itter's* bay.

"Do you ever get tired of this?" he asked Thorvald, who was in his customary place two steps behind him.

"Formal events are part and parcel of any Genevan's duties," Thorvald said. "They will become second nature to you."

"Or not," Gage said. "If Lady Christina…if she is the rightful Regent, then I can bow out of most of the pomp and circumstance. But if she is…"

"Her reputation is known to Albion's Genevan guard," Thorvald said. "We have no preferences. Only the assigned order of succession."

"God help us all," Gage said.

Red lights activated on the side of the cargo doors and the ramp lowered with a hydraulic hiss.

Black-armored Reich soldiers were in formation at the foot of the ramp. Larger and more imposing than the Indus troops, the full facemasks and small round mirrors over their eyes erased any sort of humanity from the soldiers. Each carried a heavy rifle slung low across their waist, robotic augmentation to their arms and torsos helping carry the load.

Klaven was there, along with a rail-thin man in a less adorned uniform and a monocle over a white eye run through by scar tissue.

Behind them was a Genevan guard, his armor red to match the hull of the ship.

"Friend of yours?" Gage asked Thorvald.

"We don't all know each other," he said. "And we aren't all friends."

"Let's get this over with." Gage started down

the ramp and stopped one step short of the ship's deck.

Klaven gave him a broad smile, and Gage could see laughter brewing behind his eyes. He looked much younger in person, barely into his twenties.

"Permission to come aboard," Gage said evenly.

"Granted, granted." Klaven opened his arms wide. "Welcome to the *Castle Itter*. She's no *Bismarck*, but then again, no ship is quite like him."

Gage walked off the ramp and set a pace for the shorter Klaven as he walked through the throng of Reich soldiers.

"It's enough of a surprise to encounter the Reich in Indus space," Gage said. "Even more so to see Albion vessels with you…"

"Yes, perhaps some explanation is in order." The younger man swept hair back from his face. "There we were, minding our own business in the Theonis system…well, inspecting a number of mining concerns the Reich has. Had." He waved a hand next to his face and blew a brief raspberry in dismissal.

"When out of slip space comes a group of Albion Navy warships. We weren't overly worried as…well, you must know this ship's capabilities."

Gage glanced at him from the corner of his eye. Did Klaven know what happened to Gage's father? Was he taunting him?

"Albion has fought this ship before," Gage said.

They walked past rows of Reich fighter craft, matte-red ships with blunt noses and double cannons. Kill markings were stamped to the fuselage—symbols for Indus, Cathay, pirate…and Albion tallies.

"Oh, do forgive this," Klaven said, his face going flush. "Heraldry is passed down through our squadrons even when fighters are replaced with newer technology. None of what you see are recent. The Reich and Albion haven't traded blows for many, many years."

Gage kept his face set. This entire walk-through was a dominance game by the Reichsman, but calling it out would only diminish Gage's authority in their eyes.

"You were saying about Theonis?" Gage

asked.

"Indeed I was. A group of Albion vessels arrived with this…insane story of some sort of a new enemy conquering Coventry and how they managed to escape by the skin of their teeth. I had a hard time believing any of it, but lo and behold, guess who jumped into the system?"

"The Daegon," Gage said.

"The Daegon…such interesting ship construction they have. While Regent Christina blubbered about the massive armada she'd escaped from, what followed through from Coventry did not live up to her story. The Daegon took one good look at my ship…and returned to slip space without a word," Klaven said.

"Nothing? No '*novis regiray*' and demands of capitulation?" Gage asked.

"It seems you have more experience with these Daegon than I do," Klaven said. "But Regent Christina," the Reichsman continued, barely suppressing a laugh, "she requested amnesty aboard my ship. And as she is a head of state…I was inclined to give it. I meant to return to Reich space immediately, but the ley lines have been disrupted. I chose not to risk a hard bore back home—who knows what we would find waiting for us after so long in slip space—and made for this system instead. Seems we beat the Daegon here."

Gage's hands clenched. The Reich and Albion had fought each other over the course of centuries. While both were led by a royal household, the two nation's internal policies—and their treatment of their neighbors—were diametrically opposed. For Lady Christina to beg for protection from the first Reich ship she came across…the Reichsmen aboard must have been laughing over this for days.

"Not entirely," Gage said. "The Daegon have made a number of probing attacks but don't have a foothold here. We escaped from the enemy at Siam," Gage said. "Our journey to New Madras was a bit more convoluted."

"I'm curious to know more," Klaven said as they approached a lift. "The Daegon…strike me as being worse than the Mechanix after their last Khan came to power."

He ushered Gage, the two Genevans and

Diaz into the lift. With Klaven, the quarters were cramped. The two guards had their backs to opposite walls, staring each other down.

"And you are?" Gage asked the man with the dead eye and monocle.

"Diaz is the Kaiserina's minder," Klaven said. "Don't…ah, mind him, forgive the pun."

"Your babysitter?" Gage asked, twisting the knife in Klaven's pride.

"Ha, ha, this is Albian humor, yes? Kaiserina Washington, in her endless wisdom, has yet to name her successor. As such, she's sent minders to tend to each candidate and compile an extensive report on fitness, temperament…all that business. Albion succession is much different, I understand," he said, glancing at Thorvald, "but likely more complicated at the moment. Given circumstances."

The lift doors opened to a wardroom with several couches, low tables and an actual stone-block fireplace. The head of a deer-like animal with razor-sharp antlers and black and white fur hung over the flames. Wagon wheels adorned the bulkheads, along with paintings of game birds and antique rifles.

Windows looked out across the dorsal hull and Gage saw the *Orion* and the rest of his ships. Seeing them from here, from the enemy's point of view, only strengthened how vulnerable his command really was.

"My quarters," Klaven said as he stepped out. "Have you ever hunted erdolchen stags? Difficult to stalk. Even harder to bring down with a bow and arrow, as the *huntmeisters* demand. Amongst the Reich we say that once you take a shot on an erdolchen, you best not miss, as the stag gets the next go."

"I've never cared for hunting," Gage said.

"Because you're common born." Klaven went to an antique globe in a stand and lifted it up, revealing a bucket of ice and several bottles of liquor. "Albion nobility are well-known for their safaris and whatnot. They tend to discourage the more common folk from taking part by putting ridiculously high fees on hunting permits and limiting the number available. Isn't that right?" He turned over a glass and gripped an ice cube with a pair of tongs, then raised an eyebrow at Gage.

"No, thank you." Gage walked to the window to look out over the *Castle Itter*.

Klaven shut the globe without fixing himself a drink and joined Gage.

"Full disclosure," Klaven said, "you are well-known to the Reich, Commodore Gage. We keep an eye on the competent leaders of all the major star nations. Your rise through the ranks was…it struck us rather impressive. And I must apologize."

"For?" Gage counted torpedo tube covers and noted the number of acceleration coils on the spine cannon running down the ship's centerline.

"For inviting you aboard my ship. I didn't realize your…history with it until you were already on your way. This feels macabre, but my condolences for the loss of your father," Klaven said.

Gage nodded to him slowly. He doubted that Klaven came across that information when he claimed, but the acknowledgement and apology struck him as genuine.

"Indeed, I lost relatives aboard this very same vessel at the Battle of Turnbull against the Albion Navy. A second cousin and a great uncle," Klaven said, "but it's no comparison. Distant relations that passed before I was born. It's like they never even existed to me. Your loss was much more personal."

"What are we doing here, Klaven?" Gage asked.

"What is that old Cathay curse? 'May you live in interesting times'? These times are most certainly interesting, aren't they? Albion and Reich ships within weapon range of each other and look…peace." He raised a hand to Gage's ships. "But even dark times can lead to something great. Do you know the history of the Reich? After the Great Winter following the eruption of Mount Edziza, the German people in central Europe were facing extinction. They did not go quietly into that good night. Rather, they remembered their ancestors…and remembered how many of their relatives settled in a place called Texas.

"With the world's governments in total collapse, a number of enterprising Germans organized an airlift out of Munich to Austin. For months, zeppelins ferried people out of the Arctic zone while the sky was choked with ash. Not one was left behind—not that there were too many after everything collapsed…but I digress. The German people settled in and around Austin and declared the

Fourth Reich at the Scholz Garten, a historic place linking Texas to Germany."

"And then the Reich went to war and conquered much of the American South and what was then Mexico," Gage said. "They tried to take Arizona and Utah, where refugees from the British Isles settled…and where Albion drew its first colonists once the diaspora from Earth began."

"So our people have never been friends." Klaven shrugged. "Back then glaciers and starvation were the great enemy…now these Daegon are here."

"The Kaiserina doesn't know about them yet, does she?" Gage asked.

"I suspect she's heard by now." Klaven leaned against the windowsill. "But she needs information, my good Commodore. I cannot return to Prussia Zwei with the name 'Daegon' and a few pic captures of their ships. It's my duty to learn more." He canted his head slightly to Gage.

"Travel back to the Reich would take weeks," Gage said. "There's no way word could have reached Prussia Zwei yet."

"There's a ley line between Reich space and

Vishuddha, and after the disaster there, she likely realizes there's a new force in the galaxy."

"What? But Vishuddha is one of the League's locus worlds," Gage said.

"We caught bits and pieces, but it seems Daegon infiltrators sabotaged the habitat domes and the shipyards. The death toll…best not to think of the number. The League's reconvening on Lantau. Cathay space."

"Lantau…is at least closer than Vishuddha." Gage got lost in thought as his original plans went up in smoke.

"But the *Castle Itter* is stuck in this system for a time," Klaven said. "Might as well make the most of it."

"Are you going to fight the Daegon?" Gage asked.

Klaven laughed and turned to Diaz, who stood next to the Reichsman's Genevan guard, and wagged a finger next to the older man's face.

"We have a very clear policy, my good Commodore," Klaven said. "The Reich never fires first, but any attack on a Reich ship is an attack on the

Kaiserina herself. She has not declared war…and as such I will not place my ship in any circumstances that may commit the Reich to a war without the Kaiserina's blessing or knowledge. You understand?"

"I do," Gage said. "Francia didn't. Though there's still some confusion over whether the Franks really did fire on the *Bismarck* before the Reich declared total war."

"Bah," Klaven said, making a face, "ancient history. The Francia planets have integrated fairly well into the Reich. After a number of pacification efforts. And resettlements. And none of that matters now. But let's focus on another matter. Regent Christina." A playful smile came across his face.

"You see," Klaven said, taking a seat on a couch and crossing his legs, "I didn't think there would be any confusion over who the Albion Regent is. Christina is King Randolph's …second cousin? By way of marriage, I believe. Maybe once removed? Needless to say, she has a blood right to the throne. Yes?"

"Albion's right of succession is different than you're picturing." Gage glanced over at Thorvald.

"I thought her claim was legitimate—if not a bit tenuous—until I saw your Genevan," Klaven said. "They don't come cheap, and they only protect those within the scope of their contract. I've never known them to abandon those they're assigned to…and you are common born, Gage. So if a Genevan is with you, then that means a member of the royal family is too…one that's incapable of wearing the crown due to injury…or age."

"You're clever," Gage said.

"I imagine you'd rather not have that walking relic with you," Klaven said, "but they are just so dogged in their duties, aren't they? I know your pain—in stereo, no less."

"Lady Christina approaches," Klaven's Genevan said.

"Thank you, Rapoto." Klaven rubbed his hands together. "This will be interesting."

The door to the quarters opened, and Lady Christina came in, her generous midsection straining the limits of her uniform. Gage had to bite his lips to keep from saying anything about how poorly she wore it.

"Sorry to keep you waiting," she said, ambling over to Gage. "All this stress with the invasion has given me something of a tummy issue." She held out a pudgy hand to Gage, then took it back.

"Wait, where are your manners?" she asked him. "I am the Regent. I am to be treated the same as if I were Queen." She looked at the deck, expecting Gage to take a knee as was customary for any Albion officer the first time they were introduced to the Crown.

Klaven wiped a hand over his mouth, his eyes wide with suppressed laughter.

"Lady Christina," Gage said, "I came to this ship as a courtesy to you to escort you back to the *Orion*. Perhaps we can discuss matters once we've taken leave of Unter-Duke Klaven's hospitality."

"You know who I am." She put her hands on her hips. "You know what happened to Albion. How does this require any sort of discussion? Don't let your rank confuse you as to your status, Gage. You're common born. You're not in the line of succession. At all."

Gage ground his teeth together so hard they

clicked.

"If I may," Thorvald said, stepping away from the bulkhead.

"Ah, Captain Royce," Christina said. "Wait…Royce? How did you get here?"

Thorvald drew his visor off his face so that Christina could see him. "Thorvald, my lady. Royce took his final breath in service to Albion," Thorvald said. "I was forced to take on his armor and his AI."

"What is this?" Rapoto asked. "Royce would never—"

Diaz cleared his throat loudly and the other Genevan went silent.

"This…" said Christina, wagging a finger at Thorvald and Gage, "this is suspicious."

"I have full faith in Thorvald," Gage said. "And he does bear Royce's AI. As King Randolph's personal guard…he carries the King's succession plan."

"You think I'm not in it?" Christina asked. "I have a blood relation. Every member of the royal family is on the plan."

"The King was known to…prune the list,"

Thorvald said. "When his brother renounced all claim to the throne to live as a commoner on—"

"Just get it over with." Christina rolled up a sleeve. "DNA test, yes? Go on."

Thorvald touched the palm of his armor to her bare skin and the mail beneath the thin plates glowed. He took his hand back and paused, head cocked to one side.

"Well?" Christina knocked gently on the side of Thorvald's head.

"Something is…off with my AI," Thorvald said. "The bonding was rushed. I've yet to gain full access to the deep systems and—you must tell them everything, Grynau—and there is no change to whom I must protect."

"Lies!" Christina turned to Gage. "What have you cooked up with him? Maybe this is some chauvinist plot between the two of you?" She pointed an accusing finger at Klaven.

"I serve the Kaiserina," Klaven said, "not a Kaiser. She would not stand for chauvinism, or even misanthropy. Rapoto? Perhaps you can help clarify this?"

The other Genevan looked at Thorvald.

"It is true that a rushed merging would limit some of his access, but the AI in the suit knows the truth, even if it will not divulge all of it. Grynau will tell us if Lady Christina is on the succession list."

"She is," Thorvald said, "toward the bottom. The very bottom."

"Still more legitimate than that commoner!" Christina shouted. "Thorvald, is it? You're my bodyguard now. Come to my quarters and carry my bags. We are leaving this ship and transferring my flag to the *Orion*."

Klaven looked away, his eyes squeezed shut as tears leaked from the sides.

"That…my AI will not allow it," Thorvald said. "It will not…it tells me that another is higher on the succession list and no change is allowed."

"Who?" Christina asked. "Who else is there?"

"Prince Aidan," Gage said. "I have him elsewhere, safe. Now that this question has been resolved, may we—"

"This is not over," Christina said. "Not over by a long shot, Gage."

"Then let us leave this Reich ship and sort it out properly," Gage said.

"I'm going back to the *Adamant*," she said as she stomped out of the room. "And someone get my bags!"

The door shut and Klaven slapped his knee, laughing so hard he had to gasp for air.

"Unter-Duke," Diaz said, running a fingertip along the edge of the monocle poised over his dead eye.

"I'm sorry." Klaven stood up and gave his belly a pat. "I am so sorry. You just…you have no idea how much I enjoyed that. She's been on my ship eating all our Black Forest cake and planning her 'government in exile' on Prussia Zwei, and to see it all get crushed like that…does Albion have a word for *schadenfreude?*"

"I'll return her to—"

"No, no," Klaven stopped Gage, "as a gesture of goodwill, I will see her back to the *Adamant*…along with her bags."

"And then what?" Gage asked. "What will you and the *Castle Itter* do after that?"

Klaven smoothed out his uniform.

"We will stay out of the way and observe until such time as we can leave this system and return home. But as you still seem to be the Albion Regent, my ship did carry out a number of repairs on Lady Christina's ships. She even opened a line of credit while she was aboard my ship. This is an expenditure," he glanced over at Diaz, "that the Kaiserina has incurred. The Reich does not help anyone for free. You know this."

Gage reached into his uniform and pulled out a small data chit.

"Here are the holo tank recordings of every battle we've fought with the Daegon," Gage said. "Scrubbed of sensitive Albion data, naturally. I was going to give it you as a gesture of—"

"Consider your debt paid," Klaven said quickly and held out a palm.

Gage tossed the chit to him and went for the door.

"It has been my pleasure, Gage," the Reichsman said. "Let there be no blood between us, yes?"

Gage stopped at the threshold, gave Klaven a nod, and left. The door shut and Klaven stuck the data chit into a port on a coffee table. A holo formed over it and he swiped through data files.

"You did well," Diaz said. "He suspects nothing."

"Why would he?" Klaven fast-forwarded through the battle at the Wicked Sisters in wild space, then paused it. "The Kaiserina wishes to know if these Daegon are as powerful as they claim. They've offered her an alliance…we're here to see if they're dealing true with us."

"They've already wiped out Albion. That should be enough for her," Diaz said.

"Albion was only ever a burr in our boot," Klaven said. "Too far from our stars to crush effectively, but when we did fight them…they fought honorably. To see them brought down like this…"

"They stopped us cold during the last war," Diaz said. "We could have had more stars for the Reich if not for them."

"But will these Daegon let us keep what we take?" Klaven brought the Daegon ship *Medusa* into focus within the holo. "Or will they stop after they have Earth, like they claim?"

"That's not for us to decide," Diaz said.

"No…not for us." Klaven waved to his Genevan. "Rapoto, a moment?"

****

Thorvald walked beneath the Albion shuttle in the *Castle Itter's* bay, scanning for any devices—lethal or nonlethal—that the Reich may have attached. He felt a slight tremor through the deck and spun around, arms up.

His forearm knocked away a blow from Rapoto and Thorvald stabbed his fingertips at the other Genevan's throat. Rapoto slapped the strike away then held up his own hand perpendicular to the bridge of his nose.

"*Benvegna,*" Rapoto said. "Truce now."

"*Benvegna* to you," Thorvald said with a sneer. "Explain yourself."

"I had my doubts you were a true Genevan,"

Rapoto said. "You wear another man's soul. House Ticino—that is yours, yes?—will have much to explain to the other Houses."

"Ticino protected their charges, kept to their contract. That matters more than disturbing the AI." He tapped his chest.

"Never has such a thing happened to House Solothern. Never in almost a thousand years of service." Rapoto tapped his own chest harder.

"May your House never go through what happened on Albion. Ticino fought and died as demanded. There is never shame in this," Thorvald said.

"I spoke harshly," Rapoto said. "My apologies."

"What do you want? Is your curiosity sated?"

"Who is the other Genevan with you? There must be one more…"

"Anything you know, you will tell Klaven if it affects his safety," Thorvald said. "I have no duty to you or him. As we say on Albion, go pound sand."

"Because if there is another, I may have a way to protect their charge," Rapoto said. "I see the lines on your face. I see how stiff you are in the other man's soul. You've been away from Geneva for so long—almost an entire contract of twenty years, if I'm guessing right. There have been developments amongst the Houses. Deep issues amongst the trade."

"I'm listening," Thorvald said.

"Trust for trust," Rapoto said. "You have the word of us both that we will keep your answer to our heart, only to be shared if it risks Klaven's blood." A rune appeared on his chest armor, the name of the AI within.

"Salis," Thorvald said. "The other House Ticino is Fiona Salis."

The rune scrambled and vanished.

"This is…good and terrible news," Rapoto said.

A pair of knocks sounded through the hull, the crew signaling that they were almost ready to leave.

"What do you mean?" Thorvald asked.

"Gage is no fool," Rapoto said. "He's considered sending the boy prince to Geneva for safekeeping, hasn't he? The Houses will never allow it, no matter what the Daegon do. We have our honor and it is better to die than live without it." He narrowed his eyes slightly at Thorvald. "The Houses will never take in the boy…but they want Salis back. She can bring the boy with her if she chooses."

"What? Why?"

"She is not of your House, Thorvald. Already…" He grasped at his throat as the AI tried to choke him off from saying more. "Said too much. Send her back *with* the boy. He'll be safe." He hacked and backed away.

Rapoto turned and ran, one hand to his throat.

The double bang came again.

"All clear on the external check. Returning now," Thorvald said into a receiver on the back of his hand, then took his thumb off the key. "No, Grynau," he said under his breath, "I don't know what the hell's going on either."

****

Gage entered his quarters aboard the *Orion*

and paused. The room smelled of toast and nutmeg, and a fresh uniform was laid out on his bunk. Thorvald stepped in front of him and drew a pistol off his hip.

Someone hummed a tune from within the attached galley and a shadow fell across the threshold between the two rooms. A female sailor carrying a tray had her eyes on the tea and crackers as she entered. She looked up and into Thorvald's muzzle and shrieked. Crackers leapt off their plate and the kettle fell over, spilling hot tea across the tray and onto one of the sailor's hand.

"Bugger me!" she shouted, trying and failing to keep the tea on the tray. Most of it sloshed out onto the deck.

"Who're you?" Thorvald asked.

"Yeoman Emma," she hissed through her teeth, setting the tray onto a desk, then wiping a burned hand on her apron. "Beggin' the lordship's pardon. I'm his steward until such time as Bertram can return. Bloody hell that hurts."

"No one cleared this with me," Thorvald said.

"Didn't know I had to have my orders

chopped off by a walking toaster, now did I?" She untied her apron and began mopping up the tea. "We're almost out of the good brand and look what I've done. You'd think the Indus would have more but I'll be a monkey's uncle before anyone can get to ground to buy any."

"It's fine, Thorvald." Gage pushed the Genevan's wrist down. "I'm glad to have more help. Emma…" Gage narrowed his eyes. "I know that name from somewhere."

"Was in the engineering complement," she said, sitting back on her knees. "Was Captain Cox's steward on the *Huntress* not too long ago, then there was a minor incident while on shore leave and I lost a bit of rank and privileges for a time."

"You were in that bar brawl. The one that ended with several 11th Fleet sailors stealing a police car," Gage said.

"I had nothing to do with that last bit…local bobbies already had me in custody when the other lads took off." She looked away, guiltily. "But other than this fine first impression and my repeat visits to the captain's mast…honored to be your steward, sire."

"I don't like this," Thorvald said.

"Well, I've not gone sticking a hand cannon in your face for no reason, now have I?" Emma asked.

"Thorvald," Gage said, going to the uniform laid out on the bed and looking it over, "I have the same twenty-four hours in a day as everyone else. I can spend that time bothering with my own laundry, meals and other tasks or I can have Emma on hand to handle these things for me. Every minute I'm concentrating on things not related to the command and operation of this fleet and the war against the Daegon…is time spent poorly. She's invaluable…unless you want to take away from your duties to me and start ironing my pants."

Thorvald holstered his pistol. "I'll keep an eye on her," the Genevan said.

"He does that to everyone." Gage gave Emma a nod and went into his restroom to change clothes.

"Captain Price will have all the other ships' masters in your wardroom in thirty minutes," Emma said. "Perhaps enough time for a nip? I could get another kettle on…"

"Too long," Gage said. "Have them over now."

With a glare, Emma tossed her wet apron to Thorvald and went to a comm panel next to the door.

CHAPTER 11

Gage and Price stood in a passageway just outside the main door to the wardroom. Armsmen from a dozen ships lined the bulkheads, all escorts for their captains. Thorvald herded them away from the two officers as they spoke.

"How are the 2nd Fleet ships?" Gage asked.

"Battle cruisers *Sterling* and *Adamant* are fully mission capable," Price said, reading from a tablet. "They weren't happy about cross-levelling their torpedo magazines, but we'll have the *Orion* and the rest of the cruisers partially loaded in another hour. Frigate *Havoc* and destroyers *Gerber and Corvo* are good for combat operations. That's all that made it, sir, all that's left of the 2nd."

"And we're lucky to have them," Gage said. "Anything from…the other matter?"

"Comms confirmed a good deal of tight-beam cross talk between the *Adamant* and the *Renown*," Price said, her face growing darker. "Seems Captain Arlyss had a long conversation with someone. I can guess who."

"There's no getting around this fight," Gage said. "Better to have it now than in the middle of a battle. Shall we?"

"I'm with you, sire," she said. "The Crown is Prince Aidan and no one else."

"Thanks…and stop calling me that." Gage keyed the door open and strode into the wardroom.

The assembled officers seemed surprised that Gage had come through the same door they had, and not the connection to the admiralty's quarters on the other side of the room.

"Room, atten-tion!" Captain Vult shouted.

The officers snapped to their feet, all but Lady Christina, who sat at a small table in the corner with Arlyss…who got up so slowly that it looked like he was in pain.

"As you were." Gage went to the desk at the fore of the room, which smelled brand-new from the ship's foundry. The last one had been wrecked by the Daegon infiltrator that murdered Admiral Sartorious and the rest of the fleet's captains.

"To our brothers and sisters from the 2nd Fleet," Gage said, his eyes looking over a faint stain on the carpet, the phantom smell of blood and smoke in his nose, "welcome aboard the *Orion*. I trust you've been…informed as to what happened in this very room."

"A tragic loss," said Captain McGowan of the *Sterling*. His chest bore several racks of ribbons and the Saint Michael's award, a medal given only for destroying an enemy vessel while in command of an Albion Navy ship. Only Gage and Commander Erskine of the *Valiant* had that award as well. "At least you survived." McGowan took a sip from his tea, his eyes on Gage.

"Not for the lack of the Daegon's trying," Gage said. "All ships have completed the blood screening?" he asked Price.

"One likely suspect aboard the *Havoc*," Price said. "Stepped out of an air lock before the armsmen could arrest him."

"I had no reason to believe there was a Daegon agent aboard my ship," said Commander Napier, who was rail-thin with sunken cheeks. Gage wasn't sure if she was naturally that thin or if stress had eaten away at her.

"They're quite adept at hiding in plain sight," Gage said. "While that issue is resolved, keep your ships at ready alert at all times. We've had to deal with more than just sleeper agents. We're on course back to New Madras but given our casualties, it's more feasible to fold the remaining ships of the 2nd Fleet into the 11th for the duration of this—"

"Preposterous," Lady Christina said and Gage's face hardened. "By custom and tradition of the Albion Navy, the older 2nd Fleet has primacy in any reorganization. And while I agree with your thought to merge our commands, it will not be you or the 11th in charge."

Gage put one hand on the desk, gently tapping fingertips against the wood. "Lady Christina," he said evenly, "may we discuss this in private?"

"We most certainly will not," she said. "You've corrupted that Genevan of yours with some very convenient errors as to succession, but the laws and regulations of the Navy are most clear in this. There's discussion over who is the true Regent, but as ranking officer of the more senior 2nd Fleet, *I* am in charge here."

Several captains from the 11th, who'd been with Gage since the first Daegon attack on Siam, shifted uncomfortably. There were a number of glances among the slightly more than two dozen officers present.

"She is of the Crown's bloodline," Arlyss said. "By right she is the Regent until such time as Parliament can confirm her as chief executive…until Prince Aidan has reached the age of maturity, naturally."

"Do you see any Parliament out here, Arlyss?" Gage asked.

**"There are millions of Albion expats across settled space," Arlyss said. "We can convene one in exile and—"

179

"Where?" Gage asked. "Would you have us hide behind the Reich's skirts, beg for a bit of space on one of their worlds and pretend it's the Exeter Palace? There is no place for us to go but back to Albion. That is our home. That is where are families are, where our history lives. We cannot retreat any further. We must turn this war around and we are not going to do it with…" he pointed at Lady Christina "…with any confusion as to who is in charge and why they are in charge. If we squabble in front of the Indus, we lose any and all authority. If we squabble, we'll be no better than the Francia when they fled the Reich. Now they're nothing better than pirates and they've abandoned all hope of reclaiming what they once had."

"Then simply let go of any notion that you have some right to be in charge," Arlyss said. "Enough playing at this, Gage. You're common born. These are Albion officers." He swept a hand across the room. "We are of the nobility, the class that made our nation great in service with the Crown. We've no desire to leave our fate in your hands, no matter how much misplaced faith Admiral Sartorious had in you.

Lady Christina is the Regent. Let that settle the matter. Perhaps you can stay with Prince Aidan as a tutor."

"If you claim Lady Christina is the Regent," Price said, "then the Genevan can settle the matter, can't he?"

"We don't need a foreigner to arbitrate over Albion matters," Captain McGowan said.

"Someone has already invited the Reich into this." Gage looked at Christina.

"Was I wrong to accept Unter-Duke Klaven's hospitality?" she asked.

A number of officers cleared their throats a bit too loudly.

"2nd Fleet owes its lives to the *Castle Itter*," Arlyss said. "The Reich defended—"

"They did no such thing," said Captain Allen of the *Adamant*. "On Lady Christina's orders we disengaged from the Daegon attack, leaving most of our frigate and destroyer complement behind in contact to buy us time to get away. The *Castle Itter* never fired a shot. The enemy broke off pursuit once we reached the Reich's engagement envelope."

Commander Erskine of the *Valiant* knocked on a table for attention. "My father served aboard the *Grand Isle* with King Randolph. He always spoke highly of the Genevan complement. Never in their history have they ever been party to a coup or revolution. They always protect the rightful leaders of a star nation, and the lines of succession are laid out for them. If this Genevan will not endorse Lady Christina, then that is the will of King Randolph, God rest his soul."

Arguments broke out, with more officers migrating toward Gage's side of the room than Lady Christina's. The captains of the larger ships—all part of the larger, more powerful noble families—seemed to favor Christina, while the captains of smaller vessels—and with few to any familial holdings—to Gage.

"Enough!" Gage picked up a tea saucer and broke it against the side of the desk and the room went silent. "Thorvald, who is the Regent? Lady Christina or I?"

"Commodore Gage is Regent," he said. "In times such as this, we Genevans have a test…the

182

Asimov Test. AIs are incorruptible. They will defend who they are programmed to defend without fail. If you all would prefer, I can remove myself from this suit and the AI can operate it."

"What good is that?" Arlyss asked. "An empty suit that—"

"Grynau," said the Genevan, touching his chest, "does not need me. I can leave this suit and then we will carry out the Asimov Test. The two under consideration, Gage and Christina, will pick a second. Then they will stand shoulder to shoulder while their seconds each take aim with a pistol loaded with one bullet. Both fire. The AI will protect the rightful Regent. The other will receive a bullet."

"That..." stuttered Lady Christina, her chubby cheeks going pale, "that can't be real. You're making all this up."

"I've heard of this," Captain Allen said, "quite common in the Cathay Dynasty. They used it in the Biafra Empire around the turn of the century. Something like a dozen of their nobles ate a bullet before they accepted the old ruler's illegitimate daughter as the new leader."

"It's ridiculous!" Christina backed against a bulkhead. "We can't let our leadership be chosen through some sort of-of-of Russian roulette!"

"There's an element of chance in that," Thorvald said. "Not with the Asimov Test."

"I agree to it." Gage pointed to a bulkhead. "Price. Get your sidearm. Lady Christina can choose who she likes. It's not like this room hasn't seen its share of spilled blood." He unbuttoned his uniform top and shrugged it off his shoulders.

"Wait. What?" Christina looked as pale as a ghost. "No…I absolutely will not be a part of this."

"Then you doubt your claim," Captain McGowan said and stepped across the room to where the officers supporting Gage had gathered. One by one, the rest of her backers moved over…except for Arlyss.

"But if she…" said Arlyss, who had gone red in stark contrast to Christina, "if she isn't then…pardon me, my lady." He lowered his head and changed sides.

"This is the end of discussion," Gage said. "2nd Fleet will be merged with the 11th. Lady

Christina, according to records, you were in command of the logistics ship *Bawiach*…which was lost to the Daegon. Return to the *Renown* with Captain Arlyss. He'll see you transferred to the *Helga's Folly* once we return to New Madras. We'll put your merchant marine experience to use there. Questions?"

The room was silent.

"Dismissed." He swung his uniform top back on as the officers filed out…all but McGowan.

"Thomas," McGowan said, shaking his hand, "all things considered, it's good to see you again. Shame about Barlow. A good man."

"He died in service to Albion. You and he were on the fencing team at the Academy, that right, Jules?" Gage asked.

"That's right. Both majored in void engineering. I must apologize for the show." He tilted his head slightly to the wardroom, empty of everything but half-empty teacups, furniture and Thorvald. "I wouldn't follow Christina out of curiosity, but some of the bluer bloods out there needed to be led by the nose a bit. You were…you were willing to get shot right then, weren't you?"

"Yes," Gage huffed in surprise.

"If the Asimov Test hadn't worked out in your favor, I'd have envied you. Better cooling on a slab somewhere than trying to clean up after that nitwit," McGowan said.

"You're the captain of the *Sterling*," Gage said. "You had command authority after the Daegon destroyed your fleet's flagship, the *Nimrod*. Why did you let Christina take over?"

"It wasn't a matter of following her orders...it was just that she had the same ideas I did when it became obvious we couldn't beat the Daegon. I'm disgusted with myself for running off." McGowan swallowed hard. "But there's no honor in suicide. And then to rely on the Reich...I half hoped they'd decide to take Christina hostage after we arrived in system, demand our full surrender."

"How would that have turned out?"

"Bad for them. They'd have had to keep feeding her as we laughed and set our own course to New Madras," McGowan said. "I'm with you, Gage. Albion's light burns."

"And we carry the torch." The two shook

again.

An alert chimed.

"Bridge to the Commodore," came from a speaker in the ceiling. "Indus void forces have gone on high alert."

"Doubt this is another pleasant surprise that's cropped up in the outer system," Gage said.

"Back to my ship," McGowan said. "Good hunting."

CHAPTER 12

James Seaver ran at a crouch, bullets striking a wall just over his head. He rolled forward and landed hard on his rifle, pain ripping up his arm and shoulder. He grabbed the edge of the wall and yanked himself forward. He came around the edge and found three men in the same matte black uniform as his, but with a red sash over their chests and red cloth tied around the stocks of their rifles.

He pulled the trigger on the unfamiliar weapon he carried and it rattled in his grasp as heavy caliber bullets ripped out. His targets jerked as the rounds hit. They fell over, limbs stiff and rifles still gripped in their hands.

"Point clear!" Seaver shouted through a window as he plucked magazines out of the fallen soldiers.

Soldiers with blue sashes rushed into the

building, panting from a quick sprint.

"Forward," the word stung his ear from a small bead implanted behind his jaw and a torque around his neck tightened, restricting his airway enough to get his attention.

"You heard her," Powell said, a young woman that looked equally terrified and exhausted from the effort.

"She knows about that machine gun position?" Inez did a quick peak over a window sill and dropped down as bullets smacked into the house.

"It knows about us," Seaver went for a stair well, stepping over a fallen man in red and bounded up to the next level. He ran for the back of the room, empty but for a few discarded water bottles and climbed out of a window.

"This isn't 'forward'," Powell said as he followed Seaver up onto an angled roof. Inez and the fourth member of their fire team, a scrawny man named Nassau, joined Seaver just below the lip of the roof.

The crack of weapons sounded through a long metal tunnel, echoing off houses and buildings a few stories tall.

"On three," Seaver jammed his rifle against his shoulder and counted down.

They stood up as one and fired down on a machine gun nest barricaded behind broken furniture and sand bags. Bullets smacked off the weapon and the three soldiers manning the weapon. There were curses as the men went rigid.

"Go go," Seaver slid back down to the window and rumbled down the stairs and out through a broken doorway. He banged against the wall of the alley next to the machine gun and waved Nassau over.

Nassau slung his rifle over his shoulder and picked up the machine gun.

"Why does the smallest guy have to carry the heaviest thing?" he asked.

"Team three is in violation," stabbed into Seaver's ear.

"No," Seaver grabbed Nassau by the scruff of the neck and pushed him forward. The four hustled forward, the torques around their necks tightening more and more until they crossed a street. The torques popped loose and Seaver took a hard breath.

"Three!" Legio Keoni, clad in flack armor pointed a knife hand at Seaver, the other held a maul crackling with electricity. "Three through the breach, now!"

"But we have—" Seaver ducked his head as the maul came down on his shoulder and he yelped in pain. Keoni grabbed the front of his uniform and threw him into a knocked out hole in the side of a building.

Seaver stumbled over bodies with blue sashes, losing his rifle in front of him. Bullets snapped past him, one hit him between the knuckles and he snapped his hand back, the pain from the maul strike forgotten as a new and much stronger agony replaced it.

He scooped up his weapon as Inez and the rest of his team came into the room.

Powell went down with a sharp yell.

Nassau opened up with the machine gun, firing wildly from the hip until he dropped it suddenly and started clawing at his throat.

Seaver struggled forward and stood up to see through a low window.

A Daegon soldier raised a pistol at him. He fumbled with his weapon, blood from his knuckles making his grip slip. The Daegon shot him twice in the chest and his pain gripped his body. He went down on one side, his jaw tight as an electric shock paralyzed him.

Inez fell face first next to him.

The pain cut out and Seaver clutched his bleeding hand to his chest.

"Feet!" Keoni came into the room and started kicking prostrate soldiers. "On your feet!"

Seaver groaned and policed up his weapon. Inez wiped a hand across a bloody scrape on his face and gave Seaver a nervous glance.

"Yeah, not good," Seaver said.

"Form up. Ten seconds to comply," Keoni put his heels together and the soldiers fell into ranks quickly. Keoni kicked the machine gun away from Nassau and hauled him up onto his knees as he kept clawing at the torque around his neck.

Centurion Juliae, the same Daegon that shot Seaver, walked down the side of the formation. She dropped the magazine from her pistol and replaced the dummy rounds with compact energy bolts.

"You obey...the Daegon," Juliae walked down the first rank, the blank eyes of her skull mask looking over each of her soldiers. Her words echoed in Seaver's ear bead. "You obey without question. Without hesitation. You," she stopped in front of Seaver and grabbed his bloody hand, "your team was nearly terminated for non-compliance. Why?"

Words caught in his throat, unsure how to answer. She'd never asked him a direct question in the weeks he'd been under her command.

Keoni popped his maul to one side and stalked towards Seaver, a neutral expression in his face.

"Tactical necessity, master," Seaver said. "I saw the chance to seize the heavy weapon, avoid casualties...we took it."

Juliae let his hand go and went to the front of formation where Nassau was on his knees, hands to the ground, fighting for breath.

"You had no control over the machine gun," Juliae said. "You struck fellow themata in the next building."

Nassau looked up at her, hate written across his face.

"Bitch," he reached to the small of his back and pulled out a crude knife made from a bit of metal, strips of cloth wrapped around the hilt. He stabbed the shank at Juliae's chest, but she caught him by the wrist, stopping him cold. She snapped her hand to one side and Nassau's fist came off at the wrist.

He looked down at his bleeding stump in shock.

Juliae raised her pistol and shot him between the eyes, blowing his brains out onto the floor and the wall.

Nassau collapsed to the ground.

"You were right about that one," she said to Keoni. "Clean them up and get that," she wagged her smoking barrel at the corpse, "to the incinerator." She glanced over at Seaver and Keoni nodded as she left.

"Our master give four hours for rest and food before we train again. First we clean weapons," Keoni said. The man hailed from a planet named Papa'apoho, some deep fringe place Seaver had never heard of before he met the cruel sergeant. "Squad leaders. Go. Team three," the man pointed his maul at Nassau's body.

Seaver and the others stood around the dead man, deciding amongst themselves how best to move him.

"You," Keoni took Seaver by the arm and put two gloved fingers on the crook of his elbow. Seaver felt a sting and the pain in his hand went away.

"Juliae thinks you do well," Keoni said, "but you think too much. Obey her. Instincts, no. This," he touched the back of his jaw where their beads were, "this yes. Or…" he cocked his head at Nassau as the other two carried him to incinerator units in the back of the training area.

"I serve, Legio Keoni," Seaver said.

"Not all," Keoni touched Seaver's chest. "You still smell of your home. Not the themata."

Seaver opened his mouth slightly, but opted to keep his mouth shut.

"I no Daegon. You ask."

"Who are they?" Seaver asked. "What do they want? What they did to Albion I—"

Keoni held up a finger and shook his head.

"Too much. See doc bot," Keoni passed him a small plastic chit. "Fix hand. Need it to fight."

Keoni rapped his maul against the side of his leg, the smell of ozone coming off as it sparked.

"Yes, Legio," Seaver clutched the chit and hurried away.

CHAPTER 13

Bucky's was something of an outlier as far as orbital way stations went. A massive holo sign of a smiling marmot in a baseball cap wrapped around the outer hull. Many smaller signs—each the size of a freighter—flashed around the main advertisement, all promoting restaurants, repair shops, the best fudge this side of the Milky Way and a number of specialty massage parlors.

The *Joaquim* had docked on a lower level, the entire ship within an atmosphere filled bay.

Tolan, his face set to the thin features, came down the gangplank from his ship to where a station official and a pair of armed guards waited for him.

Geet and Loussan followed behind him, the captain with a breather mask over his mouth and a pair of sunglasses over his eyes.

"Welcome to Bucky's," the official said. She stepped back from Tolan as he came off the gangplank, her eyes watching his hands and darting back and forth between the three of them. "This station is under Concord common law. We don't have many laws, but if you break any, it will be unpleasant. You all going to be any trouble?"

"No trouble at all," Tolan said. "Nothing to declare. Here for repairs and a bit of hospitality. I'm used to docking on the upper decks. Station's a bit crowded for this time of the year, yes?"

"Concord's under emergency." She held a tablet out to Tolan. "Traffic to the planet's restricted. ID scan."

"Scan? I thought this was Concord space. Behave and it doesn't matter who you are," Tolan said as he waved his palm over the tablet.

"How long have you bunch been in slip space? You heard what happened to Albion? These Daegon?" she asked.

"We heard, we heard." Tolan motioned for Loussan to touch the tablet. The captain did so, and the official frowned at him.

"What's with the atmo gear?" she asked, glancing at the tablet.

"Found him on some deep hole of a colony. Lousy immune system. Eyes aren't used to so much light. Had to hose him down a couple times before he was ready for civilized company," Tolan said.

"No issue with him…or you. Your turn, skinny," she said to Geet.

Geet smiled, revealing a few missing teeth.

The tablet went red when he touched it, and the two armed guards readied their rifles.

"Public charge of petty larceny," the official read from the tablet. "Public indecency. Failure to pay for contracted services. Public indecency. Public indecency. Public—"

"What's the fine?" Tolan asked. "We don't mean to stay here for too long. Just need to purchase a number of major end items and be on our way. No need to go through all the magistrate hullabaloo."

The official glanced over one shoulder back

to a customs stations. "Five troys," she said. "And three for my associates to compensate for their time. Each."

"Eleven? He's not even getting paid that much for this cruise. Maybe we're better off picking up someone else that's less trouble while we're on station," Tolan said.

"Wait…" Geet went pale. "Wait…I'm getting paid—"

Tolan slapped him on the back of the head.

"Make it eight and then get off the station as soon as you can," she said.

Tolan swiped a hand against the inside of his coat and shook her hand. She gave him a half smile then took a small chit from her tablet.

"Pay your docking fees at the kiosk. Don't try and take off with the boot still on your ship. You do, you'll leave most of it behind." She winked and went away with her guards.

"Really?" Loussan asked. "You could have paid eleven."

Tolan pressed a button on a fob and the *Joaquim* buttoned up.

"Always negotiate with Concordies. You accept the first offer, they get suspicious," Tolan said. "All right…you know where to get the IFF?" he asked Loussan.

"I do…but it won't be cheap," Loussan said.

"Fine, fine. Call me when you've got the item and a price. Geet. Commissary run. And everything else the ship needs." Tolan handed him a pack of troys, slips of gold in thin plastic bills.

Geet's jaw dropped at the sight of so much money.

"I also put a neat little explosive device in your body while you were asleep," Tolan said. "This ship leaves and you're not on it?" He mimicked an explosion.

Geet shoved the money into his pockets, nodded frantically and took off at a jog.

"You didn't," Loussan said.

"I didn't," Tolan said. "But he doesn't need to know that. Bet he'll beat us back to the ship with a cleaning bot and a steak dinner. Off we go, Loussan. Try not to get noticed and don't forget where we parked."

****

Tolan walked down a line of garages, small shuttles in various states of disrepair in each. The air smelled of ozone and grease. His gaze flit from sign to sign until he found one bearing a Maltese cross. Above, level upon level of the station reached to Bucky's lit dome, the uppermost reaches behind thin clouds.

He ducked into an alley and signaled to a young woman in skintight latex over little of her body, black fishnets and lace over the rest. Her eyes seemed to swim in their sockets.

"Looking for a good time, handsome?" she asked.

"What do you call bliss on this rust bucket?"

"None of that here," she said. "No shipments from wild space in the last few days. Fiends for that stuff cleaned me out. I've got stardust, apple cores—"

"I need a nerve-system dampener. A fuck-it-all pill."

"Got edibles," she said, shrugging.

"Do I sound like an amateur to you?"

"This strain's amazing. Concord has the best hydroponics setup for ten systems. Best I got. You want them or not? Cherry sour flavor." She put her hands on her hips. "Twenty troy-pence."

"If it's shit, I'm coming back here." He waggled his fingers and a small bill appeared. He handed it to her.

"Kid in a blue cap back on the street has your stuff. Watch for pigs. They want everything sold through the licensed places all of a sudden." The money disappeared into her top.

"Fascists." Tolan walked out onto the main street and a boy in his early teens brushed passed him and pressed a small wrapped bag into his hand. Tolan sniffed it and grimaced. "Just to keep me level."

He pocketed the drugs and went over to the shop with the Maltese cross where small drones worked across a sleek shuttle with a chrome hull.

"Owner's looking to sell," said a burly man in coveralls from behind Tolan. He was bald and a blond beard was braided down both sides of his mouth, dangling and tipped in small beads.

"Everyone's looking to sell and then buy one-way tickets to free space. I'm Dieter."

"Who would ever part with a Daimler-Ewing 9000? Finest machine to come out of Dallas Secundus in the last ten years," Tolan said.

"You know your Reich's made." Dieter reached into the air and thin wires embedded in his hands glittered as he tapped out commands on an unseen screen.

"I also know luxury models like this are supposed to go back to the factory for all but the most routine maintenance. You're replacing the suspensor coils." Tolan wagged a finger at him.

Dieter huffed. "The Kaiserina thinks she can keep every last blueprint to herself," he said. "It never works that way. They sold this yacht to a Concordian. Did they think the buyer—from this planet—would let their choices be restricted? Waste of time."

"Which is why they hired you, a former engineer at the Imperial Academy, to come out and service their shiny toys." Tolan winked at him.

"What? That's ridiculous." Dieter looked to a workbench where a heavy wrench lay, the handle protruding over the edge.

"But you were a plant from Kaiser Washington…the 28th? His Secret Police sent you here to report on black-market tech moving through the system. Someone as knowledgeable as you would be much in demand to verify what was a fake and what was the real item. But that was decades ago. You really must like this station to have stayed on here after you were recalled…or forgotten about. Given the dustup after 28's…accident, I'm guessing the latter."

"How do you know all this?" Dieter put a hand on the wrench.

"Please, you're not the only one out here with a past. We have files on you," Tolan said.

"And which 'we' is that?"

"Doesn't matter. What does matter is that I have some tech aboard my ship that I need you to repair. How about you let your robots finish that up and you come do a little freelance work for me— under the table, naturally." Tolan flashed a stack of troy bills.

"Why tip your hand?" Dieter asked, his

demeanor relaxing.

"Because when you see what's on my ship, you'll either be amazed or angry, probably a bit of both. And that will beg a number of questions. Best to answer them now so we fully understand each other." Tolan set the stack down on a tool chest and a drone scooped them up and flew around a corner.

"Which tools do I need?" Dieter asked.

"What am I, a mechanic? Bring them all."

CHAPTER 14

Seaver pulled his boots off and got a whiff of feet and unwashed socks. He was on the second of four bunks, the third—Nassau's—was empty. The lights were low, but the rustle of men and women struggling to sleep on canvas bunks carried around, along with coughs, mutterings and passing gas.

A clear suture on his hand sat in a numb patch in his hand. He could flex his fingers easily enough, which was a surprise, given that the Daegon medical bot had just dug out a small dummy round from between bones in his hand.

"You," Keoni's voice buzzed in his ear. *"All team three. Office."*

Seaver stuffed his foot back into the boot as Powell and Inez sat up, groggy but moving quickly to obey the sergeant. He pulled his uniform top on and they went through a door at the end of the barracks to a small inner room where Keoni had his office; little more than a cot and a small nightstand. Keoni's armor hung on a wooden cross. The man sat on his bunk, pants rolled up to his knees and a vape pen in one hand.

"Legio," Seaver said.

"News," Keoni opened the top drawer of his stand and took out a bottle of grey liquid and two slivers of what looked like coconut shells. He poured the liquid into a shell and handed it to Powell. She smelled it and hesitated.

"Bula," Keoni motioned for her to drink and she took a sip. She shrugged and downed the rest.

"Oh…my tongue is numb," she frowned and passed the shell back.

"Good stuff," he gave a drink to Seaver who downed it in one swig.

"Bula," Keoni said again.

"That's what this is called, Legio?" Inez asked.

"No, it's kava. You say 'bula' when you drink it. Bula," he put the bottle to his lips and turned the end up.

"I feel…nice," Powell said.

"You three go to shaping," Keoni said. "Juliae favors you. Shaping for best themata."

"Shaping? Is that more advance training?" Seaver asked. A gentle calm came over him as the kava took effect.

"Training, sure," Keoni sniffed and leaned back against the bulkhead. "We second force to take planet. First has problem. Place called Concord, you know?"

"The masters attacked Concord?" Seaver asked, his face full of surprise. "Even the Reich wouldn't attack that place. They fight hard against everything."

"That why first army have trouble," Keoni scratched his face. "That why shaping open."

"How long have you served the masters? Why?" Seaver asked.

"Masters came to my home…they don't give choice," Keoni said. "Serve here," he raised a hand high, "or serve here" he lowered his hand. "I can fight," his hand wavered between the two levels.

"Why do they have blue or green skin?" Powell asked.

"So you know who the true masters are," Keoni said with a smirk.

"Where did they come from?" Inez asked.

"Far," Keoni brushed his hand away. "Beyond ke kai sky river. You call the Veil, yeah?"

"Slip travel's impossible through the Veil," Seaver said.

"Can I have more?" Inez asked.

Keoni tucked the bottle next to his body.

"Beyond ke kai," Keoni said. "They the old kings, come back to be the same kings. Not kings we remember, but kings. Juliae…she from the low village, no strength in her family. She pledge to Lord Eubulus. Be part of big name. Remember that. Help her name and she help you. My themata all from Papa'apoho…I'm last. Rest all dead, or go to the suits."

"Suits?" Powell asked.

"You go shaping, not suits," Keoni chuckled.

"Only those not worth the bullet go to the suits. But you go now. I see you again."

The door opened behind them, and a Daegon male soldier in full armor was there. He motioned them out of the office and put cuffs on their wrists, all connected to a line he held.

"Wait, where are we—" Seaver's question caught in his throat as the torque tightened. The Daegon led them away with a jerk on their restraints.

****

Seaver pulled at the straps holding him down on a gurney. A bright light overhead washed out most of the room he was in. All he could hear were muffled screams through the walls.

A Daegon in medical scrubs, his sky blue skin shone around a mask over his eyes, nose and mouth, held up a syringe filled with silver liquid.

"Stop," Seaver said. "Just stop. What are you going do to—"

The Daegon slapped a gloved hand over his mouth and held head down and jabbed the needle into his carotid artery. Seaver's vision blurred and the feeling of his body faded away. The Daegon turned away.

"Faaaa," Seaver's lips felt like rubber as more babbled out of his mouth.

The Daegon lifted up a rack of glass vials and attached IV tubes to them. The first went into his leg and fire coursed through his veins.

Seaver tried to scream, but he was paralyzed.

More needles entered his body, each more agonizing than the last.

CHAPTER 15

Tiberian gripped the deck of his bridge with the talons built into his battle armor. The needle pains up and down his spine from the armor prompting him into combat helped sharpen his mind as his ship came out of slip space.

A dome rotated up and around his command seat and a holo field formed around him. His *Minotaur* hung just in front of him as the rest of the Daegon armada snapped into existence in a field of icons and data feeds.

He reached out and New Madras appeared, the pale blue of the Indus ships and defenses already visible to him. He grasped at the *Amritsar* fort then plucked at the defenders' formations one by one.

"Looking for a decent target?" Gustavus

asked from over his shoulder.

"There is only one target that matters to me," Tiberian said. "The buoys have all been destroyed...where are the Albion ships?"

"A hard-bore slip journey," said Gustavus, scratching at the fresh scar tissue on his face. "If Gage chose that as an escape...they could be on their way to anywhere in feral space."

Tiberian snarled, then barked commands to his bridge crew on the other side of the dome. Torpedoes erupted from the Indus star fort and converged on the leading ships of the Daegon force.

"You're worried about the wrong thing, Uncle," Gustavus said. "You know my father's been hailing you for the last ten seconds?" The younger man motioned to a pulsating icon.

"When I need your help, I'll ask for it." Tiberian stabbed a finger at the icon. "What!"

Eubulus appeared in the holo, his form so perfectly rendered Tiberian could almost smell him.

"I almost doubted your Albion strays had made it here," Eubulus said. "The Indus fight the way they've been taught—ready for an incursion from the outer system, not a knife to the gut."

Tiberian held his arms to the side, then brought his palms together. The entire battle space around New Madras appeared in the holo, with Eubulus standing next to him as he examined the same data.

"We're within their lines," Tiberian said. Icons for Daegon ships on the planet-side edge of their formation went amber with damage as more and more torpedoes struck home. "Let us defeat them in detail and bring this world under our control so I may continue my—"

"Tunnel vision will be the end of you," Eubulus said. "I *almost* doubted you as to the Albion ships being here...yet they are." He reached to one side and the holo shifted to the outer moons, where Gage and his ships had sprinted ahead of the much larger *Castle Itter* on their return trip to New Madras.

"Such an easy target," Tiberian said. "Helm! Bring us about and—"

"No," Eubulus said bluntly, "no, you remain here under my command."

"My writ—"

"Can. Wait." Eubulus looked up from the battle, his heavy jowls working as he stared his brother down. "You would break formation now and show your belly to the Indus? No. We break the defenders first, that is my writ. I'll allow you to play in the aftermath once it suits me."

"Eubulus, it would be so easy if I just—"

Gustavus put a hand to his hilt.

"Then let us break them," Tiberian said. "Perhaps the Albians will give in to despair and simply surrender. I'll have my fun with their crews, but Gage is mine."

"One thing," Eubulus said, "that larger vessel with them…the *Castle Itter*. It is not to be touched. Baroness' orders."

"She mandates mercy now?"

"She does as she likes, and we obey. I want the *Minotaur* to engage and destroy this formation." Eubulus gestured at a group of six Indus cruisers, all on a straight-line course for the Daegon's troop transports. "Simple. Clear. Do it, then return for more orders. Don't make me regret tolerating you."

Eubulus vanished.

"Too easy," Tiberian said. "Helm, set the following course." He stretched a line away from the Daegon formation and curved it over the Indus cruisers' projected path. His ship turned within the holo and he felt the slightest pressure through the soles of his boots through the deck.

"Why not charge them head-on?" Gustavus asked. "Less time. Same result."

"Eubulus chides me for myopia, while his child fails at the same lesson," Tiberian said. He zoomed out slightly, and projected courses from all the nearby Indus ships appeared. "What do you see?"

Gustavus walked around the holo, hands clasped behind his back, eyes sharp. "The Indus…are moving about like roaches in a sudden light. I see no direction. No strategy. A better commander would have tightened around us, hammered us into the anvil that is their star fort."

"You do see," Tiberian said. "We already landed themata soldiers on the planet. More than anything, they're afraid of what's in our troop transports now. And a fearful enemy makes mistakes. Guns," he said to one side, "ready the turrets. Finish them in one volley. Any crew that misses will feel the whip."

"By your will!" came back.

"By now the Indus commander knows I'm coming for him," Tiberian said. "What will he do..."

Bombers launched from the Indus ships, along with a fighter escort. The smaller craft did not vector toward the *Minotaur,* but leapt forward on afterburners toward the Daegon troop ships.

"Well?" Tiberian asked.

"They are desperate," Gustavus said, "fixated on the threat within the transports and not this ship. They think either the bombers will take out the transports...or they'll run our gauntlet and manage it themselves. I would have set the bombers on our ship in the hope of slowing us down."

"I prefer they have hope," Tiberian said. "It is more satisfying to crush it and see their will to fight crumble. These Indus have their back to the wall...and they're going to fight to the end for it. Same result, just more work for us. Shall we kill them now or let them suffer a bit?"

"Their systems are still largely intact."

Gustavus's head tilted from side to side. "Let's see if we can make them panic."

"Good instincts," Tiberian said. He focused the holo on the Indus fighters and bombers, nearly sixty craft carrying enough ordnance to gut the Daegon landing force.

"We're within firing range," came from the bridge crew.

Tiberian held up a hand.

One of the troop ships nearest the oncoming Indus force rotated around and made straight for the bombers. Hull panels exploded off and a swarm of missiles twisted into the void and streaked toward the attackers.

Tiberian smiled as the bombers vanished off the holo like candles snuffed out by a gust of wind.

"Q-ships," Gustavus said. "I didn't know we were using them."

The Indus cruisers held their course…then their courses wavered as their prows angled away from the troop ships.

Tiberian chopped his hand down.

Energy cannons fired up and down the

Minotaur, pounding the dorsal shields and weakening their energy fields with each strike. The reverberations across the shields grew stronger until the barriers failed and the first cruiser was hit in the bridge superstructure. Two of the Indus ships managed to return fire, and both were crushed by the Daegon's answer. The rest of the ships succumbed within minutes.

"They will be ruled," Gustavus said with a smile.

"That they will." Tiberian turned his attention on the Albion fleet, still many hours away. He put a hand on the hilt of his sword and looked at Gustavus, whose attention was on the unfolding battle.

"Why are they so determined to return to a fight they can't win?" Tiberian asked.

"What was that?" Gustavus glanced up.

"The Albion ferals…" He stalked toward the edge of the holo dome and pointed at a crewman. "Get me contact with our infiltrators already on the surface."

"By your will," the Daegon woman with deep-purple skin lowered her head in submission.

"Something catch your attention?" Gustavus asked. "My father will need our firepower for the assault on the star fort."

"Set the course yourself." Tiberian sat in the command seat and brought up a menu with a wave of his hand. He tapped on an icon within Theni City and waited as a connection went through.

"I may have a scent."

CHAPTER 16

"Bank left! Left!" Wyman shouted into his mic as a Daegon fighter closed on Ivor's Typhoon. He rolled his plane to one side as Ivor cut across ahead of him and opened fire with a quick burst of his cannons. A bolt clipped the Daegon's tail and it went into an uncontrolled dive, corkscrewing into a city block and exploding on impact.

"Ah…damnit," Wyman said, looking down at the growing flames.

"Thanks for the save," Ivor said and looped around to join his wing. "Civilians are all supposed to be in bunkers by now. Blame the Daegon for the mess. Let's not add ourselves to it, yeah?"

"Yeah." Wyman scanned around the virtual glass of his cockpit, looking for more enemy fighters.

"Cobras, this is Marksman," the squadron commander said over the radio. A waypoint appeared on Wyman's HUD, pointing well east of the city. *"Indus request we run interdiction on a track of landing pods. Given that the locals are holding their own, and we're just plinking stragglers from the main fight in the upper atmosphere, we're going to oblige them."*

"Then who's going to run top cover for the embassy?" Wyman asked. The Albion government building sheltering Prince Aidan was marked by a golden square on his HUD.

"Did I stutter, Freak Show?" Marksman asked. *"Indus have things under control. Killing their ground troops during descent is a hell of a lot easier than trying to root them out of the streets."*

"Daegon have been playing rope-a-dope with the Indus Navy since they came out of slip space," Ivor said on a frequency shared with Wyman only. "If we peel off now and they push the screen the Indus fighters have—"

"He didn't stutter," Wyman said and banked

toward the waypoint. "Form up and link targeting computers with the rest of the squadron. Two missiles from every Typhoon should do the trick."

Red diamonds appeared on his HUD, Daegon pods arcing down from orbit to landing zones outside the city.

"Fish in a bar—that's funny," Ivor said. "No fighter escort at all."

"The Daegon in there have a death wish?" Wyman asked. "Planetfall with no—"

A yellow light flared overhead and he banked hard out of reflex. An Indus Chakram fighter plunged between his and Ivor's planes, ablaze and disintegrating all the way down.

"Holy—no chute! No chute," Ivor said.

Wyman looked straight up to the gray abyss of a flat cloud layer. Flashes of light from explosions and brief contrails from missiles lit up the cloud like a thunderhead.

"Doesn't look like everything's 'in hand' to me," Wyman said. He looked back to the tracks of the incoming landing pods, then back to the fight above.

"All ships set to cruising speed and ready missile salvo," Marksman ordered.

"Break break," Wyman said. "Permission to close and go to guns."

His fighter settled into a double-line formation just as they passed over the outer edge of Theni City.

"Not the time to be a glory hound, Freak," Marksman said.

"I think the pods are decoys. No escort. The landing zone's too far from their other LZs to support their invasion. Let me pop one and see if it's even carrying troops. If I'm right, we save missiles for whatever's next. I'm wrong and I just look stupid," Wyman said.

"Damn it…punch it, Freak. Be prepared to get the hell out of there if you're wrong because we'll unload to keep them from hitting the ground in anything but a flaming mess."

"Accelerating." Wyman pushed his throttle forward and he slammed back against his seat. Color bled from his vision as the force of roaring engines pooled blood in the back of his head. His cheeks pulled to the side in a horrific smile beneath his air mask and he struggled to keep a hold on the throttle.

Target icons grew larger in his HUD and he made out the pods with his naked eye as dawn crept over the horizon. He eased the throttle back and his face flushed as blood flooded back to where it was supposed to be.

Radar alerts pinged on his canopy as the targeting computers from the Albion fighters kept trying to target his Typhoon. His IFF broke the radar locks, but he didn't want to risk being downrange from the rest of the Cobras if and when they launched. He'd had enough close calls today. Dying from a friendly fire wasn't going to do any good.

"Switching to guns." Wyman flipped the guard off his trigger and dove in behind the nearest Daegon pod. He fired twice, both shots missing, but lighting up the pod as they passed.

"No reaction…" He fired again and hit the pod dead center. It wobbled and fell out of formation. The pod flashed, then exploded with enough force that it slapped Wyman's fighter up.

"That's not right," Wyman said. "What the hell was in that? A bomb?"

"Freak!" Ivor shouted. "Pull up. Pull up!"

The Daegon pods had veered toward the Cobras with sudden bursts from thrusters, a maneuver that would have killed any soldier inside from the g-forces of the turn.

New radar-locks alerts popped up across his HUD, none of it from the Albion fighters.

Wyman uttered a long string of obscenities and pulled his fighter's nose straight up, slamming the throttle. As he shot upwards, he pulled the emergency override on his electronic defense suite and his fighter's entire supply of chaff and IR flares spat from their housings.

On his canopy's holo display, his fighter appeared, trailed by dozens of Daegon missiles, all closing on him.

The clap of exploding ordnance sounded beneath him, bursts of light casting shadows down the length of his Typhoon. Wyman wasn't sure what would happen first—either he'd black out from lack of blood to his brain or the missiles would catch up to him.

The whoosh-snap of missiles faded away and

he flew into the cloud layer. His hearing died away and his breathing became more and more labored. His head lolled to one side and he felt a bit of peace as he started drifting away.

"Freak!" Ivor shouted.

He snapped back and killed his engines. The Typhoon continued on momentum and broke through the clouds. The sky was a mix of stars and the encroaching dawn as his plane came to a stop, then flipped back and dove nose-first to the surface.

"Freak Show, status report," Marksman said.

"Happy to report I'm not dead," Wyman said. "Zeroed out my chaff and flares to—"

"Whatever you did worked," Marksman said. *"Those pods were a trap and you went in face-first. Dumping all your EW in one go must have done something to the Daegon trackers as they all locked on to you and your flares. Well done. I'm going to pretend you meant to do that."*

"Yeah, totally intentional." Wyman came out of the clouds and reformed on Ivor's wing.

She looked at him through their canopies and shook her head very slowly.

"Bhagadara!" came over the radio. *"Bhadara!*

Badukam vala bhajo!"

"That's coming in over the clear," Wyman said. "Is it…Daegon?"

"I heard 'run' in there," said another pilot, call sign Vulgar. "In Indus. What? I've been watching a lot of their movies and picked up a couple words."

"It's bedlam in their channels," Marksman said. *"Translation software's off-line to protect bandwidth and…mother of God."*

Wyman looked up as Indus Chakram fighters streaked out of the clouds and made a beeline to the city center and the golden Gurdwara. A glow grew in the clouds.

"Oh, this is not good," Ivor said.

"Freak show, this is Cita-che, *I mean, this is Ranbir,"* came over the channel he shared with Ivor.

Wyman wagged his wings to get Marksman's attention.

"I read you, Ranbir," Wyman said.

"Get below the air defense zone, now! Two thousand meters, now! Now!"

Wyman repeated the warning and angled his nose down. Cobra squadron followed in a disorganized descent, two Typhoons almost bumping wings ahead of Wyman as they flew. The altimeter on Wyman's HUD ticked down.

They just crossed three thousand meters above ground level when the Daegon ripped through the clouds. Hundreds of teardrop-shaped fighters dropped, multiple formations in the shape of a guillotine's blade. They opened fire as one, and yellow energy bolts rained down on the city and ripped past the Cobras.

On the ground, air defense nests spread across Theni joined the fight. Rockets and proximity fused cannon shells stitched across the sky, and the Albion fighters were stuck in the middle.

Wyman rolled his fighter around, desperately trying to avoid the ground fire as a Daegon bolt cut down the seam where his canopy met the fuselage. He pulled level just as an Indus shell burst overhead.

"Goddamn it, don't shoot me!" Wyman shouted.

He roared over a high rise and wagged his wings at the gun crew in an air defense nest. When the barrel of the weapon didn't slew to track him, he was reasonably sure they recognized the St. George's Cross on the underside of his wings and realized he wasn't Daegon.

Dashed lines rose from bunkers and strong points across the city, all converging on the dark blades made up of Daegon fighters.

"Cobras," Marksman called out, *"kick up and let fly. Missiles set to first lock."*

"But sir," Vulgar said, *"if there's any Indus still up there—"*

"Just do it! Reform over the embassy once you're empty."

Wyman bore down on his abdomen and tightened his thighs. He cut power to his engines and brought his nose straight up. His Typhoon felt like it hit a wall as he lost forward momentum. He flipped off safety controls on his missile panel and beat a fist against a yellow and black striped button.

Every one of his missiles ignited and slid off the rails, shooting up toward the Daegon formation on a trail of fire. More missiles from the rest of the Albion fighters joined the death blossom.

Wyman cycled power back to his engines and

swung the plane level with the ground. He descended to a few hundred meters above ground level, low enough to run the risk of hitting a building—and to avoid the Indus air defense artillery.

Fireballs burst to life as the Albion missiles struck home. More and more Daegon ships exploded as the ground fire found their range.

The Daegon formation shifted, pointing toward the Golden Temple. A ripple of energy bolts aimed right at the building.

Indus fighters—already holding over the temple—didn't break formation as Wyman thought they would, closing ranks instead and taking the hits meant for the Gurdwara. Chakram fighters flamed out and crashed into the icy river. Bolts struck the water, kicking up tall gouts. A series of Daegon fire hit the temple…and dissipated against a shield.

"They put a ground shield on that thing?" Vulgar asked. "You know how much those cost?"

"They're breaking up!" Marksman shouted. Overhead, the Daegon guillotines flew apart into small groups of fighters and accelerated toward the ground, eager to get beneath the air defense artillery's

fire. *"Embassy. Keep them off the embassy."*

"Roger that," Wyman said. "Ivor, any missiles left?"

"Empty as my wallet after shore leave," she said.

"Same here. Guns it is."

"Behind us." She pulled into an Immelmann turn and Wyman followed, pulling up hard and rotating his fighter level to the ground as he came about the opposite direction he'd been going.

A Chakram fighter jinked from side to side, a Daegon ship on its tail. Wyman and Ivor opened fire, their bolts forming interlinking bands of fire just ahead of the enemy's nose in time for it to fly through and get wrecked.

"Thank you," Ranbir said as he brought his fighter up to join them. *"Just be careful where you shoot because—"*

"You want to tell the Daegon that?" Ivor snapped. "Because they seem to have run out of shits to give and are just using plasma bolts to communicate."

"Two bogies, four o'clock." Wyman banked

to engage.

"The rest of my squadron…they are gone, I believe," Ranbir said. *"I'll fly with you."*

"Less talking, more shooting." Ivor opened fire, the blasts from her cannons lighting up her nose as they left the barrel. Her shots went wide and loped toward the surrounding mountains.

The pair of Daegon fighters sped away from them, then one spat ahead with a push from its afterburners. It angled to one side and the jet wash disrupted the flow of air over its fellow. The other fighter flipped over in the turbulence and fired.

Wyman, caught flat-footed, lost a wingtip to a passing bolt as he struggled to get out of the line of fire. His fighter lost control and went into a nose dive. The controls were sluggish one moment and too loose to control anything the next as his onboard systems fought to regain aerodynamic control through adjusting his flaps and rudder.

He put one hand on his eject lever as he pulled back on the stick…and the Typhoon finally responded to his commands. He shot over a neighborhood of low houses, positive the boom of his engines had shattered windows for blocks around.

An energy bolt cut past his canopy and he realized he had an enemy on his tail.

Wyman jinked from side to side, his Typhoon sluggish with battle damage. He had seconds before the Daegon realized what an easy target Wyman was.

Out of the corner of his eye, he saw a skeleton of an incomplete stadium. The gap between metal beams looked just wide enough for something insane, but not guaranteed to be suicidal. He banked hard, fishtailing, and flew straight for the stadium.

"Freak, what the hell are you—"

He didn't hear the rest of what Ivor said as he shot through the structure. The tip of a rudder clipped a beam and it tugged his fighter back.

The Daegon came through too fast and cut over the field of materials. The pilot tried to thread his way through the other side…but construction was more complete there and the fighter ripped apart into a wave of flame and ripped beams, leaving an ugly exit wound in the stadium.

"I'm OK," Wyman said as he leveled out and Ivor and Ranbir came up on either side of him.

"We got the other," Ivor said. "Can you still fly? You look like you're holding it together with spit and wishes."

"Systems are…" Wyman tapped a blank screen. He smelled ozone through his mask, and a shower of sparks spat out from his weapon controls. "Not OK. Only way I can keep fighting is as a target to buy you two time to get a shot or I turn this crate into a human guided missile."

"You're worth more alive," Ranbir said. *"Follow me. I'll escort you back to the airport near the embassy…emergency crews are already waiting."*

"That's…that's probably for the best," Wyman said.

"Freakish Show," Ranbir said, *"that was going to be the new cricket stadium."*

"It'll still be the stadium," Ivor said. "Still under construction…just under a bit more construction now."

"Can we cut the chatter," Wyman said as another panel blanked out. "I know we're not far from a landing strip…but everyone just think positive thoughts right now."

He glanced up and saw golden skies as the dawn chased away the clouds. The Daegon attack had ended, but this was far from the last battle for Theni City.

****

An Indus soldier hurried into a hastily fortified building where steel plates were propped up against the inner walls and held in place by hydraulic braces. A machine gun pointed out a window and down the street, passing in front of the Albion embassy.

A sergeant looked up from a steaming mug of tea at the new arrival. A half-dozen other soldiers were positioned around the room, all looking tired and stressed out.

"Who're you?" the sergeant asked.

"Major Malhotra sent me from strongpoint East-19," the soldier said and tucked his hands beneath his arms. "He wants me to get an M37 anti-tank weapon from you and relocate it to the other position."

"Does he now?" The sergeant frowned and looked the soldier up and down, his eyes lingering over his wrists. "Why didn't he call it in? Putting you on the street in all this mess is dangerous."

"Officers, what can I tell you?" The soldier shrugged. "Do you have the M37? Because if you don't then I'm supposed to go down the whole line of strongpoints until I find one."

"Of course we have the M37." The sergeant put his tea onto a weapon case he was using as a desk and tapped the cup against the hard plastic. "But how can I trust you with a weapon like that when you've lost your kara." He touched a metal ring around his own wrist. "You can't do the work of God if you've lost your hands."

"That is an M37 case. All I needed to know." The soldier's hand flashed forward and the sergeant felt a thump in his chest. The hilt of a knife with a crystalline blade guard and handle stuck out from a seam in his battle armor.

The sergeant's knees buckled as his vision swam, and the other soldier yanked the blade out and threw it into the eye of one of the machine gunners, killing him instantly.

The sergeant fell to the ground, his mouth moving but saying nothing. He watched as the Daegon infiltrator slaughtered his men with the knife and his fists in seconds before he slipped into darkness.

The Daegon looked over the dead Indus, then kicked the sergeant's corpse away from the weapon case and popped it open. He took out an olive-drab cylinder the length of his arm and popped a handle and optics off the side with a slap of his palm.

"Well, Glycas?" he asked as he turned around. Coming down from the stairs, blood dripping from a knife, was another Daegon in Indus dress and a crow with a white back and breast on his shoulder.

"Roof is clear, link set up." Glycas tugged at his beard. "Can we end this charade, Pegarius? I feel sullied, dressing as these ferals."

"Eubulus was told to send infiltrators, not simple foot soldiers." Pegarius touched the side of his ear and rapid clicks of Daegon battle code sounded in his ear.

"*Lord* Eubulus has reavers that sow terror

behind enemy lines. We don't skulk about. I'm still shocked he seconded my team to you and your liege lord."

"Tiberian carries a writ from Assaria. Would you contest that?" Pegarius tossed the other Daegon a rocket launcher.

"Never." Glycas looked the weapon over with scorn. "This some kind of a toy?"

"It will get the job done," Pegarius said. "Your drone surveyed the target?"

Glycas touched the bird's foot and a 3D scan of the Albion embassy appeared, projected from the crow's eyes.

"The blueprints don't match what we got from the city database…not a surprise," Pegarius said. "If the target is here…then he will be in this bunker." He touched a solid block in the projection. "No external air vents. Smart. We'll burn them out with *purka.*" He touched a pouch on his belt. "The other teams are in position. You understand your orders?"

"Take him alive…if possible," Glycas said. "Dead is just as good."

"Alive, or Tiberian will throw us to the

themata regiments as penance," Pegarius said.

"He'll throw *you*," Glycas sneered. "Lord Eubulus prefers targets dead. Easier to deal with."

"Then let this be a challenge to hone your skills," the Daegon said and touched his ear. His eyes rolled back and his lips quivered. He shook his head quickly. "The rest have their instructions. For Assaria's glory."

"For the great masters," Glycas said and put the rocket launcher to his shoulder.

****

"What was that?" Bertram asked, cocking an ear to the vault's ceiling. Prince Aidan sat in a chair, feet dangling over the edge, a small stuffed tiger doll on his lap.

"Likely just another ordnance strike or a plane crashed nearby," Ambassador Carruthers said. Her dress and jacket were at odds with the Spartan interior of the emergency shelter, as if she expected to waltz out of the embassy and to a cocktail party soon as the fighting was over.

The shelter was little more than a reinforced cargo container with integrated life support, a few cots, and a crate full of supplies. The sole toilet had a few boxes of freeze-dried food stacked around it for modesty. A large safe took up a back corner.

"No." Salis put a hand to the metal wall and the interlocking plates of her armor shifted up and down her arm. "Something hit the outer wall."

"What do the Marines say?" Bertram brushed the front of his uniform off and edged closer to Salis, not wanting to frighten Aidan with their talk, as the boy was engrossed in a cartoon show featuring a cat and three ill-behaved mice.

"They're not saying anything." Salis touched the side of her helmet. "But there's shooting. I feel the frequencies through the wall. A good deal of shooting."

"Then what—" Bertram looked quickly at the boy and lowered his voice, "then what do we do? There's one way in and out of this box, and if…if it's *them* then we—"

"Too dangerous to try and evacuate now." Small plates spun around Salis' forearm. "The entrance is well hidden. Carruthers said this place was built clandestinely and the Indus shouldn't even know about it. Our best bet is to stay quiet and wait for…"

She turned her face up to the ceiling.

"*Miarda*. Ambassador," Salis said, pointing at the safe. "What's that made of? Graphenium and ultra-dense diamond composites, correct?"

"That's an Albion state secret and I—" Carruthers backed into the wall as Salis stalked toward her. "Yes. Yes! It's proof against tampering for days. We keep certain documents in there that—"

"Open it. Now." Salis went toward the door and stared at the ceiling. "Something's burning through the ceiling."

"Did feel a bit warm, now that you mention it," Bertram said.

"Gas masks." Salis opened a drawer and tossed the other two adults a pouch each. Then she went to Aidan and lifted his chin up with a finger.

"I don't want to," Aidan pouted.

"My Prince, it's time to be safe," she said. "You remember what I told you about principal externalized life support?"

"Your special mask, young master," Bertram said.

"It's too scary," Aidan said, pulling his knees up to his chest.

"I know, but now is not the time for negotiation." Salis put the palm of her hand on the top of Aidan's head and plates slid off and formed a helmet over Aidan.

"No!" Aidan slapped at the plates, tossing the stuffed animal away, and Bertram had to pin his arms to his sides as more plates interlocked over Aidan's face, muffling the boy's cries. Salis reached behind her back and removed a small cylinder, which she pressed to the back of Aidan's helmet where it sank into the metal. Eye holes lit up on the helmet.

"Thirty minutes of air for him. Put your damn mask on," Salis said to Bertram as she picked up the squirming boy and carried him to the back of the shelter. "Activate the emergency air flush if needed."

"Tigey!" Aidan screamed and reached for the doll laying by the door.

"Ms. Salis will get Tigey." Bertram maneuvered Aidan into a corner and looked at Salis.

Though his face was covered by the emergency hood, she could see his eyes were full of worry.

Salis handed Bertram a pistol from off her hip, then detached the carbine locked onto her back.

"You're no Genevan, but you will fight to your last dying breath, won't you?" She didn't wait for an answer as she hurried to the front of the crate.

Carruthers had her hood on and the safe was open. Salis swept an arm inside and emptied the papers and several gold bars onto the floor.

"Now just a moment," Carruthers protested.

"Shut the safe as soon as you can." Salis stopped beneath a red glow forming in the ceiling. "You'll know when."

"And what're you going to do?" the ambassador asked.

"They won't get past me." Salis saw the stuffed tiger in the corner by the vault door. She almost went to retrieve it to toss over to Bertram for some sort of comfort for Aidan, but her AI tightened the armor around her legs, keeping her from moving.

Salis raised two palms up to the ceiling as the red spot changed to yellow, then white. Drops of molten metal fell between her hands and spattered against the floor, sending up thin lines of caustic smoke.

Her AI shifted thin plates from her back and shoulders up onto her hands and forearms, forming mitts, just as something slammed into the vault door. A vibration from a drill sent a tremor through the floor.

"Really wish Thorvald was here," she said. "Double the Genevans for double the problems."

+Focus+ her AI sent. +We are all+

"That we are." Salis swallowed hard.

A white-hot puck melted through the ceiling, black smoke roiling off it as it fell into her grasp.

Salis gasped with pain as the extreme temperatures fused the plates of her thick gloves. She swung the breaching device around, fearing she wouldn't be able to release it and get it into the safe. Her AI severed the links on her forearm armor and both fists went flying. The mass of smoke and melting metal hit the back of the safe and oily smoke poured out.

"Close it! Close it!" Salis fell to her knees,

both palms blistered and blackened.

Carruthers pushed the door shut, her face passing through the smoke. Hydraulics within the safe squealed and the smoke ceased. Carruthers sank against the side of the safe, then slumped over.

There was a whoosh as emergency air vents kicked on.

+This is nothing+

A chill ran down Salis' arms as her AI injected her with painkillers. New armor plates shifted down her bare skin and covered her burns.

There was a loud crack, and the vault door went ajar. A small cylinder was tossed in and rolled to a stop at Salis' feet. She stomped a foot over it and her armor formed a seal around the device as she picked up her carbine.

The flash bang went off with a muffled crack, and she winced in pain as her armor absorbed the blast.

Salis jammed the muzzle of her carbine into the space between the frame and the door and opened fire. In two seconds of sustained fire, she emptied the entire magazine of flechette rounds.

When she jerked the weapon back, it was flecked in blood and gore.

The vault door flew open and an Indus soldier, his entire front covered in blood splatter, jumped over two bodies and went right for her. Salis grabbed him by the wrists and swung him like a sack of potatoes into the vault wall. He hit so hard a red print of the impact remained after he crumbled to the ground.

Shots fired and struck Salis in the arm holding her carbine where the plates had thinned. Instead of having little to no effect on her like a fully armored Genevan would expect, the bullets hit with enough pain that she dropped her weapon.

Glycas tossed his empty rifle at Salis' face and lunged at her with his crystal knife. She let the barrel bounce off her helmet and sidestepped the stab, snapping a kick into the Daegon's chest and stomach hard enough to stop him in his tracks.

He switched his grip on the knife and slashed it at her face. The tip caught her forehead and cut through her armor, leaving a gash over her left eye. Her AI tightened the press of her helmet over the

wound, but blood ran into her eye and she lost half
her vision.

Salis caught the arm and bum-rushed Glycas
into the wall, pinning his arm there. She brought one
palm back and slammed it into his shoulder,
dislocating it with a wet pop.

Glycas clenched his jaw in pain and stared at
Salis with pure malice.

"We want him alive," the Daegon said,
spitting blood. "Resist and we'll see the boy suffer."
His gaze flinched to the side for a split second.

Salis swung Glycas around as Pegarius opened
fire from the doorway. Bullets thumped into Glycas'
back as Salis used him as a human shield. When
Pegarius adjusted his aim higher, she ducked down
and shoved Glycas away. He hit Pegarius in the chest,
sending them both down in a heap.

Pegarius threw Glycas off and went for a
pistol on his hip.

Salis raised an arm and a punch dagger
snapped out of her armor plates. She stabbed
Pegarius in the throat and sent his head flying with a
twist of her wrist. She spun back around and found

Glycas leaning against the wall, his breathing fast and shallow.

"You will...be ruled," the Daegon said, smacking his dry lips. "Tiberian...he has you now." His head tilted back and his eyes quivered rapidly.

"Send him." Salis put a boot to Glycas' neck. "He'll get the same." She snapped his neck with a sharp kick.

The sound of gunfire echoed down the stairs leading to the vault. Salis picked her carbine back up and braced herself against the door. She slapped a new magazine into the weapon and raised it up as a head peeked over the top of the stairwell.

"Friendlies!" a man called out. "Albion Marines. We've killed the last of the attackers. Indus already have reinforcements coming."

"Stay up there until we have this sorted," Salis said. "No Indus in the embassy. Do a visual confirmation of any Albion personnel that should be in here. Shoot any fresh faces."

"Understood. But do you need any medics?"

Salis looked back. Bertram was next to Carruthers, a hand checking for a pulse. The steward shook his head quickly.

"Negative. Stay up there until I tell you otherwise," Salis said to the Marine.

"Mr. Berty!" Aidan shouted. "Mr. Berty, I want my Tigey!"

Bertram touched the bottom of his emergency hood and looked at Salis.

"Air's clear. Good work on the emergency vents." Salis looked at the corner next to Glycas' body and saw the stuffed animal. "Get that for him."

She shut the vault door and went to Carruthers's body. The front of her hood had melted, succumbing to whatever toxic fumes had come off the Daegon breaching device. Salis hoped her passing had been quick. She put a hand to the safe and felt its temperature rising.

"Not a lot of time." Salis found Aidan cowering beneath a cot. She touched the helmet and the armor plates returned to her.

Aidan wiped tears from his wide eyes. "Are you OK?" the boy asked.

Salis felt pain creeping up from her burned hands and her forehead throbbed. She willed the face mask of her helmet off and wiped her blood-covered eye with the edge of a blanket.

"It's nothing," she said. "Just a minor laceration. I have sutures that can—"

"Just a boo-boo, my Prince," Bertram interrupted, brushing the stuffed tiger off on the blanket and thrusting it into Aidan's arms. "She'll be just fine. Won't. She?"

Salis reformed her mask. "Yes. I'm fine."

"The ambassadee-or…" Aidan craned his head up to look around, but Bertram moved to block his view.

"We have to leave very soon," Bertram said, "don't we, Ms. Salis?"

"This location is compromised." Salis pulled up a map of the city on her internal HUD, and her AI picked out several other secure locations. "But…Albion has a number of safe houses across the city. We might be safer there."

"Might?" Bertram rustled Aidan's hair and gave Tigey a pat. "Can we do better for him than *might*?"

"This is…we're in a city under siege and there

could be more of these Daegon anywhere. I'm…I'm trained for this, but I was trained to be the junior agent, not in charge of the whole protection detail…of just me. Genevans work best in teams. Our AI's link data and—"

"And what does your training tell us to do right now?" Bertram asked.

"We evacuate under disguise and do our best to blend into the populace. Avoid hostile contact until we can signal for evac." Salis flexed her fingers, fighting the pain that stiffened them.

"Then let's best be going," Bertram said. "We need coats and perhaps a snack and…Master Aidan, can you do something for me?"

"What, Mr. Berty?" the boy asked.

"We have to go, and there are some scary things on the way. Will you keep your eyes closed as tight as you can for me? And don't let Tigey see either, OK?"

"OK." Aidan's face fell, and Salis felt a strange twinge of emotion. The child wasn't falling for simple excuses anymore. He knew what they didn't want him to see.

Bertram scooped the boy up and flung a blanket around Aidan's head and shoulders.

"Best you go up first," he said. "I made sandwiches earlier. I'll get them."

Salis nodded and hurried to the door.

Aidan buried his face against Bertram's shoulder and squeezed his stuffed animal tight. He felt something small and hard in the left leg, like a grain of rice was in there. He'd have to tell Mr. Berty about it later, but when he had to keep his eyes closed, he had to be quiet too. Those were Ms. Salis' rules.

CHAPTER 17

In the command holo of the *Orion*'s bridge, Gage watched as ships died in the void. The Indus fleet had contracted against the Daegon incursion, but the enemy had maneuvered toward the southern pole and tore through an entire Indus fleet.

The numbers were nearly equal in terms of ships, but the Daegon had massed their forces in one mutually supporting sphere, with their smaller vessels forming layers around the battleship analogues carrying the fleet's commanders. At the same time, the Indus were sending in more and more ships piecemeal…and losing them rapidly.

"XO, why don't we have comms with the

Stiletto or the *Cutlass* yet?" Gage asked.

"The Daegon are jamming all the channels," she said with a shake of her head. "The bandwidths are chock-full of noise and we're too far away for a tight-beam IR to our ships…or even the Indus. At least they should be able to form a beam relay and talk to each other."

"Doesn't look like it." Gage zoomed in on a slugging match between Indus heavy cruisers and the outer Daegon sphere. "The Indus are default aggressive. When they realize they're within engagement range, they attack. No one's coordinating this defense. It's like they're hoping the Daegon will run out of munitions before they run out of ships…this is…"

He gripped the edge of the control ring.

"What would we do if we were there?" Price asked.

"If Chadda had listened to me and brought his perimeter rings in closer to the planet—doesn't matter. We only have the tactical problem in front of us. Show me the Daegon's projected course," Gage said.

A dashed red arrow traced ahead of the enemy fleet and wrapped around the planet, coming close to the *Amritsar* star fort and Theni City. The low orbitals were awash in red haze from the holo, showing Gage that data from there was so fragmentary that it was unreliable. Two blue diamonds of Albion ships pulsed—the last-known location of the two destroyers Gage had left behind for repairs.

"They'll pass over Moga and Sunam, major population centers, before they get back to Theni," Gage said. "My guess is that they'll launch more ground assaults and come in for the killing blow on the *Amritsar* once they clear the horizon."

"I concur," Price said. "At current velocity…we'll reach the planet half an hour after the Daegon reengage the star fort." Her face fell. "It may well all be over by then."

"Commodore," said Ensign Clarke as he ran up to the command dais. "Sire, I think we have a way into the Indus comm network."

"Then what are you waiting for?" Gage asked. He reached into the holo and flipped a screen toward

Clarke, showing broken connections back to every ship in the Indus fleet.

"One of our techs found a backdoor to their alert network on Harihara, the inner moon. It really is almost sloppy of the Indus to—"

Price slapped a palm against her station.

"An old signaling station on the planet's surface. Visible wavelength semaphore to—we can get in, but it's technically an act of war for us to hack into their system," Clarke said.

"I doubt the Indus will open fire on us," Gage said. "Get in there and get me connected."

"Aye aye." Clarke turned and waved a hand and sailors at his station went to work.

"Some good news," Gage said and opened a channel to the *Castle Itter*.

"Commodore…" Price did a double take as the connection went through, "what are you doing?"

"Long shot," Gage said.

A screen with Klaven came up.

"Ah, Commodore, I was curious if you knew just why the Indus seemed determined to piss away all their combat power while the—"

"I need your spine cannon in this fight," Gage said. "The *Castle Itter*'s main gun can destroy the Daegon's capitol ships. There's an engagement envelope where a miss won't endanger the planet coming up in—"

"Impossible." Klaven shook his head. "The Reich is neutral in this conflict. We are simply here to observe and report, not intervene."

"Klaven," Gage said, leaning closer to the Duke's screen, "you see those cities burning? The Daegon aren't here to wage war on just Albion or just the Indus or even the Kongs. They are here to conquer all of us. If the Reich sits on the sidelines now, it will be even worse for your people when the Daegon come for you. And they will."

"I'm afraid there's no evidence of that happening." Klaven crossed his arms over his chest. "And there is no way I would ever fire the spine cannon with a habitable world in the firing arc. One strike to the arctic ice would be catastrophic to the environment."

"The Indus would rather worry about a too-long winter than a Daegon occupation, Klaven,"

Gage said. "You know how to command a war ship. You know what the Indus are doing wrong—they're fighting with too few ships at a time because they can't coordinate a counterattack that has a chance of succeeding. All of settled space is like this right now." Gage held up a hand and tugged at his fingertips. "We come together and we can beat them." He closed his hand into a fist.

"I cannot," Klaven said, then looked away slightly. "I will not. The Kaiserina has spoken."

"She doesn't even know yet," Gage said. "How will you look in her eyes if you go back to Prussia Zwei with a clean hull and no battle honors? When she decides to fight the Daegon—and she will—you won't—"

Klaven's screen cut out.

"Stuck-up, blue-blooded, little…" Gage trailed off.

"I've got the *Cutlass*," Price said. "The connection is bad but—"

"Give it to me," Gage said, and a grainy picture of Lieutenant Commander Timmons came up on Gage's console.

"Commodore?" Timmons had her void helmet on, and sparks leaked down from a rent in the roof of his bridge behind him. "The skies over Theni are a mess right now. The Daegon attack—"

"Are you mobile?" Gage asked.

"The *Cutlass* is limping like a dog hit by a car," Timmons said. "We can break orbit, but there are Daegon everywhere."

"And the *Stiletto*?" Gage asked.

"Lost with all hands when the Daegon destroyed the void dock," Timmons said, then look up suddenly. "Guns, slew to starboard forward. The bombers just broke off from their vector on us and— yes, I see the torps! Counter fire! Counter fire!"

"Do you have the VIP aboard?" Gage asked.

Timmons didn't reply, his focus elsewhere. The commander stood as panicked shouts filled the channel. Timmons twisted back to the camera.

"I don't have him. He's still down on—" The channel washed out with static, then died.

"Heaven receive them," Gage said and crossed himself quickly. He looked down for a moment, then back to the holo. "I need Chadda,

261

Price."

"Comms is working it," she said. "All the Indus channels are a mess. There's...there's some sort of data loop that keeps breaking into the comms."

A new screen came up, showing a burning building beneath flame- and smoke-strewn skies. A sea of low rubble stretched across the ground. A single, frightened voice speaking Indus kept repeating the same phrase as the picture bobbed up and down as whoever held the camera moved forward. The video panned down, and Gage realized that the cameraman wasn't walking over debris, but bodies.

The building, the walls once majestic and gold plated, were stained with soot, the bottom stained red with blood from executions still being carried out by Daegon soldiers.

"This is the Malout Gurdwara." The translation was sterile, carrying none of the fear and pain Gage heard in the speaker's voice. "The Daegon will rule us. Surrender. We will be ruled or we will die. This is the Malout—"

Gage cut the feed.

"Bastards," Price said. "That's a house of worship. Not even the Mechanix or the Reich are so low."

"Get me the *Amritsar*," Gage said. "Then have the ship captains on deck."

"Working," Price said as she looked up at him through the holo.

"This is all on me," Gage said. "I put Aidan down there because I thought he'd be safe…now we're the ones out of danger. Lady Christina would've high-tailed it into slip space with him and the rest of the fleet by now."

"And they all would've starved to death between stars," Price said. "The Indus are still fighting. Theni City…the fighting isn't as bad there. And the Prince has Salis with him. She's better trained for this than anyone on that planet."

Gage looked over at Thorvald.

"She will protect him," Thorvald said. "She may abandon the embassy if it's under threat…So long as she lives, Aidan will live. And so long as she lives, I can find her."

"I sent him down there to be safe while I

defended him in the void...but now the *Orion* is the safest place in the system." A wry smile crossed his face. "Irony."

"We'll be back within range to New Madras in five and a half hours," Price said.

"The fight looks like it'll be over before that," Gage said. "If the Indus surrender, getting Aidan back aboard will be...more difficult than I can imagine right now."

"Then how do we keep the Indus in the fight?" Price asked.

"Get Chadda on the line," Gage said.

****

"There." Tiberian looked over a map of Theni City, a perfect holo recreation compiled from sensors and cameras from all across the Daegon fleet. With the claw tips of an armored hand, he plucked a pulsating dot moving out of the Albion embassy.

"You can't be sure," Gustavus said. "Your agent failed his mission. If the ferals know he planted a tracker, this could be a snipe hunt. Something to lure us away from the boy."

"Glycas' last message said the boy was alive and that the tracker was locked. That's Aidan." Tiberian zoomed in on the dot. "But he's moving slowly…on foot. An easy hunt."

"If your agent was able to plant a tracker, then why didn't he simply kill the boy?" Gustavus asked. "Your obsession with taking him alive serves no one but your own ego, Tiberian. It's time to put an end to this. A saturation bombing will suffice." The younger Daegon traced a circle in the holo and a command wheel appeared.

Tiberian snarled and grabbed Gustavus by the wrist. "How long?" Tiberian asked. "How long have we planned our return? How long have we watched these mongrels rut about, killing each other, perverting their bodies with technology…suffering under their own impulses. All of this is part of the plan." He let his nephew go.

"The Baroness has her own writ, and that is to break the will of Albion," Tiberian continued, "to see the once mighty and defiant star nation brought to its knees and surrender completely. As Albion goes, so will the rest of the feral nations. If they defy us, then that will spread to the rest of the ferals and our re-conquest will take even longer, be even bloodier…and even we do not have the resources to grind down every planet. Would you rule a graveyard, young one?"

"Killing the boy serves the same purpose." Gustavus swiped the back of a hand through the command wheel, dismissing it. "This last fleet under Gage is nothing. When the rest of the ferals learn of the prize we took at Coventry, then the Baroness' writ will be complete. You're wasting time and lives—lives that matter, at any rate."

"No, Gage is more of a problem than we first anticipated," Tiberian said. "He's known to the rest of the ferals for rising above his low-born status, for winning against the odds."

"If there's one enemy I hate," Gustavus said, touching his scarred face, "it's the competent ones."

"Gage has the reputation that can rally the ferals against us. Killing him is too easy, and his legend as a martyr would hurt us in ways we can't destroy. Once I get the boy prince…he'll either surrender to keep him alive or I'll slit Aidan's throat while Gage watches. He's no hero if he chooses to let the boy die. Both ends serve our needs."

Gustavus stroked his chin. "Or we just kill them all and be done with this," he said.

"Heh. You've too much of your father in you," Tiberian said. "We must rule these people, and slaves must accept their collars. Learn to love the lash. Eubulus understands this. Why else hasn't he simply erased Theni and the rest of this planet's cities with atomics?"

"The Indus on this world are a warrior breed." Gustavus frowned, then he narrowed his eyes at Tiberian. "If these surrender, the rest of the Indus will lose the spine to fight us."

"So you can be taught," Tiberian smirked. He scratched the air in the holo with two fingers and Eubulus appeared, standing at a command semicircle at waist height.

"What?" Eubulus grunted. His face was worn, an edge of worry to his otherwise imposing stature.

"I have my quarry," Tiberian said. "I'm going to Theni City to fulfill my writ. Leave it intact until my work is complete."

"Your Albion pets are up to something," Eubulus said. "Their fleet has grown larger, and they're on an intercept course." He touched a panel and flicked his hand to one side. A new holo of the planet showed the *Orion* and more ships closing fast.

"They are of no concern," Tiberian said. "Once I have the boy, they will kneel to us."

Eubulus raised an eyebrow to his brother. "We're in the end game. The star fort of theirs has been enough of an issue and I was just about to resolve it…but I grow tired of placating you," he said. "Go. Gustavus will command the *Minotaur* in your absence. Better to have a commander that's focused on the task at hand. You fail to return and the ship is his. You fail to get the boy and I'll take you back to Assaria in chains to remove your stain from the family—and the ship will still be my son's."

"Don't get too comfortable," Tiberian said as he removed a command bracelet and tossed it to Gustavus. He marched out of the holo sphere to a waiting lift.

CHAPTER 18

Wyman squeezed his eyes shut and opened them wide. He nudged his control stick to one side as he drifted too close to Ivor's wing.

"Hey," she said.

"Sorry." Wyman tapped fingertips of his left hand against his thumb. His brain was raw. Loose thoughts ran circles through his mind and the distant mountains surrounding Theni seemed to warp slightly if he stared at them too long. "Been a long day."

"If only the Daegon would ease up so we could have a couple hours of crew rest," Ivor said. "I'm going to send them a strongly worded letter. On an energy blast. Which won't work. I'm tired too,

OK? You had a whole hour on the ground while they put your fighter back together. Ass."

"New orbital track," Ranbir said and a trio of Indus fighters joined their formation. "Troop carriers. Projected landing zone is Rambagh Park. This one's got a fighter escort."

"So probably not more murder balls," Ivor said. The Daegon had sent several of the missile-laden pods at the city, and the Indus and Albion fighters had grown weary of trying to intercept any after several devastating losses. "Whose turn is it to be the rabbit?"

"I did the last one," Ranbir said and Indus language filled the channel. "The others say they lost half their squadron to a murder ball and they refuse."

"We're not up here for show," Wyman snapped. "Hostiles are coming down in our sector and we're dealing with it. I'll be the rabbit. Again." He looped around and nudged his throttle forward.

"Anyone have any missiles left?" he asked.

"Two," Ivor said.

"One…and three total with the other Chakrams," Ranbir said.

"Didn't…didn't they just do a turn and burn at a FARP?" Wyman said. The availability of forward air rearm/refuel points had decreased as the battle wore on, but the Indus had fought hard to keep them open.

"The city's main depot is off-line," Ranbir said with a huff. "Computer systems are haywire. They're having to do everything by hand and missiles aren't getting to where—"

"Fine. Complaining up here isn't going to make more magically appear. We have seven total air-to-air missiles with the last one I have." Wyman marked targets on the approaching wave of drop pods and assigned them to the other fighters.

"Freak Show," Ivor said, "don't go rabbit on this one. Feels off to me."

"Why's that?" Wyman asked, his mind too tired to pick up on what she suspected.

"Pretty decent fighter complement with this wave," she said. "Haven't seen fighters with murder balls, have we? They loose off that many missiles, they're sure to hit their own fighters. Daegon don't seem to mind losing troops, but they don't throw their fighters away for nothing."

"Yes, I was just about to say this," Ranbir added.

"Don't go running the gauntlet? Twist my arm, why don't you?" Wyman cut his speed and the rest of the fighters caught up to him.

"Freak, where's Marksman and everybody else?" Ivor asked him on a private channel.

"Hell if I know," Wyman said. "Command and control's gone to absolute crap. Daegon are jamming long-range comms. Repeater stations on the ground keep getting taken out. Just fly straight and shoot anything that doesn't look like us. Or the Indus. Or…that about covers it."

"Yeah, yeah…tone!" Ivor said as their targeting systems locked onto the Daegon fighters escorting a half-dozen landing craft.

"Firing," Wyman said, loosing his last missile, his fighter jolting as it leapt off the rails. He kept a lock on his tear-shaped target, his systems communicating directly to the missile to guide it in. White streaks traced a line from his ship to the oncoming force.

"Come on…hold this time," Wyman said under his breath. The missile closed, but the enemy ships made no evasive maneuvers, as if they didn't even know they were under attack.

A flash of light so bright his canopy activated emergency screens left an artifact band across his vision. One hand went up over his eyes, but the light cut out as suddenly as it arrived.

"The hell?" Ivor asked over their channel as it filled with static.

"I've lost my fish," Wyman said, his missile gone from his scope. The rest of his systems blinked on and off, then stabilized. "Where are their fighters? I can't—"

Energy bolts snapped past his canopy and he gunned his fighter forward into a steep climb.

There was a panicked transmission in Indus that cut out. Wyman looked down and saw an expanding fireball and two Daegon fighters speeding away.

"Lost one," Ranbir said.

Looking to one side at the oncoming troop carriers, Wyman said, "Hold them off. I'm going to run rabbit anyway."

"We just decided—shit! That was close!" Ivor said.

"I've got a hunch. Be prepped to run their escorts down." Wyman turned to the landers and increased his speed. Even in his exhausted state, the Daegon defense against his missiles piqued his mind. Using a wide-spectrum energy burst—if that's what it was—to break his guidance systems was something new. And using something like that to protect rank-and-file soldiers—already under a fighter escort—struck him as being off.

There was someone important in those troop carriers.

He opened fire with his cannons just beyond the max effective range. His bolts fizzled just before they reached their targets, but one hit home and sent a carrier lurching to one side. Two sped forward, putting themselves between him and the rest of the landing force.

"Not you two." Wyman pulled into a high, tight loop and dove down on the transports, bolts from ventral turrets blazing past him. He angled to one side and pulled his trigger, sending a long line of plasma bolts through the landers' formation. Most missed, but he managed three solid hits before he sliced between two Daegon ships on their left flank.

His comm channel went crazy with English and Indus, but he ignored whatever warning was coming and hit his port-mounted maneuver thruster. His Typhoon spun around and he opened fire again, his bolts crossing with incoming fire and hitting a lander in the belly.

A bolt hit his right wing and shook him like a pea in a can within his cockpit. He got to see the wing holding on by a few metal spars before it ripped away completely and he fell down in a flat spin.

"Ejecting!" Wyman slammed his back against his seat and held his spine as straight as possible as he grabbed two emergency handles behind his head and pulled.

His canopy ejected and a rocket beneath his seat shot him out of his stricken fighter. He held on for dear life as his seat tumbled end over end through the frigid sky. Glimpses of a dogfight, burning wreckage, and a war-torn city swam around him.

Just why his ejection seat's parachute hadn't deployed became an immediate concern to him.

Wyman grabbed one of the handles by his head and yanked on it with no effect. He found the other one whipping around his face and fought to catch it, the centripetal force of his fall and the wind making something so simple almost impossible. Finally, one finger hooked on the line and he pulled them both as hard as he could.

There was a click and the parachute deployed. The silk composite canopy caught the air and yanked him so hard his neck felt like it was about to snap. He looked up at the risers, checking that they had deployed properly, then he looked around him. Daegon fighters had no qualms about shooting him. He'd seen them do it to other ejected pilots.

Fighters swirled in a dogfight not far from him, and he counted more Chakrams—and one Eagle—in the fight than Daegon ships.

"Ha. I was right," he said as cold air stung his eyes. "Escorts tried to break contact when I went for the VIP. Ranbir and Ivor took them from behind. Not that I feel all that smart right now." He looked down, wondering if he'd land in a power line, a burning building, or someplace that would break several of his bones on impact.

Then he noticed hunks of ice flowing past the island with the Golden Temple.

"Not the river, not the river, not the…oh no…" Wyman looked up at a new sun forming on the horizon. A massive fireball made up of hundreds of distinct pieces blazed down from the sky. There was only one thing in the void that size.

The *Amritsar*.

He watched as the star fort broke apart, sections exploding as they overheated, like a comet dying as it entered a star.

At least it's going down over the ocean, he told himself.

A tone grew in his helmet as the ejection seat's sensors read that his descent was almost over. He looked down at a row of blocky houses passing beneath his seat.

"And here we go…" He braced himself against the back of his seat and put his arms over his head.

The seat twisted itself around and the back slammed into a wall. Wyman's world became dust and splinters as he crashed through the second-story floor and came to a sliding stop on a rug. The seat tipped over on its side, his helmet smashing through a small wooden footstool.

Wyman opened one eye and looked up through the gap he'd come through. He patted himself down, checking to see if pain told him where he'd broken bones.

He heard a man yelling, and an Indus with a thick gray beard and wielding a ceremonial kirpan knife ran at him from a doorway.

"Albion! Albion!" Wyman held up his arms to ward off a blow.

The old man, wearing little more than an overly long tunic and a small turban, waved the knife over his head and kept screaming.

"I'm your friend! Really!" Wyman slapped at the release on his straps, but they wouldn't open. Keeping one arm up and using his other hand to remove his helmet, he smiled at the old man, who looked more confused than frightened.

"See, I'm not blue or green like the Daegon." He dropped the helmet and gestured to his pale, sweat-soaked skin. "See? You know that's what they look like, right? I'm not Daegon."

"Daegon!" the man raised the knife higher.

"Nahim Daegon!" a little boy said from the doorway. *"Nahim Daegon, Dada."*

"Nahim?" The man shuffled back to the boy.

"Yeah, nahim Daegon, pal." Wyman tried twisting his strap latch open, but it moved painfully slow.

"You…are Albion?" the boy asked in halting English.

"Albion." Wyman nodded furiously and slapped his chest.

The boy and old man spoke to each other, then the old man sheathed his dagger and helped Wyman unlock his straps. The pilot fell onto the floor and gave the dusty, splintered-covered surface a quick kiss, then he pushed himself up to sitting and wiped his brow.

"Sorry about the mess," he said.

"Tea?" the boy asked, a small saucer and

steaming cup in hand as he came through the doorway. "We having tea. You?"

"Sounds great." Wyman took the cup by the handle, raised it slightly in toast, and took a sip. "Thanks, you guys don't know where there's another air base with a spare Typhoon around here, do you?"

"More tea?" the boy asked as an old woman peeked around the doorframe.

"One more...then back to the fight," Wyman said.

****

An Indus soldier crept over the wreckage of a warehouse, the sheet-metal siding of the walls torn and scattered about like a ripped-up letter. A Daegon lander was crushed against a collapsed shelf that had almost reached the ceiling before it was brought low. The soldier's footsteps cracked broken pottery and small pewter plates as he went closer. Boxes spilled down the lander, covering it like a fractal dune.

"Spread out," he said to the squad behind him. "There were other landings nearby. More controlled than this one. They might be here."

"No one survived that, Chowaniec" said another soldier, motioning with his rifle barrel.

"The captain wants to know for sure," Chowaniec said, "so we're going to find out. Just cover me."

He slung his rifle over one shoulder and tossed boxes aside, each landing with a crack of porcelain.

"Careful, the captain will make us pay for all that," said a young soldier with a thin suggestion of a beard from the doorway.

"Shut up, Silvas. The Daegon broke everything in here," another said.

"But—"

"You want to do this?" Chowaniec heaved a box at the protestor and nothing else was said.

Clearing away a pile of metal plates, Chowaniec found the Daegon lander's hull. It was hot to the touch, the onyx surface scuffed and cracked.

"Anyone know what their doors look like?" Chowaniec asked, sloughing away more broken merchandise.

"I heard they're eight feet tall with no beards—like they're all women or something," Silvas said.

"So you're a Daegon?" a soldier muttered.

"And they're green with three eyes—"

Chowaniec craned his neck around to look at the frightened soldier, who promptly shut up. Touching the hull, Chowaniec felt a seam that he couldn't see. He ran his fingers down the side and jerked his hand back when he felt a tremor, backpedaling and bringing his rifle up.

"What? What is it?" an Indus asked.

"Damned if I know." Chowaniec went to one knee and aimed his weapon as a hum filled the air.

A section of the lander's hull exploded outward, the circular edge of the hull catching Chowaniec just above the neckline and decapitating him instantly.

Shots rang out as a Daegon in deep-purple armor leapt out of the ship. He flinched as Indus bullets sprang off his armor, denting it and knocking off fragments. The Daegon grabbed his chest and threw his hands out, and four tiny spheres hit the ground.

The explosion from the grenades threw Silvas against the wall and his head cracked against it, his helmet and turban absorbing most of the blow. His rifle went flying and he struggled up to his hands and knees, ears ringing.

The first Daegon fell forward, blood pooling beneath his body.

More Daegon climbed out, each armed with a rifle fixed with a serrated bayonet. They swept over the injured Indus, finishing them off with a stomp to the neck or stab to the base of the skull.

A final Daegon emerged, a pistol bedecked in thorns in one hand, a short sword held in the other. A short, regal-blue cape hung heavy in the cold air.

The other Daegon soldiers collapsed to form a perimeter around Tiberian as fresh Indus soldiers charged into the warehouse, guns blazing.

Tiberian shoved his men aside and dashed forward, so fast that Silvas thought the man had transformed into a spirit as he closed the distance to the Indus reinforcement. Tiberian shoulder-charged a soldier, knocking him back so hard his boots, turban and weapon went flying away. The Daegon spun, slicing his blade through two soldiers, cutting a line that began at one's hip and ended at the other's shoulder.

Tiberian fired a single bullet that hit an Indus in the chest. The wounded man backpedaled, clutching at the wound, then his entire upper body exploded into gore. Tiberian cut down the rest of the Indus with ease, stabbing the last in the sternum and lifting him up off his feet. He swung his blade aside and the dead man crashed down next to Silvas.

Tiberian walked up to Silvas, blood dripping off his armor and blade. Silvas was frozen in shock, his jaw open as he stared up at the skull motif of Tiberian's helmet. Tiberian lay the flat of the blade on Silvas's back, then drew it away to wipe it clean of blood. He repeated the motion for the other side, all the while looking at Silvas, his head tilting from side to side as if he didn't know what he was looking at.

"Please," Silvas said, holding up trembling hands.

Tiberian poked the tip of his sword into his turban, then flicked it up ever so slightly.

"Off? Take it off?" Silvas pressed his hands to its sides, his breathing shallow. He was about to push it all the way up, when his eyes fell on his dead comrades. Silvas's eyes hardened and he let his hands fall to his sides.

Tiberian kicked Silvas in the face, crushing his skull and killing him instantly.

"My lord," said a Daegon soldier who approached Tiberian as he looked down at the corpse. "We've lost direct contact with the *Minotaur*. Interference from the destroyed star fort."

"It will clear in time," Tiberian said.

"Yes, my lord, but we've lost the orbital fix on our prey." The soldier lowered his head slightly. "We still have a direction link to the tracker. They're here…somewhere." A holo map projected off the Daegon's forearm. A line traced from the warehouse where they'd crashed across several city blocks to the river.

"Last-known location was here." Tiberian touched a space not far from the line. "At least we landed on the correct side of the river. Fortune favors us that way."

"The target is between us and the freezing water…" the soldier said.

"Have the other packs spread out," Tiberian said, making for the door. "Triangulate where they are and run them down. The kill is mine and mine alone. There's a traitor among them. Leave that one to me."

Tiberian ran a thumb down the side of his arm and his armor shimmered, mirroring the colors and textures around him. The rest of his soldiers slipped away from view.

"Let us hunt."

****

"I'm cold," Aidan whined as he, Salis and Bertram hurried down a street. No cars were moving. A fire truck and emergency crews sprayed down a burning building as others pulled peopled out from a wrecked apartment complex, the remains of a Chakram fighters strewn across the road.

"What did we say about speaking in public?" Bertram adjusted a scarf over his mouth to hide his

lack of beard, then pushed down hard on his turban.
"We mustn't be noticed, young master."

"Stop making it worse." Salis, wearing a
padded sarong, picked Aidan up and put him on her
hip. Her armor had retracted from her face and head,
but Bertram could still see hints of it along her wrists
and neck. She pressed Aidan's face to her shoulder as
they hurried past the disaster.

"We should…I feel like we should help,"
Bertram said. "Everyone else is helping. We'd blend
right in, yes?"

"Until someone asked you something in Indus
and your beardless mouth couldn't answer," she said.
"We have no duty to them, only to the Prince."

"Yes, of course, of course," Bertram said.

"This street leads directly to the Duja Bridge,"
she said. "The safe house is just on the other side."

"I still think we should have gone to the one
on the outskirts. No bridge. Just factories along the
way that—"

"Factories with no civilians to blend into."
Salis gave him a hard look. "Factories that are all on
fire from bombardment." She tilted her head to a wall

287

of smoke rising over the other side of the city.

"Then can we rest? Aidan needs to warm up," Bertram said.

"Keep moving," Salis said and took a few more steps, then she came to a sudden stop.

"But you just said—"

Salis grabbed him by the shoulder. Armor plates slid down the back of her hand and wrapped around her fingers.

"Something's wrong." Salis yanked him toward a doorway. "No soldiers at the checkpoint a block away."

"Maybe they're getting warm. Spot of tea, perhaps," Bertram said as he half stumbled along with Salis.

"They wouldn't have left their rifles on the ground," she said.

"They what?" Bertram leaned back to look, and a sniper bullet snapped past his face and clipped his jacket, sending a bloom of down feathers into the air.

Salis kicked in the door and tossed Bertram onto a couch. Her armor ripped through her sarong and Aiden climbed onto her back as a cocoon of plates covered him, forming a hump over her back and shoulders. She swung her carbine up as a blur crashed through a window. Shots sparked off the Daegon's armor, then the field failed as a bullet punched through his helmet and exited out the back of his head.

The infiltrator slid to a stop next to the couch where Bertram was still struggling to get out of a mass of pillows.

Salis brought a fresh magazine off the small of her back and was about to slam it into her carbine when a blurry hand grabbed her by the wrist. She reared back and slammed a head butt into the Daegon, sending a ripple across the infiltrator's cloaking field as he stumbled back, his grip still firm.

Salis punted him in the groin hard enough to lift his feet off the ground, then grabbed him by the forearm and twisted, sending him sprawling. A ghost image of another Daegon tripped over the other and a crystal blade appeared out of nowhere, swinging at her wildly. The blade hit the cocoon and Salis gasped in fear for Aidan.

The blade bounced off and the Daegon slammed into her, pinning her against a bookshelf taking up the entire wall. The blade flipped over and stabbed at her neck. With her forearm, she blocked the arm holding the blade and held it there as the Daegon tried to use brute strength to drive the weapon home.

The infiltrator's cloak failed, and Salis looked into a flat visor over the man's face. The Daegon wagged the blade from side to side...then let it go. Salis knew instantly what he was doing—the other hand would catch the blade and ram it into the hump on her back...killing Aidan in the process.

Bang.

The Daegon flinched and the blade clattered to the floor.

Bertram, pistol in hand and still enmeshed in pillows, fired again and hit the infiltrator in the shoulder.

The Daegon turned around and Salis saw blood dripping from wounds on his back. She slammed two palms against the side of his head and twisted, snapping the neck and turning the visor around one hundred eighty degrees. The Daegon fell to his knees, then chest-first to the ground, feet twitching.

Bertram swung his pistol to the side and fired. The last infiltrator suddenly appeared where he was trying to get back on his feet, a bullet through the temple. The Daegon collapsed to the ground.

"Forgot about that one," she said.

"That's two…for me," Bertram brushed the pillows away and got to his feet. "Wait until Commodore Gage hears about this. I got two…and just one for you."

"You try fighting when you've got a monkey on your back." The cocoon retracted off Aidan and he lashed out, squirming and fighting as he sobbed.

"Now, now…" Bertram held out his arms and Aidan practically leapt onto him. "Shhh, we're almost there. Almost there." He stroked the boy's hair as Salis reloaded her carbine.

"Issue is," she said, "did they find us by accident or did they know where we were?"

"Neither answer is good, is it?" Bertram asked.

"One less bad than the other." Salis chambered a bullet.

"Tigey! Where's Tigey?" Aidan whined.

"Here." Salis bent down to pick up the stuffed animal…and her grip tightened on something in the foot. She squeezed hard and the tracker inside cracked.

Her armor formed a helmet over her face and a wave of static assaulted her ears and eyes. Everything went dark and her body froze in place.

+Unauthorized code+ her AI told her.

"Reset, get me loose." Salis fought to move, but the suit was like a vice.

+Overriding. Motor function enabled+

She fell against the bookshelf, bringing down a cascade of antique hardbacks as shelves broke beneath her weight. She struggled to right herself, then pulled Bertram from the building as she ignored his panicked questions.

"…*mo te comdenavis.*" Sounded in her ears. *"Quid na…who is this?"* Tiberian asked.

"Morgaten, break the connection. Do something," she said.

+System processing.+

"Anything!"

"We know what you all are, you cowards," Tiberian said. *"You should have come with the rest of the True Rulers to beyond the Veil. You should have suffered with us, been made pure through the pain."*

"You're monsters. Tyrants." Salis pressed a thumb to the back of one hand to initiate a hard reboot, but her AI used her armor to pull her hand away.

"We are what humanity deserves. We are the whip that will bring you all back into the fold," Tiberian said. *"Geneva is too far gone. We won't bother with your false Houses. We'll just turn your planet to glass."*

+Keep him talking+

"How do you know anything about my House? I am of the Guards. There's no stain on our honor like the Daegon."

"Fool. You are the Daegon…or at least you were," Tiberian said.

"What?" Salis stopped and looked back at the building from where they just escaped.

+Sending+

293

There was a scream over the connection and Salis ripped her helmet off. The transmission cut out and her AI prompted her to put the helmet back on.

+System cleared+

"What did you do?"

+Sensory feedback loop. Don't ever make me angry or you'll feel it too. Eighteen minutes to the bridge if you continue at normal pace+

She shifted the helmet off her face and head, then dragged Bertram over to a department store. She broke a glass with her elbow and took a sarong off a mannequin.

"Miss Salis…" Bertram and Aidan looked at her with wide eyes. "A bit of an explanation, perhaps?"

"I don't…I really can't. In fact, I'd like one myself. There was a device in…" She looked down at the stuffed animal in her hand and reached back to throw it. Bertram plucked it out of her grip and gave it to Aidan.

"Not anymore, I assume," Bertram said. Aidan clutched the doll to his chest, staring daggers at her.

"No…no, it's gone. But when I broke it, my AI and the programming in the device…merged. Which is supposed to be impossible."

"And then?"

"And then…nothing else that matters right now. Keep moving. We have to get to the bridge before they catch up."

****

Tiberian was on his hands and knees, a small pool of blood beneath his face as he spat out a bit of his inner cheek. The pattern struck him as somehow beautiful, the vivid red against the white snow of the rooftop.

"Master?" one of his soldiers asked. "Do you require an evac?"

"No." Tiberian wiped tears of pain from his eyes and held up a hand. A soldier pressed the edge of his skull-faced helmet against his palm. Tiberian shook blood out from the inside and put it back on. He rose to his feet on rubbery legs, then keyed a drug cocktail that his suit injected directly into his spine, making all the pain vanish into a pleasant haze.

"All of you," Tiberian said, "disconnect your compliance protocols from your suits. My voiceprint is your authorization. I forgot how much those things hurt."

"How did—"

Tiberian marched away from the questioner and went to the edge of the rooftop. He looked out across the river to a bridge.

"I know where you're going," Tiberian said, touching the side of his helmet. A static-filled channel sounded in his ears.

"Fighter echelon nine nine. What are your orders, my lord?"

CHAPTER 19

Gage took a sip of tea, noting a faint taste of lemon and honey just the way he normally took it. Emma either had good instincts or Bertram had left her specific instructions. Gage was too tired to decide.

He set his tea cup down on a small tray built into his command console and rubbed his eyes. Hours of watching the battle over New Madras while reworking an idea again and again as the operational picture changed had worn him out.

"Progress, sir," Price said. "Comms broke the firewall on the Indus internal network. They're parsing for Chadda's personal lines now."

"Well done," Gage said. "Don't wait to patch

me in. We've no time for subtleties."

"Aye aye."

Gage tapped in a command on his console and Captain McGowan appeared in the holo tank.

"Commodore?" McGowan looked like he'd just stepped out of a barbershop, his face clean shaven but for a pencil thin mustache and hair that would look impeccable even after removing his void helmet after a long battle.

"The *Sterling* received a cross level of torpedoes…three hours ago. Any integration issues?" Gage asked.

"I've got my sailors working nonstop to rebuild the tube housings," McGowan said. "Next scheduled update isn't for another hour. I was saving my report until then."

"Wait…your battle cruiser has twenty high yield tubes. Why are you—"

"Commodore," McGowan smiled slightly, "my magazines have a precisely zero count of standard Mark XII torpedoes. You've loaded forty nine Mark XXI hot runners onto my ship. With the reconfiguration, I can loose a volley of twenty four hot runners in one go. If I'm going to throw a punch, it will be one the Daegon will feel. And if we need to conserve munitions, I can always launch fewer."

Gage was silent as his mind reworked numbers.

"Good initiative," Gage said. "I'll have the *Adamant, Storm,* and the rest of the ships carrying the hot runners do the same."

"I made the suggestion to them," McGowan said. "All very receptive…with the exception of Captain Arlyss and the *Renown.*"

Gage glanced at Price, who nodded quickly and opened a comm channel to the recalcitrant officer's ship.

"I've a concept of an operation," Gage said. "You're the most experienced captain in the fleet, as all our original ship masters were killed by the Daegon, and I want your take on it."

"My pleasure, Commodore," McGowan said.

Gage reached into the holo, squeezed his fingers to shrink the projection of New Madras and the close orbitals and a dizzying array of maneuver graphics, then tossed the holo ball at McGowan's window. The holo snapped back into place.

McGowan's eyes glanced around, absorbing the information as Gage watched him.

"This requires buy-in from the Indus that we don't have…yet," McGowan said.

"That's correct," Gage nodded.

"And you've left out a key weapon system," McGowan said. "If the Reich will use their spine cannon, then—"

"How much interaction have you had with the Unter-Duke?" Gage asked.

"Very little. Lady Christina kept him all to herself."

"The Reich aren't a planning factor," Gage said. "They're going to watch from the sidelines."

McGowan's lip twitched with repressed anger.

"The Reich's *causus belli* has always been that the chaos on their borders is a risk to their nation," McGowan said. "Now there's an existential threat to every settled world from the Daegon and they're sitting this one out?"

"That's correct," Gage said.

"That's…out of character. Klaven is young.

Ambitious. He's at the helm of the biggest hammer this side of the solar system. Everything should look like a nail," McGowan said.

"He may come around," Gage said. "But I'm not going to beg for the Reich's help."

"Nor should you." McGowan raised his nose slightly. "I'll add that the *Castle Itter* didn't save us from the Daegon when we left the Coventry system. We were simply going the same direction as the Reich and they traveled with us."

A new window opened and Admiral Chadda appeared. He spoke rapidly, one hand chopping up and down at someone off screen.

"Admiral," Gage said and the Indus commander did a double take at him.

"Gage?" Chadda's brow furrowed and he looked down at his own control screens. "How did you get this channel?"

"My people will speak to your people so you can plug the gaps," Gage said.

"You're not part of this fight, Gage. At least not yet. I'm trying to keep several fleets in this fight. All have had significant casualties, and I don't have time for—"

"Albion can win this battle for you, Chadda, but you have to hear me out," Gage said.

"You're three hours and…seventeen minutes from high orbit. How exactly are you going to do that? I can barely anticipate what'll happen in the next thirty minutes," Chadda said.

"The Daegon are making a complete orbit around New Madras." Gage zoomed in on the holo and shared his projection with Chadda. Dashed lines extended from the Daegon force and looped around the planet. "They'll be able to bombard Theni City again in two hours."

"At which time the governor will offer our surrender," Chadda said. He shook his head slightly. "I can't stop the Daegon. They'll seize the sky soon enough and then we won't be able to stop them from annihilating our cities like they did on Malout. The governor won't trade our people's lives for the pride of fighting to the last."

"You're wrong to believe the Daegon will spare the planet just because you've surrendered," Gage said. "They want to break your will to fight. Not just yours, but all of the Indus. This is a Neo Sikh world. If you give up, then what chance do the rest of the Indus have?"

Chadda snarled, not at Gage, but at his implication.

"I have a plan that can end this fight, maybe not with an all-out victory, but it'll give the Daegon enough of a bloody nose that it'll slow their advance down," Gage said.

"Tell me," Chadda said.

Gage reached into the holo and tapped in a code. The same graphics he'd sent McGowan popped up.

Chadda's head bobbed from side to side.

"You're insane," he said.

"Hammer and anvil, Admiral. Works even better when the target doesn't know about the hammer," Gage said.

"You want me to pull my forces from over Mahali? There are a quarter million people in that city. They'll be defenseless," Chadda said.

"You must hold Theni, Admiral," Gage said. "The *Amritsar* and your navy are the anvil. My ships are the hammer. This requires both parts to work."

"And a bit gravity well maneuvering that I would never attempt," Chadda said. "You commit to the attack and there will be no way for you to abort. Not without tearing your ships apart trying to fight your momentum."

Gage stood up straight and clasped his hands behind his back.

"Albion stands ready."

Chadda plucked at his beard.

"I'll take a chance at victory over surrender," Chadda said. "The Reich?"

Gage shook his head.

"I can't sell a promise to the governor. Once you enter Harihara's gravity well, then it will be easier to convince him."

"We do that—and your fleet doesn't do their part—the Daegon will tear us apart," Gage said.

"And we pull our forces back over Theni without you to do your part, and I'll have sacrificed most of my planet's population for nothing. Albion and Indus have trusted each other for longer than either of us have been alive, it would be a shame to throw that all away now," Chadda said. "It's not like you're asking me to accept a Reichsman's word."

Gage chuckled.

"We'll begin our maneuver in…nine minutes," Gage said.

"Good." Chadda stroked his chin. "And it seems I have a number of communication security issues to deal with. Shame if I lost contact with the governor's bunker if he orders me to surrender after you commit to the attack…"

"Tragic," Gage said. "An issue no doubt caused by my communications techs. We'll accept full responsibility."

Chadda winked at Gage and the channel cut out.

McGowan chuckled, which grew into a full-bellied laugh moments later.

"Something amusing, Captain?" Gage asked.

"My apologies, sir." McGowan wiped a tear from his eye. "I just tried to imagine Lady Christina making the same pitch to the Indus."

"Can your crews work under acceleration?" Gage asked.

"For the chance to kill more Daegon? They'll do anything," McGowan said. "You've my full support, Commodore."

"Then let's show the Daegon what Albion can do when it's time for a stand-up fight." Gage cut the channel and looked at Price.

"Fleet wide address, sire?" she asked.

Gage nodded and waited as icons for every ship pinged green in his holo tank. He flicked a tab and another channel opened, direct to the *Castle Itter*.

Price waved at him and pointed at the anomaly in the holo. Gage waved her down.

"Albion," Gage said, and his words went to every sailor and speaker in the fleet. "It is time for us to teach the Daegon a lesson. Show them that the free nations of humanity will not bow to them, that they may have hurt us with a surprise attack, but when they face us toe to toe, they will pay dearly. This is where we fight back. This is where we make them pay. Our fleet will perform a low gravity well sling shot around the moon Harihara and then…then we will hit the Daegon harder than they can imagine. We must commit to this attack and trust in our allies. We falter and we will fail, and to fail now will mean the loss of everything. The *Orion* will be at the tip of the spear. Albion's light burns. Gage out."

****

Aboard the *Castle Itter,* Klaven sat on a couch in his wardroom, watching a holo over his coffee table as the Albion fleet accelerated toward New Madras' innermost moon.

Diaz poured coffee from a tall metal kettle into a ceramic mug. Klaven didn't seem to notice, his attention full on the Albion fleet. His Genevan guard stood sentry at the door.

"It only tastes good while it's hot," Diaz said.

"They're insane." Klaven leaned forward, elbows on his knees. "If their vector is off by even two degrees when they hit atmo, they'll either bounce off or scatter out of formation or nose dive into New Madras. Spectacular failure or spectacular success…and that's if the Daegon don't…know what can they do…"

"Valuable information to bring back to the

307

Kaiserina," Diaz said. "Perhaps if the Daegon were warned…it might curry some additional favor down the line with them."

Klaven sat back, his face firm. He picked up a small tablet and touched a button. The holo changed to Albion, a recording captured by Tolan's ship just before it escaped from the system. Klaven swiped the screen and the view changed to infrared, and bright red patches appeared along the coasts and rivers.

"You see all those hot spots? You know what those are?" Klaven asked.

"Population centers." Diaz set the kettle on the table. "Saturation from orbit is a viable threat and tactic to a planet that refuses to surrender once they've lost control of their skies. It's been done to Reich worlds, and we've done it to places that did not have the decent sense to know when the battle is lost."

"You think the Daegon ever offered Albion the chance?" Klaven asked.

"It's neither our concern nor our business." Diaz scratched a cheek, activating the recording device within his monocle.

Klaven touched his tablet again and the holo reformed into the Daegon video from Malout. Klaven sat stone faced as line after line of civilians were put up against the wall of the gurudwara temple and shot.

"We fight without mercy to end wars quickly," Klaven said. "This is a mercy in and of itself. But what the Daegon are doing…should we be party to this?"

"That is for the Kaiserina to decide."

"My father told me stories of the Francia occupation." Klaven sniffed at his coffee, then pushed it away. "Of how he took part in the divestment of Montelblanc. You know what happened there?"

"Kaiser Washington 28th had placed that information under imperial quarantine," Diaz said.

"Three million—at least—civilians dead." Klaven stood and walked behind his couch. "Officially, they died when a dam damaged by the fighting failed and wiped out the city. But you know what my father knew? He knew that the city had been sacked by the 22nd Legion. He walked those streets with Crown Prince Esparza before he became the twenty-ninth Kaiser. Want me to tell you what he saw?"

Diaz didn't answer.

"It was enough that he needed extensive psychological treatment for many years. Even with the neuro conditioning, he'd have nightmares. Ones so bad he'd come into my room with his pistol in hand and stand over me. Know what he said when he did that? He had to protect me from the beasts. Too many times, I woke to see my father there, eyes locked on the door, terrified of the ghosts of the past. Reich ghosts."

"There was an inquest," Diaz said. "Those responsible were held accountable."

"The hangings weren't public," Klaven said. "And that the Kaiser at the time of the massacre…suffered a fortuitous accident was just a coincidence, yes?"

Klaven turned to his Genevan.

"What say you, Rapoto? Curious that a Kaiser would die of anything but natural causes with Genevans around?" Klaven asked.

"Our contract…was in renegotiation,"

Rapoto said. "The Kaiser's chief finance minister missed a series of payments and our protection detail was withdrawn until such time as the books were corrected. While we were away...the Kaiser suffered his accident."

"Imagine that." Klaven raised his hands.

"What are you getting at, Unter-Duke?" Diaz asked.

"There was a marked shift in imperial policy after Montelblanc," Klaven said. "Not that the Reich was ever averse to the summary execution of a terrorist or partisan, but we stopped being what the Albion and other nations accused us of being. Still...the memories remained."

"And?" Diaz sighed.

"And," Klaven pointed at the holo, the mass executions now playing on a loop, "and I don't believe the Kaiserina would ally with this. Her father and my father walked the same streets of Montelblanc together. The 29th Kaiser was a good man. I refuse to believe that she—the 30th Kaiserina—is any different."

"It is not for you to decide," Diaz said. "You

311

have your orders."

"Observe and report, yes." Klaven waved a hand in annoyance. "Don't engage in hostile acts. Self-defense only. But if we see enough with our own eyes to know what—"

"Willful insubordination does not please the Kaiserina," Diaz said. "We serve the Reich. Not ourselves."

"Our empire wide and glorious," Klaven said. "We stand supremely blessed. I serve the Fatherland and to the Kaiserina." He smiled for Diaz's monocle. "But…but there's no use staying here after all the shooting and screaming has died down, yes? Perhaps the Daegon can give us slip space data to leave sooner?"

Diaz raised an eyebrow.

"What are you suggesting?" he asked.

"The Albion fleet will be off the Daegon's sensors for quite some time now that they've entered the moon's gravity well. We know what they're up to…the Daegon don't. A trade of information. They give us a way out of the system, we save them some trouble."

"That's…acceptable," Diaz said. "Keeps to the Kaiserina's instructions."

"Naturally, we can't simply transmit this to the Daegon; the Indus and the Albion would be more perturbed. I need you to go in person to the Daegon fleet. A high g shuttle with a cloaking field will get you there just in time, but you have to leave very soon. I'll have a team of Reichmarines with you for protection."

"This isn't without risk," Diaz said. "A Reich shuttle will look like an enemy to the Daegon and the Indus fighters."

"Then make sure you're not detected on the way in. We have Daegon hailing frequencies. You'll be fine. I'm sure." Klaven smiled broadly.

Diaz bit his bottom lip then clicked off his monocle. He bowed slightly and left the wardroom.

Klaven slapped out a beat on the back of his couch.

"What do you think, Rapoto?" he asked the Genevan.

"We have a saying amongst my House," Rapoto said. "'To catch a falling knife, one must have sharp eyes and deft hands.'"

"That…isn't helping me at all."

"I'm not here to help."

Klaven wagged a finger at him.

"And you're…doing great at that." Klaven drew a small device from a pocket and held it to his ear. "Hauptmann Richthofen? This is your Unter-Duke. I have a task for you… Afterwards, we can discuss a number of your relatives—specifically your two brothers—imprisoned for circumstances I believe need to be reexamined by a magistrate."

****

The light from explosions cast against Eubulus' face as he paced slowly through his holo sphere. Daegon officers at their stations formed a ring around their commander, like silent spectators watching an angry bull await the matador.

"Fourth themata squadron reports forty-nine percent losses after annihilating the Indus over Mahali," one called out.

"I expected higher." Eubulus swiped a thick hand across the void battle and the projection centered on a loose formation of Daegon destroyers spreading over the city. Their hulls rolled to one side, orienting their cannons toward the planet.

"The ferals withdrew their main force over the city; two carriers and one battle cruiser successfully disengaged. Last projected course was to their star fort before we lost them over the horizon," the officer said.

Eubulus grumbled and zoomed in on Mahali. The main highway snaking through a mountain pass to the city was jammed with vehicles and the undulating stream of civilians on foot.

"They're evacuating…different," Eubulus said. "Have the Fourth saturate the escape route. Then finish off the city. No survivors."

"By your will."

The corner of Eubulus' mouth turned up as fireballs stitched down the highway.

"Father." Gustavus appeared in the holo sphere, his shoulders tight and his eyes wide with emotion.

"Not the time," Eubulus said.

"Father, the Albion fleet has gone off our scopes," Gustavus said. "They entered the inner moon gravity well and—"

"And what? Likely they made for slip space in a hard bore. Less for us to mop up." Eubulus wagged a finger at an officer and the holo shifted over to the moon Harihara. The *Castle Itter* was just beyond the inner satellite's orbit, still on course to bypass New Madras. He touched the Reich ship and the projected effective range of the spine cannon stretched out over the battle space. His mouth watered at the thought of controlling such a weapon, but the Daegon needed to rule over humanity, not watch it wither and die from a mass driver strike that could send a planet into an Ice Age.

"We shouldn't under estimate them." Gustavus scratched the scars on his face.

"Just because they got the better of Tiberian doesn't mean I'm the same fool." Eubulus crossed his arms over his chest. "Sensors, launch a suite of drones ahead of us and toward the moon."

"Yes, my lord," an officer replied and thin

tracks leapt out from the Daegon fleet to curve over the horizon while others fired toward Harihara. Eubulus's brow furrowed as the drones sent to the moon blipped offline.

"The Indus electric counter measures are better than we've encountered before." The officer shrank slightly. "Our other drones are more successful, as the interference in the upper atmosphere from auroras and—"

Eubulus slashed his hand across his throat as drone data came in. The Indus ships were converging over Theni City, forming a dome over and around the *Amritsar* star fort.

"Hmm…finally." Eubulus rubbed his palms together.

"But the Albion ships." Gustavus' projection walked up to his father, arms out slightly at his side.

"We're in the final moves of this game, boy." Eubulus zoomed out to see both the Indus force and his own fleet. "Maul formation," he announced.

His officers replied with a unified "By your will" and the Daegon fleet reoriented, with the four battleships forming a center as smaller ships aligned into layers around them.

"Now we crush them," Eubulus said. "One orbit to bleed them dry, one strike to break their backs."

"Why didn't you do this when we first entered the system?" Gustavus asked.

"This planet is a military outpost. They were too spread out for us to take them in one fell swoop when we arrived. I wanted them all in one place to destroy them. If I'd destroyed the star fort at the outset, their ships may have fled. Hard bore journey or not. My plan gave them something to defend, disincentive from running. No loose ends. You and Tiberian would appreciate that," Eubulus said.

"Yes, of course," Gustavus said, somewhat sheepishly.

"Now…who had eyes on the Albion ships when they entered slip space?" Eubulus asked.

"We don't know if—the Reich. The Reich did…I'll hail them." Gustavus turned in the sphere and tapped commands into the air.

Eubulus paced around the holo, acknowledging a casualty estimate with a nod as it came up. The themata ships would suffer, but the battleships crewed by true Daegon would emerge with minor damage.

"No answer." Gustavus frowned.

"Doesn't matter," Eubulus said. "They'll have a fine vantage to watch us finish off these ferals. Then they can go back to their Kaiserina with news of our total victory. They'll bend the knee to us soon enough."

"And what am I to do with the *Minotaur*?" Gustavus asked.

"I expect you to rack up a kill tally worthy of our name. Bloody your blade. It will make giving you official command over the ship easier once I report back to the Baroness."

"What of Tiberian?"

"What of him? He'll succeed in his task on the surface and go back to being a court pet with no need of that ship, or he'll fail and then he will have no need of the ship when the Baroness melts his writ and pours it down his throat."

"I understand." Gustavus smiled. "Permission to take the lead of the formation?"

"Denied," Eubulus said. "Fools rush to glory, son. The patient commander wins the day." He held a hand out and a slave brought over a void helmet fashioned into a lion's head, complete with diamond studded fangs.

"Let the slaughter begin. Gunnery! Full missile launch. Set their sky on fire."

CHAPTER 20

The *Orion* shook as flames danced against the shields. The battleship tore across the planet's upper atmosphere, using the friction to slow its velocity after the tight slingshot around the inner moon.

Gage, strapped into a crash seat, gripped the armrests as another jolt sent the ship undulating up and down as the helmsman called out orders. Bile stung the back of his throat, and he was thankful he'd skipped out on the meal Emma offered just before the maneuver began.

Price sat in a seat next to him, HUD projections visible through her visor.

"Anything on sensors?" he asked.

"Nothing, sire. We're inside a fireball, in case

you haven't noticed."

"Then what are you looking at?"

"Anything that isn't the fireball around the hull," she said. "No need to worry, right? Helm misses a course correction through an air current and it'll all be over before we realize there's a problem. So why worry?"

"A decent way to look at it," Gage said.

"But we are sensor deaf," she said. "Only…ninety-three more seconds until we've decelerated to target velocity. Not long after that before we cross the horizon and engage the Daegon. Assuming…assuming a good number of variables: the Daegon committing to the attack, Indus falling back to—"

"Hell of a time to raise concerns." Gage put one hand on his buckle.

Thorvald stood nearby, his boots mag-locked to the ground and one hand gripping the frame of the doorway to the emergency escape pods. Whether or not the Genevan could get Gage into a pod before the ship burned to a crisp was debatable, and Gage didn't want to know the answer.

"Almost…there," Price said.

Gage unbuckled his straps and leaned forward as the *Orion* lurched up. The motion sent Gage pitching forward, and Thorvald caught him under the arms just before he could smack against the deck. The Genevan lifted Gage up and set him on his feet at the controls of the holo tank as the ship leveled out.

"I didn't see anything," Price said as she slipped into her station opposite of Gage.

Ahead, the orange glow of the burning atmosphere faded away. Bands of blue gave way to stars and the void as the ship angled up and away from the planet.

In the holo, Albion ships blinked into existence as their telemetry data feeds linked together. The ships packed in tight around the *Orion* so close, Gage could see the prow of the *Sterling* off his port side.

"We're…" Price swallowed hard. "…we're missing the *Perilous* and the *Xiphos*. Two IR plumes behind us…they must have hit debris from the battle and—"

"Why is the *Renown* in high orbit?" Gage

stared hard at the ship's icon. It was on a course to join back up with the *Castle Itter,* far removed from the battle that was just over the horizon.

"Shall I hail her?" Price asked.

"Arlyss, you little coward." Gage beat a knuckle against the control panel. "Three warships down and we haven't fired a single shot yet. I'll deal with him later."

"Data coming in from the Indus." Price swiped up from a panel and a mess of fragmentary images populated the holo. There was a scrum of Indus and Daegon ships over Theni city, the edges of the two fleets bleeding together as missiles and energy bolts made a murderous cross fire. Gage refreshed the data, and his heart sank.

"The *Amritsar* is gone," Gage said.

"We're not too late," Price said. "The Indus are holding their own. For now. If we—priority message from the governor. Coming in on several channels."

Gage touched a blinking icon and a solemn-looking governor, flanked by well-dressed men and women, bowed his head slightly.

"It is with great regret that I must accept our situation," he said. "The Daegon forces have seized control of the skies over our home. As such, I hereby order the immediate and complete—"

Gage killed the feed.

"The Indus fleet seems to have missed the message," Price said. "Are we going to ignore it too?"

"I don't need the governor's permission to kill Daegon," Gage said. "So long as the Indus keep fighting..."

He adjusted his fleet's course, moving their projected path just behind the Daegon armada to directly through their center.

"Commodore, we do that and—"

"It'll be a knife fight. Gunnery! Work up firing solution for a hot runner launch and send it to all ships. All cannons load and be prepared to fire at will once we're in the thick of it. Helm, ready for manual control. We can trade paint with the Daegon, but no more." He turned to Thorvald. "Shuttle bay three. A fighter escort will get you to the planet. Find Aidan and keep him safe. Disappear into the population as best you can if our attack fails."

"My duties are to you, Regent," Thorvald said.

"There's not a damn thing you can do for me if this ship goes down. Aidan is the Crown Prince. He is the priority. Now get moving before I kick your ass and throw you in the shuttle myself," Gage said.

Thorvald took a halting step away, as if his armor wasn't under his control, then he entered the bridge's lift with a nod to Gage.

"That was easier than I thought it would be," Gage said.

"Hail from the *Arjan Singh*," Price said.

"Torpedo solution nearly done, sire," the gunnery officer called out.

Gage held up a hand to acknowledge the update, then turned his attention to a new window in the holo.

An Indus naval officer with a cracked visor crouched against a damaged seat. The camera wobbled as he picked up an armrest and turned it to him.

"Albion ships? You're still on your attack run?" he asked.

"We'll open fire with hot runners in…forty

seconds," Gage said.

"I am Captain Birbal Singh We can…we can last that long." The camera feed shook as the ship took a hit and Singh dropped the armrest with the camera. He picked it back up and shouted commands over his shoulder as fire spread across the ceiling.

"Admiral Chadda said there might be a surrender announcement to confuse the Daegon, and that we must keep faith that Albion will perform their part of the battle." Singh gave Gage a knowing smile. "We will hold, Albion. Make it worth the price we pay, yes?"

Gage nodded.

"Guns." He raised a hand. "Fire!"

He chopped down and torpedoes launched from his ship, streaking toward the maelstrom raging over Theni City.

****

"My lord!" a Daegon cried out.

Eubulus snapped his head around, anger at the officer's breach of decorum hidden behind his lion mask. Surprise and fear did not belong on his bridge. Such emotions meant he'd lost control of the situation, and such a situation should have been beneath his capabilities.

"Control your tongue or I will rip it out and—" Eubulus made for the officer, and came to a sudden stop when one of his cruisers exploded in the holo next to him. "What? What just happened?"

"Albion drive signatures," another crewman said, and Gage's fleet appeared in the holo, more and more salvos of high velocity torpedoes bent towards Eubulus' force with each passing moment.

"How did they…" Eubulus looked to the moon in the holo, and he made the connection. "Bold. Very bold, Gage," he said. "Perhaps Tiberian is right to despise your abilities."

The *Medusa* rumbled as Albion weapons hit home.

"Minor damage to aft shield emitters. Themata squadrons can't engage yet. They're asking to fall back to our point defense perimeter and—"

"No." Eubulus watched as eight of his slave-crewed ships exploded almost as one. "Bring the port

squadrons in behind what's already under attack."
One hand double-tapped an icon on the screen on
the opposite side of the force from the Albion
advance, and he dragged the ships to where his four
battleships and attending Daegon crewed cruisers
were. He pushed his own ships away, swapping places
with the outer screen. The holo for the ships began
moving toward their new positions.

"Put more space between us and the Albion,"
he said. "They want me? They're going to go through
the thorns first."

"What of our forces engaged with the Indus?"
an officer asked.

"They can die in place. I'll finish the Indus off
once I teach the Albion a lesson. Fortune favors the
bold, but the battle goes to the side with the heavier
firepower. Bring the prow cannon to bear on the
Orion. Kill her first."

****

"Energy spike!" a bridge crewman shouted.
"Brace!" Gage shouted as the *Orion* lurched to

one side. A blast of yellow light ran through with red streaks flashed to one side of the ship, so close it left an after image on Gage's vision.

The sky over Theni city was a maelstrom of energy bolts, wrecked Daegon and Indus ships, and contrails of torpedoes and missiles swirling to engage targets. The battle had devolved into a slugging match, and the Albion fleet charged straight through it all, heading for the Daegon battleships at the core of their formation.

The Albion torpedo salvos had ripped a hole through the Daegon perimeter, leaving a gap for Gage and his ships to charge through. Wrecked hulls of Daegon destroyers slowly drifted toward New Madras, a handful had already succumbed to the gravity well and become flaming comets over Theni City.

The surviving enemy ships on the outer spheres were contracting toward the Daegon battleships, but the Albion fleet had come over the horizon with enough velocity after the atmosphere brake that they'd reach their targets at the center of the Daegon formation before the smaller ships could join the fray.

The Daegon that had been stuck in against the Indus were attempting to disengage, but the surviving defenders didn't let them get away easily, punishing any ship that turned its unshielded aft toward them and scoring kills so fast that the flank of the battle was turning in favor of the Indus.

The four enemy battleships at their center had turned their prows to face the Albion head on, but were holding their positions. A final ring of Daegon ships of the line stood between Gage and Eubulus' flagship.

"Helm, shift course to one-four mark two-nine," Price called out, and the *Orion* turned toward a Daegon cruiser. Its smaller energy cannons couldn't throw the same firepower as the battleship lance they just dodged, but the enemy ship still could hurt the *Orion*.

"*Valiant,*" Gage said. "I need your task force to deal with this." He tapped the nearby cruiser within the holo. "I spend the *Orion*'s spine cannon here and I won't have anything for their flagship."

"I don't need convincing, sire," Captain

Erskine said. His portrait appeared next to his frigate as his ship and the *Huntress* and *Firebrand* sped up to flank the *Orion* and the rest of the Albion ships.

Gage scanned the status of the other capital ships. The *Ajax, Concordia, Storm*—and two recent additions with the *Sterling* and *Adamant*—formed a nucleus around the *Orion*. Their joined shields absorbed much of incoming fire, but the hits from the Daegon battleships' massive prow energy beams had taken a toll. The impact of the enemy beams dropped off against more distant targets, and each moment Gage closed on the flagship and its three cohorts meant an even bigger hit should Eubulus score a direct hit.

But the *Medusa* had yet to fire, biding its time for a perfect strike against Gage. Two of the Daegon battleships alternated strikes on Gage's spear thrust, but not Eubulus' vessel or the *Minotaur*…Tiberian's ship.

"Not a word from Tiberian," Gage said.

"Sire?" Price glanced up at him as the *Valiant* and her fellow frigates cut ahead of the *Orion* in the tank.

The *Valiant*'s smaller spine cannon fired and struck the Daegon cruiser's shields, sending a ripple through the energy field. The *Huntress* and *Firebrand* fired as one a moment later, their shells striking in the valleys of the cruiser's shield disturbance and punching through. The twin hits split the ship into three, its turrets overloading and exploding like faulty bulbs on a string of lights.

"Well done, *Valiant*," Gage said. "Fall back and—"

A blast from a Daegon battleship erased the *Huntress* from existence and sent the *Valiant* veering to one side.

"Cut power to the starboard thrusters before they overload!" Erskine shouted, then his portrait cut out next to his ship in the holo as a slew of damage reports popped up next to the *Valiant*.

"No lifeboats from the *Huntress*," Price said.

Gage nodded quickly and touched the nearest Daegon battleship.

"Their shields…you saw the frigates' spine cannon hits on that cruiser…if our shells create some sort of resonance frequency when they strike, we can punch through without having to batter them down," Gage said.

"All for it, sir," Price said, "but is the middle of this fight the time for experimenting?"

"Our ships of the line barely out mass two of their four battleships," Gage said. "Any advantage we can—"

Twin prow energy beams converged from the Daegon battleships and hit the *Orion*'s shields. White light blasted through the bridge's windows and Gage crashed into the holo ring, knocking the air out of his chest. The holo tank fizzled then snapped back into focus.

"Shields at sixty percent," Ensign Clarke called out from the engineering station. "We can't take another hit like that, sire. Permission to redirect power from the spine cannon to—"

"Denied!" Gage took in a hard breath and pulled Price back up onto her feet. "Gunnery! Target the nearest battleships and prepare to fire. Stagger hits from the rest of our battle cruisers."

"We're still beyond max effective range," the gunnery officer said. "The plan called for three strikes

334

from the *Concordia* and—"

"All spine cannons fire," Gage said. "We need to take out at least one to give the Indus a chance."

"We fire every spine cannon and we won't be ready for another volley until…until we're almost on top of the *Medusa*," Price said. "We'll take every shot they have on the chin…"

"We don't have to survive to win this fight, XO," Gage said. "Not a word from Tiberian or from his ship. That bastard loves the sound of his own voice. If he could taunt me, he would. Which means he's not aboard his ship."

"He's on the surface. He's after Aidan, isn't he?" Price asked.

"We need to push them back, convince them this planet isn't worth the blood anymore," Gage said. "Anything to give the prince a better chance."

He looked in the holo for Thorvald's shuttle, but everything was chaos.

"Commodore." McGowan of the *Sterling* appeared in a window. "My bridge crew noted something unusual from the frigate's strike on the—"

"There's a shield resonance, yes," Gage said.

"No need to mince words, then. We've worked up a firing solution that may work against their battleships. I'd bet my rank on it, if Arlyss hadn't turned tail with the *Renown* and taken her firepower with him," McGowan said.

"Send it." Gage hovered a finger over the *Sterling* and swiped the data file toward his gunnery station when it appeared. "It's not rank that's on the line here, McGowan. It's lives. We mass our fire and I know we can take out at least one of their battleships. This doesn't work and we might—"

"It does work and we can take two of them, likely damage a third before we die," McGowan said. "History will not remember this day as a lackluster charge from Albion. I believe you're with me?"

"New firing solution checks out, sir," Gage's gunnery officer called out.

"Send it and make ready," Gage said.

"I'll see you on the high ground, sire." McGowan's portrait snapped off.

"I really wish they'd stop calling me that," Gage said.

"All ships report ready," Price said, and a

cross hair appeared over the nearest Daegon
battleship.

"Fire," Gage said.

The *Sterling*'s spine cannon fired, shooting a
hypervelocity slug at the Daegon battleship. Before it
could hit, the *Ajax* and *Concordia* staggered the next
volley. The *Sterling*'s shell hit, sending a ripple of
disruption across the battleship's fore shields. The
Ajax's round struck a rising wave, but the shields
held. The *Concordia*'s strike hit…with no reaction
from the shields.

"Didn't work. Guns! Fire our cannon on the
same target and—"

"No, wait!" Price swiped her hand over the
target and infrared readings from engines rose higher
and higher. The ship exploded into a fireball that
formed a momentary star over New Madras.

"Golden BB got through their shields," Price
said with a smirk.

"Guns, ready for the next target," Gage said.
"Bring our spine cannon into the firing solution and
keep the *Storm*'s—"

A swirl of light formed at the *Medusa*'s prow

and a tight energy lance struck out from Eubulus' ship and punched through the shields protecting *Orion*'s formation. The lance traced down the flank of the *Adamant*, leaving a trail of fire and explosions as it eviscerated the ship. The lance punched through the aft of the ship and hit the *Storm* at the base of her superstructure.

The *Adamant* ripped in half, spilling sailors and twisted metal into the void.

"Shield overlap failing!" Price shouted. "Rest of our cruisers need to—"

Cannons from the remaining Daegon battleships opened fire, pummeling the *Orion*. The forward shields failed and the dorsal hull took hits. A turret exploded, sending a geyser of fire up into the void before it snuffed out.

The ship canted to one side and Gage felt the engines sputter.

"Damage report," Gage looked to the gunnery officer.

"Main cannon's offline, sire," the man said.

Gage looked out the newly repaired windows to Eubulus' ship, cannons still firing. The *Orion* couldn't reach that ship anymore. Not with its weapons.

"Helm, transfer control to my station," Gage said. "Price. Abandon ship. I'll take the *Orion* in and distract them long enough for the rest of our ships to—"

"I will not," Price said. "None of us will leave you, sire. You know who you are. We will not abandon Albion."

"You can survive without your pride," Gage said.

"Then you abandon ship and I'll ream the Daegon myself." Price raised an eyebrow at him.

"Damn you." Gage pulled up the helm control and the rest of the bridge crew turned to look at the commodore as he set a collision course. The *Orion* lurched forward, deck vibrating from the overworked engines.

Gage concentrated on the holo, his heart sinking as the *Sterling* took more damage as it had to drop back from the formation.

Then…a single hailing channel appeared in the holo. From the *Castle Itter*.

"What do they want?" Price asked.

Gage jabbed the icon with a finger and a text box opened. It read: ADJUST 19X-7Y-20Z-KLAVEN.

"About time you bastards came around." Gage entered the course adjustment and put full power to the engines.

"Commodore," Price clung to the control panel as the *Orion* swung to one side, "you're giving our flank to the Daegon. Their next shot will—"

"Kill us. No different than if we'd kept to ramming," Gage said. The *Orion*'s projected course took it away from the Daegon ships and sent it over the horizon. "The enemy thinks we've lost our nerve. And...come on..."

In the holo, the three Daegon battleships shifted to point their prows at Gage and his ship. Gage drew back the holo. The *Castle Itter* closed on the battle, and Gage was shocked at how happy he was to see the Reich's black and silver colors.

A spine cannon shell erupted from the *Castle Itter* and bore down on the Daegon ships. The Reich attack hit the flank of a battleship, tore through it like it wasn't even there, then struck the *Medusa* in the top of a diamond segment, cracking the ship's keel and sending the engines spinning away.

"I'll be damned," Price said.

"All ships," Gage transferred helm control back to the bridge, "all ships come about and form a perimeter over Theni. Protect the city. Comms, get Singh back on the line. The Daegon are broken. We need to finish them off."

A video hail from the *Castle Itter* opened up in the holo. Klaven, in a Reich void suit with silver rank badges on his neck, bowed slightly.

"Commodore…Regent," the Reichsman smiled slightly, "my apologies for not coming into the fight sooner. But the Daegon had the audacity to attack a diplomatic shuttle en route to New Madras. Such an assault on the Kaiserina had to be addressed."

"You sent a diplomatic mission during this fight?" Gage held a hand inside the holo, ready to issue new orders as his ships formed around the damaged *Storm*. Captain Haywood signaled that he was still in command of the ship, but it had taken severe damage.

"And I am most heartbroken to say that my imperial minder, Esteban Diaz, was killed in the attack," Klaven put a hand to his chest. "Tragic, wouldn't you say?" The noble narrowed his eyes slightly.

"Tragic," Gage deadpanned.

"Not to get into too much of my ship's capabilities," Klaven said, "but my spine cannon will not be available for...some time. There's little else the *Castle Itter* can lend to this fight."

In the holo, the Daegon ships pulled away from New Madras and made for a slip space point. Shuttles and escape pods emerged from the mortally wounded *Medusa* as the forward section pitched toward the planet.

"Klaven." Gage put knuckles to his chin. "This diplomatic mission of yours had an armed escort, I'm sure. Where is it now?"

"My good Commodore," Klaven's eyes sparkled, "are you about to ask the Reich for *another* favor?"

CHAPTER 21

Salis led Prince Aidan by the hand as they joined a throng of civilians walking over Duja Bridge. The boy had one hand up next to his face, blocking the chill wind blowing off of the icy river beneath them.

Bertram tried interposing his bulk between the bow and the elements. He readjusted the scarf over his face, catching glances from bundled-up families all around them.

The gurudwara gleamed with golden light from the sunrise further down the river.

"Act. Normal," Salis hissed.

"This bloody weather. Bloody clothes." Bertram looked back to the near end of the bridge not far from them. Smoke rose from out of control fires throughout the city behind them. "This whole bloody mess. Should've stayed on the *Orion*. I will not have stern words for the commodore, but I may embellish our predicament the next time he bloody well thinks the safest place isn't in the heart of an armored ship of the line."

"Bloody cold." Aidan rubbed an ear. "Bloody rubbish is what it is."

Salis gave Bertram a hard look, and he busied himself with his scarf.

A siren wail rose in the air, and the civilians on the bridge froze, their heads peaked up, searching the sky for the noise.

Salis' AI whipped her head around and forced her eyes to focus on three Daegon fighters swooping towards the bridge. The wail grew louder as they closed.

Panic erupted from the Indus, some running for the far side, most turning back to the near river bank. One of the fighters eased away from the other two. Red lines of light formed around their edge of their teardrop-shaped hulls.

"I'm such a fool." Salis pulled Aidan close,

then forced him to the ground. She hunched over him and grabbed Bertram by the sleeve.

"We can make it!" Bertram tried to pull away, gesturing to the near side of the bridge just a few dozen yards away.

Salis yanked him down and used him as a shield over Aidan as the Daegon fighters opened fire. Her armor refolded around her head and bare skin and formed a dome over Aidan.

The bridge shook with impacts and screams from dying civilians filled the air in the wake of the explosions. Salis looked up. The way to the other side of the river was blown out, smoke and pulverized dust rising off the jagged amputation of the bridge. Dead civilians were strewn about, survivors wandered around in blood-soaked shock.

The other side, leading back to the where they'd came, was half gone. A crater, the ends crumbling into the river, took up almost two-thirds of the only route back.

"You OK, Prince Aidan?" Bertram half shouted, his ears damaged by the concussions. His eyes were wide, tiny trails of blood leaking down the side of his head and from his nose.

Salis got to her feet and unlocked her carbine from off her back. Aidan hugged her leg, his face buried against his shoulder. She scanned through the crowd retreating back over what remained of the bridge. She backed up and raised her weapon, moving slowly toward the blown out edge.

"What're you…what're you doing?" Bertram fumbled with his scarf, then threw it aside. "The bridge is out. We need to go…back."

The crowd of civilians lessened. Blurred outlines emerged from the back, knocking aside any that got too close. Tiberian materialized, flanked by several of his hunters.

Tiberian strode forward, one hand on the pommel of a sword, the other held open to his side.

"Give him to me, Genevan," Tiberian's voice boomed across the bridge.

Salis' heel scraped over the edge. She looked down past the bent metal spars. Hunks of ice swept along the current, along with loose bits of metal from crashed fighters and more than one floating corpse.

+Too cold for him,+ her AI sent.

Salis hefted Aidan onto her hip and leveled the carbine at Tiberian.

He stopped ten feet away and gestured for her to come to him with a claw-tipped hand.

"You will not let him die," Tiberian said. "I know your oaths. As my prisoner, he will live, that I promise. You can stay with him as a nurse maid, but without that abomination in your mind or the metal around your body. A pain torque. Rags. You can have those and the boy's life. Last offer."

"Albion's light burns!" Bertram shouted, fumbling with his pistol. "We will never give in to you monsters. You—"

The rest of the hunters raised their weapons up and small laser dots shone off of his heart and the bridge of his nose.

"You claim to know my House." Salis gripped Aidan tight. "You know nothing of us, tyrant. I have my orders, and any free Albion would rather die on his feet than live on his knees."

Bertram looked at her with a moment of confusion. She dropped her carbine to the ground and grabbed the steward by the belt. His eyes grew wide and he opened his mouth to protest.

"Prince Aidan will never be your slave. You cannot have him!" Salis jumped off the bridge, taking the boy and Bertram with her. They hit the water as one, sending up a splash, and sank into the current.

Tiberian rushed to the edge and looked down, catching the last of their ripple. His grip tightened on his hilt, the anger contorting his face hidden behind his mask.

"The water temperature," one of his hunters said. "If they haven't drowned yet...they'll be dead in minutes. Your writ, master, your writ is complete."

Tiberian grabbed the man by the front of his armor and swept him to one side, holding his dangling feet over the river.

"When I see the body, that is when my task is done! You wish to test the waters yourself?" Tiberian tossed him back onto the bridge. "Alert the other packs. Search downstream. Find the bodies. We're not leaving this place until I have proof that they're dead."

****

Cold lanced through Salis' body as the river flowed over her. She lay in a submerged debris field, wan light wavering through the water from the sky, teasing at warmth. A faint sensation of heat glowed through her midsection, where Aidan was enclosed in a cocoon in her armor. She'd got the protective layer over the boy right as they hit the water, and he was fully enclosed by the time they hit the riverbed, but he'd still gotten wet and she felt him shivering as her suit struggled to keep his core temperature high.

One of her hands gripped the edge of a bridge section, the other was over Bertram's mouth. Her plates shifted over his face as a respirator.

Bertram jerked like a fish caught on the end of a line. She looked at him and her heart sank. He had nothing to fight the frigid embrace. Already his limbs were jerking haphazardly and she could see the deep blue of hypothermia flooding his exposed skin.

+Air left.+ A timer reading 4:12 came up over her vision. Another number, more subdued, next to it had 17:23.

"I can't do it," she said.

+He is not our principal. Do not risk the life that matters.+

Her hold on Bertram's face slipped ever so slightly and she tightened her grip and a moan escaped the steward and fed into her helmet.

"He...matters to me." She willed the words to the AI rather than waste air speaking.

"S-S-Salis? Can you h-hear me?" Bertram asked, teeth chattering.

She nudged the hand holding his face up and down.

"C-can't keep me." He tried to grab her arm, but his fingers were frozen stiff. "Air. For the boy. Let me go."

She shook her head side to side.

+Do it.+

He'll die!

+Your oath.+

A stab of ice hit her heart, one that had nothing to do with the river.

"Let me go." Bertram tried to kick at her, pulling away from her hold. "Tell him...tell him Master Berty loves him. You know...know what he likes to eat. Take care of him…take care of…my Prince." The fight went out of Bertram and his face went slack.

Salis pulled him close and touched his face.

"Forgive me." She put one hand to his chest and thrust him away. The current caught him and he vanished into the murk.

CHAPTER 22

Tiberian sprinted across a roof top and vaulted over the gap to the next building. One hand caught the ledge and he continued on, barely breaking his stride. Hunters followed, like wolves struggling to keep up with the alpha on the scent.

"Uncle!" Gustavus' static-laced voice cut into his ears. "Uncle, the...the *Medusa*...she's dead in space. My father is injured."

"Not my concern, boy." Tiberian dove off the building and hit the wall of a half–wrecked factory, catching it with claws in his gloves and feet. He slid down, leaving gouges in the façade.

"The orbitals are—tenable...Reich...have to leave!

Retreat, retreat now...you have command," Gustavus said.

"The ferals put up a fight and you fold this quickly?" Tiberian looked up. Contrails of burning debris traced across the sky. He glanced to one of his hunters.

"Shuttle and escort can be here in eight minutes," he said.

"Summon them." Tiberian trotted around a corner to a supply yard next to the river where one of his packs was huddled around a body. "I may have my answer." He touched the grey metal box hanging from his neck.

"The feral still has brain function," a hunter kneeling next to Bertram's half frozen body said. Wires and tubes snaked from the hunter's armor to Bertram's open mouth, nose, and into his clothing. "I've stabilized him, but a full resuscitation might—"

"Do it," Tiberian drew his sword.

Electricity jolted Bertram and his chubby body went into spasms.

A neon blue liquid ran down a tube and into Bertram's chest, just over his heart.

Bertram inhaled deeply and sat up, gagging on

the line in his throat. They snapped out with an ugly sound from the steward.

"By the grace of the Lord, thank ye," he sputtered and held up a hand. "Where am I? What…happened?" Bertram looked up at Tiberian's face. "Ah…hell."

Tiberian grabbed a fistful of Bertram's top and hoisted him up in the air. He stabbed the tip of his sword into his solar plexus, the metal pierced the fabric and scraped at the flesh beneath.

"Where is the boy?" Tiberian asked.

"Dead!" Bertram looked down, his face flush from the drugs that revived him. "I saw…saw him slip away into the current. The Genevan…the water did something to her armor, she froze up. Malfunction—ah!"

Tiberian let the point slip into Bertram's flesh and a thin line of blood ran down the blade.

"Are you lying to me?" Tiberian snarled. "Why don't I rip out your tongue to be sure?"

A single shot rang out and the sword shattered. Tiberian tossed Bertram aside and whirled around, the broken hilt of his weapon still in hand.

Hunters on the perimeter of the supply yard opened fire, and the crack of heavy caliber weapons answered.

"What is this?" Tiberian asked as a half dozen reports flooded his ears all at once. "Fall back and hold until our extraction arrives." He looked down at Bertram. The man lay on one side, the tip of the sword impaled an inch deep in his chest. Bertram had both hands on the edges, pulling weakly and wincing in pain.

"I'm not done with you," Tiberian said.

"Master, look out!"

Tiberian looked up at the third floor of the nearby blown out factory as someone crashed through the glass and came down at Tiberian like a missile.

Thorvald landed feet first on a hunter, crushing the man to death. Reichsmarines crashed through the bottom level and charged. Their matte black armor and glowing eyes gave them a demonic air.

Thorvald pointed at Tiberian.

"You," the Genevan said.

"Kill them!" Tiberian sprang at Thorvald and struck with the broken sword. Thorvald rolled forward under the blow and swept a leg out, catching the Daegon commander across the ankles.

Tiberian tucked his head and shoulders and took the fall on his back, flipping around onto his feet and slashing across his body as Thorvald closed to attack, a punch dagger molded out of the Genevan's armor over his right hand.

The too short blade missed Thorvald's neck by an inch, and he stabbed his own weapon at Tiberian's sternum. It glanced off to one side, leaving a deep gouge in the metal.

"Dog!" Tiberian punched the pommel into Thorvald's visor and popped the Genevan's head back. He brought the hilt up and smashed it down towards the back of Thorvald's head.

Thorvald swooped his head to one side, then snapped it back up, the back of his helmet catching Tiberian on the chin.

Thorvald punched his blade arm at the Daegon's heart.

Tiberian took the blow on the forearm, and

the blade pierced through both sides of his arm. Deep purple blood spurted out and hit Thorvald's visor. Tiberian brought his other arm up, flipped the grip on his sword, and stabbed Thorvald in the shoulder. The jagged end squealed as it gouged deeper into the armor.

Plates shifted up to the damaged area, wedging themselves beneath the point of impact and inching the blade up and up.

Tiberian and Thorvald locked eyes through their masks, both straining to finish the other.

"Finally…" Tiberian said, "a decent fight."

"Your last." Thorvald's punch dagger retracted, earning a snarl of pain from Tiberian, and ducked forward. The broken sword skidded down his back as he drove a shoulder into Tiberian's stomach.

The Genevan drove forward and lifted Tiberian up behind his knees, driving the Daegon's head and shoulders into the concrete with a loud crack. Thorvald drew a hand across his body and the armor formed a curved blade along the edge of his hand.

He swiped at Tiberian's neck, only to have the

blow stopped dead by the Daegon's bleeding forearm.

Tiberian cocked the thumb on his other hand out, and a long nail telescoped off the tip. He drove the nail up and into the bottom of Thorvald's jaw. The nail pierced through the armor and into Thorvald's mouth, stopping against the bottom of his skull.

Thorvald pulled back, blood gushing from the hole.

Tiberian rolled to his feet and hooked a punch at Thorvald. The Genevan ducked, taking a glancing blow, then hit Tiberian in the middle of the damaged line on the armor across his torso. The armor buckled and air whooshed out of Tiberian's lungs.

Thorvald slammed an elbow into Tiberian's jaw, breaking the mask and sending the bottom half flying away. Tiberian stumbled back and Thorvald pressed forward. Thorvald kicked out, but Tiberian turned and deflected the blow with an arm.

Thorvald landed with a wide stance and caught a fist to the chest. He struck back, hitting Tiberian in the temple and knocking the Daegon's head from side to side like a swaying bell.

Tiberian grabbed Thorvald by the shoulders, reared back, and slammed his forehead against Thorvald's visor.

Thorvald's world went dark as the blow shattered the front of his helmet. He didn't see the kick Tiberian aimed for his stomach, but he felt it when the blow sent him flying. His AI ejected the ruined visor and he looked up to see Tiberian being dragged back by several of his hunters to a Daegon shuttle coming down for a landing just behind him.

Tiberian ripped off his mask and threw it at the Genevan.

"We're not done, you traitor! I'll have your head on a pike before this war is done!" Tiberian shouted.

A hunter raised a rifle at Thorvald, but Tiberian beat the barrel to one side.

Thorvald opened his mouth and spat out a mass of blood. His tongue had a decent slice across the front side, and he felt a loose tooth wedge between his cheek and jaw.

The Daegon shuttle roared away.

Thorvald crawled over on his hands and

knees to his broken visor and slapped it against his armor. It folded around the damaged piece.

A Reichsmarine, bleeding from bullet strikes to the shoulder and thighs, came over and helped Thorvald up.

"You dying, Genevan?" the Reichsmarine asked.

"Hod ye." Blood dribbled over his lips as he attempted to speak.

"Your man's over there." The Reichsmarine pointed behind him.

Two Reichsmarines, one with a white band with a red cross on one arm, knelt next to Bertram.

"On three," the medic said. "One…" The medic yanked the broken sword point out of Bertram's chest and tossed it to one side.

"Ah! You kraut-slurping, cow-patty-eating, goose-stepping arseholes," Bertram wheezed. "And liars!" he added as the medic patched up his chest.

"You're lucky you're so fat," the medic said. "You'd have a sucking chest wound if it weren't for your padding."

Thorvald, one hand pressed into the wound

beneath his chin, looked over the medic's shoulder.

"You hear that, Thorvald?" Bertram asked. "We're both armor-plated."

Thorvald huffed through his nose and shook his head.

"Where's Salis and—" Bertram looked at the two Reichsmarines. "—and the other refugees? What did those Daegon bastards hit me with? I feel kind of good. Great, really. Someone give me a gun, I want to keep fighting." He tried to sit up, but the medic forced him back down.

"An adrenaline cocktail of some kind," the medic said. "You'll crash soon, and when that happens, you don't want to be in a firefight."

"Salis?" Bertram asked as the medic ran a cauterizer laser across the puncture wound.

Thorvald picked up Bertram's jacket, removed by the medics, and plucked out a single Genevan armor plate.

"What's that? It…it must belong to Salis. She slipped it in there when I blacked out. Why?"

Thorvald squeezed the plate between his fingers and a pulse of light emitted from the contact point. A line with an arrowhead shone off the plate, and Thorvald followed the point toward the river.

"Oh." Bertram got up, ignoring the cold and his wide belly exposed to the elements. "Oh, she put a tracker on me. But if the Daegon found it, then—"

Thorvald shook his head and tapped the slate against the side of his helmet.

"Genevan only…smart," Bertram said. "Is there a transmitter in there for you to send her the all-clear?"

Thorvald nodded.

"All's well, then. She in the water? I could fancy a swim, get that Daegon stench off me." Bertram reached down to untie a boot, then froze. He swayed and tipped over.

"Mister…Thorv…I think it wore…wore off," Bertram said. The steward lay there, fingers still in the laces. The Reich medic pulled a small square off his belt and unfurled a foil blanket with a flick of his hand. He tucked it around Bertram then touched the bottom of his helmet.

"Let me look at you," the medic said. Thorvald took his hand away and tilted his chin up.

Blood ran down his throat and over his chest.

"Sorry we couldn't take out the rest of the Daegon," the medic said as he sprayed the wound with an antiseptic mist. "The hunters put up more of a fight than we imagined. Lost some good Marines in the process."

Thorvald lifted a hand and put it on the medic's shoulder.

"Yeah, you did pretty damn well yourself." The medic drew out a thin metal line from a spool. "This'll hurt and you'll look damn ugly until you get to surgery, but it's the best I can do."

"Hurr," Thorvald swallowed a glob of blood and looked down at the tracker. A single dot moved a fraction of an inch across the surface. He looked out over the icy river.

"Hurr-ee."

CHAPTER 23

Tolan looked over a railing to an open section of machinery aboard the *Joaquim*. Dieter had stripped down to his pants, and sweat covered his muscular back as he reached deep into the inner workings.

"Are you done yet?" Tolan asked.

"*Fick deinen hund.*" Dieter looked up and thrust a finger at Tolan. "You're lucky I'm here. The next time you activated this stealth drive, you would have exploded into atoms. What have you done to this beautiful thing? Such elegance in design and you..." he paused to pick up a bit of slate-gray ribbon, "you used *tape* to fix it!"

"Are you done yet?" Tolan took a sip from a

bottle.

"Come down here and I will fix it with your-your-your ass! I want more money," Dieter said. "More for a tax against your insult to Reich technology."

"If I say yes, will that make you work faster?" Tolan sighed and then ducked as a nut whizzed past his head. "Fine! Fifty troys."

"*Siebzig!*"

Tolan tapped on his fingertips, gave Dieter a thumbs-up, and then he left, the Reichsman cursing up a storm behind him.

Tolan made his way back to the bridge, noting that much of the grime on the floors and walls had vanished. Geet was on his hands and knees just outside the door to the bridge, scrubbing off an old bloodstain that Tolan wasn't exactly sure who had provided.

"Not bad." Tolan reached behind Geet's ear and flashed a small black disk with a bit of sleight of hand. "Got the bomb off you. You're safe now."

Geet slapped the back of his head and neck in a near panic, then his eyes narrowed. "Hey…wait a minute."

Tolan shut the door to the bridge behind him, then unwrapped the chocolate that had substituted for the "bomb" and ate it. The bridge smelled faintly of lemon and the pile of trash below the console was gone.

"I should've hired him years ago. This is great," Tolan said.

He tapped a console to check the ship's docking-fee balance and received an error message. He looked up and out the bridge's windows. The nose of his ship faced the force field between the dock and void, but he could see the cockpits of other ships to either side of him. The crews on every bridge were gesturing wildly at each other, more agitated than anyone had any right to be at the same time.

"Loussan," Tolan said into the conn, "think we've got a problem. Need you up here."

Tolan wired entirely too much money to the customs station, but the boot—the hydraulic grips on his ship—didn't budge.

A mechanical arm swung off the boot and locked next to his cockpit. A blank screen flipped over, then flashed with static.

NOVIS REGIRAY emerged from the noise on the screen, then hardened into plain text.

"Loussan!" Tolan yelled over his shoulder and the pirate captain barreled onto the bridge.

"That doesn't look good," he said, elbowing Tolan to one side and working the controls. "The central system is off-line. The safety protocols should release the boot but they're—"

"Get Dieter and use the plasma torches to cut us free," Tolan said. "Time to skip town."

"Fine by me." Loussan turned to go, but stopped when a flash of light cast his shadow across the bulkhead. He stopped and heard Tolan sit hard in the command seat.

"Well…shit," Tolan said.

Beyond the force field, a Daegon fleet hung in the void, hundreds of their smaller ships forming a loose cloud around three giant battleships.

One merchant vessel—the boot clamps still on the ship but the heat of freshly cut metal glowing from the shorn edges—slipped out of the docks. Tolan shook his head as it accelerated slowly and a white bolt of energy from a Daegon ship destroyed the merchant vessel without warning.

NOVIS REGIRAY flashed several times on the screen outside the bridge, then vanished.

"My God, I've never seen such a fleet," Loussan said.

"I have." Tolan formed a steeple with his fingers beneath his chin. "Didn't end well for the planet where I saw it."

"What is going—" Dieter rushed onto the bridge and froze in the doorway. Geet tried to jump up and peek over his shoulder.

"YOU WILL BE RULED. HOLD POSITION OR BE DESTROYED" scrolled by on the screen.

In the void, drop pods fell from the ships and streaked toward Concord.

"What do we do?" Dieter asked.

"Are the stealth drives fixed?" Tolan asked.

"So many ships…" Dieter put a hand over his mouth.

Tolan threw a half-empty plastic water bottle at Dieter and hit the bulkhead. "The stealth drives!

Sooner I have answers, the sooner we can make an informed decision and survive!"

"Hours," Dieter stammered. "I need hours."

"You have the new IFF loaded?" Tolan asked Loussan.

"Yes…Coventry registry just like you asked." Loussan swallowed hard.

"Decent, at least we won't stick out like a sore thumb if the Daegon are looking for the *Joaquim*," Tolan said. "Dieter, get back to work."

"Just 'get back to work'? That's your plan?" the Reichsman asked.

"That the Daegon didn't blow this fleabag to pieces the second they arrived was a miracle." Tolan waved at the fleet, which was taking fire from the ground. Several of the smaller ships had taken damage and were spiraling down the gravity well.

Salvos flashed from the attacking fleet and Tolan looked away.

"They want this station for some reason," the spy said. "They just might want all the ships aboard it too. We're not ready to make a break for it, so it's best we *do* get ready while we have the time…and see if another path presents itself."

"This is that famed Albion bravery?" Loussan asked. "I expected better from you jackboots."

"I'm an intelligence professional," Tolan said, rolling his shoulders forward. "That makes me a coward and an opportunist doing everything I can to avoid being caught. You pirates should appreciate that. Now, let's…let's do our best to act like just another tramp ship caught in a war zone. You get all that, Geet?"

"I don't know what's going on," he said from behind Dieter.

"Exactly. That's the exact attitude we all need to have when the Daegon come looking for us. So let's everyone get back to work." He took a small red gummy candy from his pocket and popped it into his mouth. "Chop, chop, boys."

CHAPTER 24

Salis moved slowly through the river, each step testing her footing as she fought the current like it was a gale wind. The timer still gave her and Aidan several more minutes of air supply, more if she cut back her oxygen mix.

She went to all fours as she reached the bank, then lifted her head up and out of the water just enough to peek over the surface.

+Grynau welcomes me.+ Her AI put a glow on a nearby building for her.

Then it is safe, Salis emerged from the river, her plates flexing like scales to expel water. The back of her helmet puffed as the air tanks refilled. She marched up frost solid soil to the remains of a school.

Reichsmarines came out of the building and

she stopped, reaching for a weapon on her back hat was long gone.

Thorvald and Bertram—the same foil blanket wrapped around his shoulders—came out onto a playground. Salis' heart skipped a beat to see the two, and she felt an involuntary smile cross her face.

She went to one knee and the cocoon opened up and she helped Aidan to the ground.

"Mr. Berty!" Aidan rushed into the steward's arms. "Where did you go?"

"For a bit of a swim, young master," Bertram said. "All's well…soon as my teeth stop vibrating and this double vision goes away, that is."

"Who're the scary men?" Aidan hugged Bertram and slunk between his arms. Salis made the conscious effort not to take the slight personally.

"They're from the Reich," Bertram said. "And they're here to help, they keep saying. I don't want to believe it, but they've not sold me into slavery yet."

Thorvald smacked Bertram on the shoulder.

"Yes. I said 'yet.'"

Thorvald knelt next to Aidan and pointed to a bloody patch on the boy's pants.

"Minor abrasion." Salis removed her helmet and slapped the side, knocking frost away. "Treated and disinfected. What happened to you?"

"Tiberian," Thorvald sent the sub-vocalization from his armor to hers. He touched his swelling jaw and winced. *"I followed the beacon you put on the steward, but the Daegon got to him first. Fight ensued."*

"You kill him?"

"We're not assassins, Salis, we're guardians. That being said…I didn't kill him this time. The commodore has the fight in orbit under control, and he's got the Daegon on the run. Extraction's on the way down. We're due back on the Orion *soon as possible."*

"Fine by me." She put her helmet back on. "I've had enough of this planet."

Thorvald touched the bloody stain on Aidan's leg, and a small line of lights lit up on his arm and her HUD flickered.

"What did you do?" She touched the side of her helmet. "My AI just took a data influx from yours."

"Files." Thorvald canted his head slightly. *"DNA contact opened a number of sequestered data*

373

sources…*my AI kept them hidden as need-to-know because of how I inherited this suit back on Albion…so much data.*"

"There's still blackouts for me." She ran her finger tips up and down through the air, scanning data. "What do you have?"

Thorvald popped to his feet so suddenly, the Reichsmarines took cover, searching for threats.

"*I have the organ donor database open. Prince Aidan has….he has a close blood relative aboard the fleet,*" Thorvald said. "*Same father. Different mother.*"

"How is that possible?" Salis asked. "How would someone not know…not know that King Randolph is their father?"

"*Because they were never told,*" Thorvald said. "*Commodore Gage needs to know about this.*"

"What will he do with the relative? He or she must be older than Aidan…that would mean a different Crown Prince, right?"

"*Salis, you don't understand. Commodore Gage* is *the blood relative. He's Prince Aidan's half-brother.*"

CHAPTER 25

Gage watched as a Reich shuttle came through the force field of the *Orion*'s only functioning landing bay and settled down on three hydraulic gears. Typhoons from Cobra squadron settled down further away.

The ramp of the Reich shuttle lowered, and Prince Aidan came down, flanked by Thorvald and Salis. Bertram limped behind them.

Aidan had a sour expression as he walked up to Gage. The boy put his hands on his hips and his bottom lip began to quiver.

"I-I-I was scared." Aidan flung his arms around Gage's legs and Gage hugged the boy.

"I know, my Prince, and you were right to be scared. It was a horrible situation…and I'm sorry,"

Gage said.

"Did you send the bad ones?" Aidan asked.

"No, but I was still wrong to send you away. This ship…the entire Fleet, it may be better for you here," Gage said.

Aidan thrust a finger at Salis.

"She lost my Tigey!"

"It was the best tactical decision at the time," she said. "The Daegon put a tracker in it."

"Well done to you both," Gage said to the Genevans. "Thorvald…what happened to you? Your face."

Thorvald shrugged.

"The scars might make him prettier, but he needs to have his tongue and jaw reconstructed." Salis touched the armor on the back of her head, then motioned to Thorvald's neck. "I can speak for him. And if we may, sire," she glanced down at Aidan, "we need a word."

"Later." Gage stepped around them and clasped Bertram by the shoulders. "Bertram…you look awful."

"I died," Bertram frowned, "but I got better.

Begging your pardon, sire. But given my actions on the planet, I'd like to ask a small boon of you."

"You may ask." Gage's brow furrowed and he looked at Salis, who nodded.

"A shower, sire. A long, hot shower. I need ration chits from you, Emma—who owes me—and Salis. Maybe yours too, by your leave."

"See Doctor Seaver first," Gage said. "Thorvald as well. Salis will get Aidan resituated."

Gage waited for them to leave, then went to the bottom of the shuttle ramp.

"I'm impressed," Klaven said as he tromped down, stopping short of setting foot on the *Orion*'s deck. He used the ramp to keep his stance slightly higher than Gage's. "I never thought I'd see the inside of an Albion ship. Looks tremendous, even with all the damage."

"You've permission to come aboard," Gage said.

"Best not," Klaven said. "I'm not here, Commodore, not officially. And I won't ask for your grace to step foot on your deck. We Reich have our own foibles, and those in line for the throne must never appear to kneel to another sovereign. Even if that sovereign is but a boy."

"At least I can thank you in person." Gage held out a hand, and Klaven grasped him by the forearm. Gage returned the hold and they shook. "The timing of your intervention was…interesting."

"Well, I couldn't very well join in the fight until after the Daegon murdered my ambassador, now, could I?" Klaven asked.

"You had me change course so you could get a flank shot on their battleships," Gage said.

"Fortuitous. I'll leave an offering at the Shrine of Saint Siegfried on New Prussia once I get home." Klaven glanced around, a bit nervous.

"That where you're off to now?" Gage asked.

"When the Daegon ran out of the system with their tails between their legs, they used a slip space frequency that we were able to capture. It opened up the ley lines to several nearby systems…the *Castle Itter* will weigh anchor for Lantau. The League's meeting there. I'm reasonably certain it hasn't fallen to the Daegon. Yet."

"We found the same frequency. We're also

going to Lantau," Gage said.

"Then we should travel together." Klaven held his arms out. "But separately. You know what I mean. Albion ships are no longer under my protection. There is the conundrum that is Lady Christina. I'd rather not have her—"

"The Indus need a new Albion ambassador here," Gage said. "The governor accepted Lady Christina's credentials."

"How does she feel about that?" Klaven asked.

"I don't care," Gage deadpanned. Christina and Captain Arlyss had both blamed the other for the *Renown*'s unexpected departure from the battlefield. Gage had Arlyss removed from command and confined to quarters until there was time for a formal inquest.

"Dodged a bullet there," Klaven said. "When will you be ready to leave for Lantau?"

"Twelve hours," Gage said, "I'm evacuating what Albion citizens I can from New Madras. The governor's sending Captain Singh and the *Arjan Singh* with me…in case the Cathay Dynasty doesn't believe what I have to tell them."

"Have you ever been to Kong space before?" Klaven asked.

"I've not."

"Best be on your toes. Imperial intelligence has heard a number of contradictory stories of court intrigue coming from the Forbidden Continent. The Indus welcomed you with open arms. I doubt the Kong will be as friendly," Klaven said.

"I did all right with a planet full of pirates." Gage touched his arm where he'd been stabbed during an honor duel on said same planet.

"My people will talk to your people." Klaven turned away. "We'll arrive at Lantau together."

"What of the Reich?" Gage asked. "Does Kaiserina Washington know she's at war?"

Klaven stopped and half turned. "It's complicated, Gage. Perhaps she'll be ready and eager to throw these Daegon back into the hell they spawned from. Perhaps she'll consider Diaz's untimely death a tragic accident and repent to the Daegon by sending them my head on a platter. While it was my decision to—I mean, my hand was forced after their dastardly attack— the Kaiserina will do what she will. I don't plan to stay at Lantau long. There's a ley line to Reich space from there."

"It was…a pleasure to fight beside you," Gage said. "Given the circumstances."

Klaven turned and bowed.

"Albion and the Reich have shed each other's blood for so long, perhaps a mutual enemy will stop us from fighting each other in the future," Klaven said. "But I have a feeling this war's just begun. As we say back home, *vaya con Dios*."

He went back into his shuttle, the ramp raising before he even made it back inside.

CHAPTER 26

Tiberian made his way down a narrow staircase aboard the *Minotaur*, Gustavus just behind him. The air was stale but still had a reek of desperation to it. He'd never ventured into the under decks assigned to the ship's thralls. Such a thing was beneath his station.

"Why here?" Gustavus asked.

"Silence." Tiberian went to a door and pressed his palm to a reader. A sensor suite passed over him and the door slid to one side. Gustavus gagged as the smell of blood and viscera washed over them.

Inside was a mock-up surgical suite. Eubulus lay on a suspensor field, clamps over the stumps of amputated legs, lines filled with blood, glowing fluid and saline solution draped from his body to vials in a brightly lit life support station hanging over his body.

Half of his body was blackened and burnt. Pus dripped from the wounds and spattered to a mat beneath.

A thrall crept out of the shadows and mopped up a bit of mess that had leaked from where a tube entered Eubulus' femoral artery in his inner thigh. She scrambled back to her place by a medical waste can and huddled against the wall.

Tiberian looked back at Gustavus, pleased at the young man's lack of reaction to the sight of his father in such a state.

"Doctor Ziev?" Tiberian asked, and a man with lime green skin and a slight hunch came out from behind a bank of work stations. "Will he live?"

"He…does not have the will for it." Ziev cringed slightly. "I'm keeping him viable as per your instructions."

"Wake him." Tiberian went to his brother's side and Eubulus groaned as fluid coursed through the lines.

"Why?" Eubulus opened his remaining eye up to Tiberian. "You should have let me…"

"This…doesn't have to be the end." Tiberian

held his brother's hand and motioned for Gustavus to come closer. "My writ is complete. The last of the Albion royal family is dead. I return to Lady Assaria in glory. Differences aside, you gave me a ship. Let me hunt them down. I owe you."

"Owe me a life like this?" Eubulus asked. "To survive just long enough to go back to Assaria—" He cut off with in a hacking cough.

"So far as the others Houses will know…you died aboard your ship," Tiberian said. "The family's honor remains intact. Your writ will fall to me or Gustavus. I can keep you aboard. Change your appearance and gene profile to—"

"No!" Eubulus reached for Tiberian's neck, but his hand flopped to one side. "Live in your shadow as a cripple? Better to send me to the golems. At least there I might forget my failings. Alive…I'm a risk. Assaria has enemies. They find me and…where is my son?"

"Here." Gustavus put a hand to Eubulus' chest.

"Do better than me, boy," Eubulus said. "You've the strength to do that?"

"Yes, Father."

"Prove it," Eubulus grasped Gustavus' hand and pushed it away. "I died at my station, carrying out my writ. See that stays true."

Gustavus unsheathed a dagger and twirled the blade around his hand before holding it in a reverse grip. He stabbed down into his father's heart and Eubulus jerked for a moment before going slack.

Gustavus withdrew the blade and wiped blood off Eubulus' arm.

"Ziev." Tiberian held a hand to one side and claws popped out of his glove's fingertips.

"I expected as much, master," the doctor said. He held up a small pill. "May I depart on my own terms?"

"No." Tiberian swiped his hand across Ziev's throat, ripping it out and splashing blood over the thrall, who began screaming.

Gustavus threw his knife and the thrall went silent.

Tiberian pulled a thermite grenade off his belt and flicked the ring off. He tossed the device onto his dead brother's chest and the two left the hidden hospital room.

They strode up the stairs together, the smell of smoke and burning flesh at their backs.

"Now what?" Gustavus asked.

"Now we return to Albion with what's left of your father's fleet," Tiberian said, not looking at the other man. "Our re-conquest must continue, even after a failure like this."

"And the Baroness?"

"Leave her to me." Tiberian touched the small amulet around his neck. "I'll do what I can for you."

"And the Albion?"

"I have unfinished business with Gage," Tiberian said. "Perhaps the Baroness will bid me to finish off the last of them. You'll join me, if that's her will?"

"Gladly." Gustavus gripped the hilt of his sword. "But save some prisoners for me. I will play my father's death game until the last of them dead at my feet."

"But the Genevans are mine," Tiberian said. "As is Gage."

CHAPTER 27

"Arriving Lantau system now," Price said as the *Orion* transitioned from slip space. "Fleet exiting the ley line in formation. Small miracles. *Arjan Singh* arriving."

"Have the *Renown* transfer Captain Arlyss to our ship and remind the other captains that court martial proceedings will begin once we've made contact with Lantau void control." Gage waved a hand through the holo tank to wake it up.

The Lantau system was heavily populated, with two urbanized planets and several outer moons boasting domed cities and deep caverns full of factories and cities. They'd arrived at a little used slip point near a gas giant, and there was a lag as their initial hails to Lantau Prime had to travel several light minutes before they received a response.

"Void Guard station at the gas giant appears

to be abandoned," Price said. "No electromagnetic activity at all. The one settle moon looks to be empty as well."

"Odd," Gage said.

"But we are picking up media transmissions from the inner planets." Price shrugged. "Those are very active. At least we haven't shown up to a system that's supposed to have ten billion people just to find it empty. Maybe we caught something of a break here."

"Don't," Gage said. "You're tempting fate."

"*Castle Itter* just emerged," Price said. "Put some distance between us and them? Let the Kongs know we're not completely buddy-buddy with the Reich?"

"Not just yet," Gage said. "Let's not spook them. The Cathay can be a bit…testy."

"Sire." Clarke from the comm station approached the command dais. "Sire, there's something you should see. I don't…I don't know how to explain it. Our systems did an automatic handshake with a satellite relay and something in their buffers—"

"You didn't hack their systems like you did with the Indus, did you?" Price asked.

"No, ma'am, nothing like that." Clarke came up next to Price and touched a panel.

In the holo, a news video played. Chinese characters filled the edges and a Cantonese language voice over began.

"Working on the translation," Clarke said.

In the video, Cathay ships traded fire with Daegon vessels. One by one, the characters switched to English and Gage saw that the battle had taken place in the Tai Po system a few days ago.

A white and red vessel, its hull very different from the Daegon's linked diamond ships but instantly familiar to Gage, snapped by in the background of the video.

"Stop, go back," Gage said.

"That's not what you need to see, sire." Clarke swallowed hard and the video sped up before freezing on a frame. More of the white and red ships were there, locked in combat with the Cathay, Daegon destroyers mixed in among the white and red.

"Impossible," Gage said.

"Those are Albion ships, sire," Price said, her face going pale. "Albion ships fighting alongside the Daegon…against the Cathay. Oh…I think we're in trouble."

In the holo, a bright red square with a black border flashed. A hail from Lantau Prime.

Gage rubbed the bridge of his nose, and watched the video as more Albion ships engaged and destroyed Cathay forces at the battle in the newsfeed.

"Sire?" Price asked.

"I don't have an explanation for this." He opened the channel and an Asian man with a wide military cap looked square at the camera.

"Albion forces, I am Governor General Jeremy Han. You are declared hostiles at war with the Cathay Empire. Surrender immediately and prepare to be boarded or we will destroy you. You have ten minutes to comply."

The message looped and Gage cut the sound.

"Commodore?" Price asked.

"We double back to New Madras and we gain nothing," Gage said. He moved the holo to Lantau Prime and zoomed in on the orbital docks circling a small moon. "Biafra, Mechanix, gold-plated Cathay ships of the Emperor's Own...a half dozen other League worlds are here. This is where we should be."

"A fleet with two dozen battle cruisers just left anchor over Lantau Prime's southern pole," Price said. "I don't think they were kidding about us surrendering."

"Pull the fleet into a sphere. Ready fighters but to not launch," Gage said. "We're going to hold right here and try and talk some sense into the Kongs." He double-tapped Han's face and a dialogue box opened.

"Cathay forces, I am Commodore Thomas Gage of the Free Albion forces. We are not hostile to you or your Emperor. We will not surrender. Do not engage my ships, as we retain the League of Stellar Nation's inherent right to self-defense. My fleet is here to conduct League business, and we demand safe passage to Lantau Prime." He cut the transmission.

"That's...a bit forceful," Price said.

"Kongs." Gage shook his head. "You show weakness and they will walk all over you."

"They have more warships in system than the

Daegon sent to take New Madras," Price said. "Just so you know."

The Cathay fleet vectored straight for Gage's ships. He watched as the clock ticked on, and waited for a response. Even with the time lag…Governor General Han had yet to send a response.

"More Cathay vessels weighing anchor," Price said and several course projections from across the system converged on the *Orion*.

"Albion does not surrender." Gage scrolled through the news video, watching as ships from his home world fought and died beside the Daegon. "We don't…which is why I can't believe what I'm seeing here."

"And the Cathay?" Price asked.

"I can't take back our home with what we have now," Gage said. "We need the League. The League is here. We're not leaving."

"Hold." Gage clasped his hands behind his back.

It took another half hour before the Cathay ships neared to the point that light speed communication was near instant.

Then a new hail arrived from the Cathay ship *Liaoning*.

"Albion ships." Han appeared in the tank. "This is your last warning. Surrender."

"The answer is still 'no'," Gage said. "No changes to my last message."

"Cathay torpedo tracking systems just went live," Price said. "And the *Castle Itter* is hailing us. As is the *Arjan Singh*."

"Hold position," Gage said.

In the holo, the Cathay ships closed in. More and more alerts from active weapon systems pulsed warnings.

Gage looked to Thorvald at the door next to the lift.

"Have Prince Aidan moved to his new bunker," Gage said. "I may...I may have misread this situation."

THE END

The Exiled Fleet returns in POINT OF HONOR, coming in late 2019!

FROM THE AUTHOR

Richard Fox is the author of The Ember War Saga, and several other military history, thriller and space opera novels.

He lives in fabulous Las Vegas with his incredible wife and three boys, amazing children bent on anarchy.

He graduated from the United States Military Academy (West Point) much to his surprise and spent ten years on active duty in the United States Army. He deployed on two combat tours to Iraq and received the Combat Action Badge, Bronze Star and Presidential Unit Citation.

Sign up for his mailing list over at www.richardfoxauthor.com to stay up to date on new releases and get exclusive Ember War short stories.

The Ember War Saga:

1.) The Ember War
2.) The Ruins of Anthalas
3.) Blood of Heroes
4.) Earth Defiant
5.) The Gardens of Nibiru
6.) Battle of the Void
7.) The Siege of Earth
8.) The Crucible
9.) The Xaros Reckoning

Made in the USA
San Bernardino, CA
02 January 2020

62573445R00241